The Pearl Fishers

by

H. De Vere Stacpoole

Double9 BOOKS

The Pearl Fishers

by H. De Vere Stacpoole

ISBN: 978-93-70815-25-4

Published by

DOUBLE 9 BOOKS
2/13-B, Ansari Road
Daryaganj, New Delhi – 110002
info@double9books.com
www.double9books.com
Tel. 011-40042856

ABOUT THE AUTHOR

Henry de Vere Stacpoole was an Irish author best known for his 1908 romance novel The Blue Lagoon, which has been adapted into several films. Born on April 9, 1863, in Dún Laoghaire, Ireland, he became an established writer, publishing works under his own name and occasionally using the pseudonym Tyler de Saix. Stacpoole's literary works often explored themes of love, loss, and human connection, many set in tropical or exotic locations, reflecting his passion for travel and adventure. His writing resonated with readers for its vivid settings and emotional depth, and The Blue Lagoon remains his most famous work. Stacpoole was married twice, first to Margaret de Vere Stacpoole in 1907, and later to Florence Robson in 1938. He passed away at the age of 88 on April 12, 1951, in Shanklin, United Kingdom. His works, though primarily known for their romantic themes, also captured an essence of escapism, making them timeless classics. His legacy endures through his novels and their adaptations into films, which continue to captivate new generations.

CONTENTS

CHAPTER I
ALONE

The sun was breaking above the sea line, and the Pacific, heaving to the swell, lay all to the eastward in meadows of gold.

The little boat, moving gently to the vast and tremorless heaving of the sea, seemed abandoned in that world where nothing moved save the swell, and, far away, a frigate bird drifting south, dwindling and vanishing at last, blotted out in the blue of the morning sky.

The man in the stern of the boat lay as though he were dead, his arm curled over a water breaker and his head on his arm; but now, at the first touch of the sun, he moved, sat up, and, clasping his head with both hands, stared about him.

Heavens! What an awakening that was from sleep, the absolute and profound sleep that follows on disaster! In a moment, as though his mind had been suddenly lit by a great flash of energy that had been accumulating since he closed his eyes, he saw the whole of the events of the last three days in their entirety; he saw the past right back to his childhood, as men see it in that supreme moment that comes to the drowning, and which lights recollection to its farther frontiers.

He saw the schooner *Cormorant* landing at Ginnis' Wharf in Frisco, and he saw himself on board of it as second mate, Harrod, the first mate, standing by the weather rail, and Coxon, the skipper, just come on board, wiping his face with a red bandanna handkerchief before giving orders to cast off from the wharf where the tall Cape Horners lay moored by the Russian oil tanks, and the grain vessels by the great elevators were filling with living wheat.

He saw the Golden Gate and towering Tamalpais and the great Pacific, violent with the ruffling of the west wind and rolling toward the coast, to burst in eternal song on the beaches of California.

They were bound for Papeetong, away down near the Low Archipelago, with a trade room well stocked and plenty of copra in prospect.

The *Cormorant* was well found, well manned, and Coxon was an A-1 schooner captain; everything promised a prosperous voyage and a quick return, when on the evening of the second day out Coxon had called his second mate down to the saloon.

"Floyd," said he, "it's not for me to say a word to the second mate against the first, but Harrod, though he's the best chap in the world in some ways, has a weak spot, and that's drink. You notice he never touches anything, but there's no knowing how long he's on that tack—it may last the voyage, it mayn't. Not that he's any way out of the common when he's on liquor, but it's never no good to have a man boozy out of port, so, like a good chap, lead him off it if he seems taken that way. He's my own brother-in-law, and as good as they make 'em, else he wouldn't be aboard the *Cormorant*. It's my ambition to break him of it, and he's willing to be broke; still, the flesh is weak, as you'll soon discover if you live long in this world and knock against men—and there you are. A word to the wise."

Coxon's own weakness was a violent temper—we all have our weaknesses—and Floyd's was a happy-go-lucky optimism that made him believe in all men. He was only twenty-two, the son of a parson in Devonshire, educated up to fifteen at Blundell's School, set adrift in the world by the death of his father, and choosing the sea, prompted by the master ambition of his life, to be a sailor.

Harrod had run straight for the first week, and then he had fallen. He would appear on deck slightly thick of speech, and sometimes he had a stagger in his walk, and he would repeat his remarks in an uncalled-for way, and tend to turn quarrelsome at the least word.

They could not tell where he got the drink from, nor did they know the fact that his condition was due neither to rum or whisky, but to samshu.

Samshu is a horrible, treacly compound made by the Chinese of the coast; it is not kept in a bottle, but in a jar, and it is the last thing in the way of intoxicants. Balloon Juice, Cape Smoke, Valley Tan vie with each other in villainy, but Samshu is the worst.

It is very rarely found out of Canton and Shanghai, and it had been brought on board the *Cormorant* by the Chinese cook, who traded it to Harrod for money and tobacco.

A gale had struck them, driving them some hundred miles from their course, and when it had passed, Harrod, one afternoon, under the influence of this stuff, had gone into the hole where paint and varnish were stored, carrying a light. A few minutes later came a cry of fire. Coxon was the first man on deck. He saw in a moment that there was no hope. The varnish room was blazing like a torch, belching smoke and sparks and jets of flame like a dragon, and just as unapproachable.

There was nothing to be done but take to the boats.

The Kanaka crew and the Chinaman whose samshu jar had done all this bundled into the longboat. Floyd ought to have been with them, but he was held back by the work of victualing and lowering the quarter boat, and they shoved off without him, so the three officers were left—Floyd, in the quarter-boat, and the skipper and Harrod quarreling on deck. Coxon's temper had overmastered him. He was the owner of the *Cormorant*, and his whole fortune was in the trade on board.

Floyd, hanging on with a boat hook, heard the shouting and stamping of the men on deck. He tried to get on board again to separate them, but the smoke drove him back, the heat was terrific, and he cast off, rowing round to the windward side in the hope of boarding her there. As he passed round the stern he was just in time to see the end of the tragedy, Coxon flinging Harrod over the weather rail and following him into the sea.

Neither of the two men appeared again, and the reason was very obvious—the water was filled with gray, flitting shadows. The tragedy of the burning schooner had made its call through the depths of the sea, and the sharks were assembling for the feast. Floyd waited. The whole of this terrible business had left him numb and almost unmoved. Tragedy thrills one most in the theater; on the real stage the imagination becomes paralyzed before the actual.

He pushed away farther from the flaming schooner; she was burning now like a torch, and volumes of white smoke passed away to leeward on the wind.

The sun was setting, and the picture of the burning ship against the glowing western sky would have been unparalleled had there been eyes to see it as a picture. Floyd, gazing at it, watched while the flames, half invisible, like the ghosts of brightly spangled snakes, ran up the masts. He saw the canvas wither away, and then he watched her lurch as the seams opened to the heat and dip her bowsprit in the sea.

She settled slowly, the sea boiling about her, and then suddenly she plunged bow first and vanished.

In less than twenty seconds there was nothing to tell that a vessel had been there with the exception of a wreath of smoke dissolving in the blue of evening.

The upper limb of the sun had just passed beneath the horizon, and in the momentary twilight before the rush of the stars Floyd saw the longboat, far away, and with sail hoisted to the wind.

Then the night came down, and at dawn next day the longboat had vanished.

As he awoke from sleep now he saw all these pictures vividly. Till the night before he had not slept at all, and it was the return to normal conditions of his brain refreshed by sleep that now gave him a full view of his past and his position.

The quarter-boat possessed a mast and lugsail; he had stepped the mast and hoisted the sail, which now hung limp and flicking to the warm, steadily blowing wind.

He rose up, and, standing with one hand on the mast, looked over the sea. North, south, east, and west it lay blazing in the sunshine, with not a sign of sail or wing on the dazzle and the blueness, an infinite world of sky, an infinite world of water all flooded by the living light of the great golden sun.

Floyd, having glanced about him, returned to his former place in the stern of the boat and began to review his stores; he had taken stock of them twice in the last two days, but had you asked him now to give an account of them he would have been at a loss to say exactly how they stood.

The water breaker was his first consideration. It was half full—enough to last him for six days, he reckoned. There was a full bag of ship's bread, another half full, some tins of potatoes, some tins of canned meat, but no can opener, and a few tins of condensed milk. So much for the provisions. There were also in the boat the ship's papers and a japanned tin box containing the ship's money. These Coxon had flung in before the quarrel between him and Harrod had broken out. There was nothing else at all with the exception of a boat hook and a bailer.

He had in his pockets a knife and one of those tinder boxes in which the flint strikes on a wheel, a pocket handkerchief, a few loose matches, and a pipe and some tobacco. It was American navy twist, and he had nearly half a pound of it. It was the first thing he found in his cabin on rushing down, and it was the only thing he had taken away.

Having breakfasted off a biscuit and a bit of meat from one of the cans which he managed to haggle open with his knife, he lit his pipe, brought the sheet aft, and took the tiller. It did not matter in the least where he steered, for Australia and China lay away to the west, the whole continent of America to the east—both were hopeless; the Low Archipelago lay to the south, and the hope of an island was just as brilliant in any given direction.

So he gave his sail to the wind, trusting in God.

As the morning wore on, the sea line became hung with light, fleecy clouds that deepened the far-off blue of the sea. This fringe of light cloud often hangs on the skirts of the Trades. Steering, Floyd could hear the tune of the water as it flapped on the boarding and rippled in the wake. The breeze was not strong enough to raise any sea, and the swell was scarcely perceptible unless to the eye.

CHAPTER II
THE ISLAND

About an hour before noon Floyd, relinquishing the tiller, stood up and, supporting himself by the mast, looked around. Then, sheltering his eyes with his hand, he fixed his gaze straight ahead.

The sea line at one point was broken, and the sky just above the broken point had a curious and brilliant paleness.

Once before he had seen a bit of sky like that, and he guessed it at once to be the reflection cast upward from a lagoon island.

The sight of it dried his lips and made the sweat stand out on the palms of his hands; then, taking his place again at the tiller, he resumed his course.

The boat was making about three knots, and he reckoned that the island could not be more than ten miles away. Were bad weather suddenly to spring on him Pacific fashion, he might either be driven out of reach of the shelter before him or sunk. But the wind held fair and steady with no sign of squalls, and now, when he looked again, he could see the palm-tree tops raised high above the water, and—what was that—a ship?

The masts of a ship, all aslant, showed thready near the palms. She was wrecked—of that there could be no manner of doubt.

The shimmer of the sea cut off everything but the palm tops, the palm stems, and the masts; they seemed based on air.

In an hour, standing up again, Floyd made out the whole position distinctly.

The island that lay before him was simply a huge ring of coral clipping a lagoon a mile or more in diameter, as he afterward discovered. It was not an even ring; here and there it swelled out into great spaces covered with palms and artus and hotoo trees. Near the break in the reef for which he was now steering, piled up on the coral literally high and dry, lay the carcass of what had recently been a schooner of some two hundred tons.

She must have been sent right up by some great lift of the sea.

As he drew near he could see that the planking had been literally stripped off her from a huge space reaching from the stern post almost to midship; there was no rudder; the sails, he thought, had either blown away or flogged themselves to pieces, taking with them gaffs and booms. Then he remembered that the masts, still standing by some miracle, would certainly have snapped like carrots had sail enough been on her to carry away the spars like that. He could not tell. The thing hypnotized him as he watched it, his hand on the tiller and the opening of the reef before him.

Though the sea was as calm as the Pacific can ever be, a steady surf was breaking on the reef. The boom of it came to him now against the wind, and the boat heaved to the short sea made by the resistance of the great coral breakwater.

It was like the bourdon note of an organ, and though it swelled and sank it never ceased, for it was the tune that ringed forever the whole four-mile circuit of the atoll.

Then as he passed the coral piers and opened the lagoon, the sound of the surf grew less loud and the boat went on an even keel.

Before him lay the great blue pond, calm as a summer lake; the shore surrounding it showed long beaches of salt-white coral sand and great spaces of foliage; palms and breadfruit, mammee apple bushes and cane, colonies of trees all moving, gently pressed upon by the warm trade wind, whose breath made violet meadows on the broad lagoon.

It was the most extraordinary place in the world.

It had a touch of the ornamental, as though some city more vast and wealthy and populous than any city we know of had decreed this great space of water as a pleasure lake, ordered the white of sand and green of foliage, emerald of shallow water and blue of deep, and then vanished, leaving its pleasure place to the wastes of ocean.

The water at the opening of the lagoon was very deep, but inside it shoaled rapidly, and Floyd, glancing over the thwart, saw the white sand patches and coral lumps of the lagoon floor almost as clearly as though he were gliding over them through air.

He swept the circular beach with a glance, flung up his hand to shade his eyes, and then with a shout put the helm over and hauled the sheet to port.

Away on the beach to the right something flapped; it was the sailcloth of a rudely made tent, and by the tent, waving its arm, stood the figure of a man; by the man, squatting on the beach sand, was another figure, small and difficult to distinguish.

Floyd instantly connected these figures with the wreck; they were evidently the remains of the shipwrecked crew.

As he drew closer the man on the beach showed up more clearly—a bronzed and bearded man in dubiously white clothes, and the figure seated on the sand revealed itself as a girl; she was almost as dark as the man, and she was seated with her hands clasping her knees.

He unstepped the mast and took to the sculls; a minute later the stem of the boat was grinding the sand of the beach, and Floyd was over the side helping to pull her up.

Before they exchanged a word they pulled her up sufficiently to keep her from drifting off with the outgoing tide. It was easy to see they were sailors.

"She's all right," said the bearded man; "and where in the name of everything have you come from?"

Floyd flung both hands on the shoulders of the other. It was not till this moment that he had borne in on him the frightful loneliness and the fate from which he had escaped.

"I'd never hoped to see a living man again," said he. "Never, never, never! You're real, aren't you? Don't mind me. I'm half cracked; your fist—there—I'm better now."

"Wrecked?" said the bearded man.

"Yes; wrecked, burned out. The *Cormorant* was the name, bound from Frisco to Papeetong; drink and fire did for us——"

He stopped short. He had been staring at the girl. She had shifted her position only slightly, and she was looking at him with eyes that showed little interest and less emotion—the eyes of a person who is gazing at shapes in a fire or at some object a great distance off.

She was a Polynesian—a wonderfully pretty girl, almost a child, honey-colored, with a string of scarlet beads showing on her neck about the scanty garment that covered her, and with a scarlet flower in her jet-black hair.

It was a flower of the hibiscus that grew in profusion in all the groves of the atoll.

"That's Isbel," said the bearded man. "Kanaka, called after the place she came from. Isbel Island in the Marshalls. I'm Schumer, trader and part owner of the *Tonga*. There she is"—jerking his thumb at the wreck. "Hove up in a gale a month ago; we've been here a month; every man jack drowned but me and Isbel. I've salved a bit of the cargo—foodstuffs and suchlike. What's your name?"

"Floyd."

"Well, that's as good as any other name in these parts, anyhow."

He sat down on the sand near the girl, and Floyd did likewise. Then Schumer, taking a pipe and some tobacco from his pocket, began to smoke. He talked all the time.

"We've rigged up a bit of a tent. Isbel prefers to sleep out in the open. Kanaka. Not much between them and beasts except the hide. Well, tell us about yourself. What's the name of the schooner did you say was burned?"

Floyd told; told the whole story while Schumer listened, smoking, lolling on his back and cutting in every now and then with a question.

"Well," said he, when the other had finished, "that lays over most yarns I've heard. And what's become of that boatload of Kanakas, I wonder? Starved out most likely. Good for you they took their hook; good for me, too, for now we've got your boat, and a boat's a handy thing. We can get across the lagoon easy, for there's no getting round on foot beyond that clump of cocoanuts on the shore edge there. There's a quarter mile or so of broken coral all that way; razors ain't in it beside broken coral. We can fish, too, and it may be handy to have a boat if we sight a ship, though this island is clean out of trade tracks. We were blown two hundred miles from our course."

"What was your cargo?" asked Floyd.

"Printed stuffs, tinware, and general trade; a missionary—he was washed overboard—and several passenger Kanakas under him. Isbel belonged to his lot. She can talk English—can't you, Isbel?"

"Yes," replied the girl.

It was the first thing she had uttered, and Floyd noticed the softness of her voice and the way she avoided the "y," or rather the hardness of it, without breaking the word or mutilating it.

"It was the storm of storms," said Schumer; "there we were, running before it with scarcely a rag of canvas set and every wave threatenin' to be our last, every man jack on deck clinging to whatever he could hold when the great smash came. I don't know how I escaped. Providence, mostlike—same with Isbel, though I guess she's so little account she escaped the way some did in the earthquake out in Java three years ago. I saw a whole family flattened out under their own roof and a basket of kittens saved. It's that way things work in this world."

"Well," said Floyd, lying on his back on the sand—there was shade here from the trees—"I'm jolly glad you were saved. Good Lord, it's only coming on me now, the whole business; it's just as if one had escaped from the end of the world. It's not good to be drifting about in a boat alone."

Schumer agreed.

Floyd had now taken stock of his new companion. He was a powerfully built man with a bold and daring face, a trifle hard, perhaps—hard certainly one would say in striking a bargain; he was tanned by sun and wind, and despite his name he spoke English like an Englishman; sometimes the faintest trace of an American accent was perceptible, and sometimes the inimitable American cast of words lending color and picture to his conversation.

Floyd liked him.

"Well," said Schumer, rising up, "let's go and have a look at the old hulk; there's some more stuff worth salving—not that if I had a derrick and more boats and a ship to lade the stuff in I wouldn't salve the lot. By the way, what did you bring off in that boat of yours?"

"There's some biscuits and canned stuff, and a tin box with the ship's papers and some money—nothing much."

"Money, did you say—how much?"

Floyd told him.

"Well," said Schumer, "money's not of any use to us here—wish it was; all the same, it's worth having, for there's no knowing the moment the door may be opened for us to get out of here."

He led the way toward the wreck, Floyd and Isbel following.

The coral islands of the Pacific may be roughly divided into two classes: compound islands—that is to say, islands made of solid land and surrounded by a coral ring or breakwater, and simple islands or atolls—that is, simple rings of coral inclosing lagoons.

Then we have occasionally a third variety, an atoll island in whose lagoon one finds several islets.

This island that Floyd had struck was of the simple variety; the lagoon was of an irregular form, circular as a whole, yet here and there making bays in the coral.

The coral ring had four definite areas upon which vegetation flourished; one might say that the ring inclosing the lagoon consisted of four islands, each joined to each by naked coral.

The *Tonga* had been lifted by one great heave of the sea right onto the raw coral of the northern pier of the reef. It was not so great a feat, after all, for the reef was lower than elsewhere, and ships before this have been lifted over atoll reefs and deposited upside down in lagoons.

The *Tonga* was not upside down, but she was broken fore and aft, and the fact that her masts were still standing formed another incident in that category of strange incidents—the story of the power of the sea.

The rudder had been plucked off and lay there like a great barn door flung down on the coral; the pintles were gone as though they had been torn from the wood by forceps; the planking, as I have already said, was stripped from the port side right to midships; she lay with a list to port, and through the great gaping wound where the ribs of the vessel showed like the ribs of a half-devoured carcass, the contents of the trade room and cabin could be seen half shed on the coral, half still contained.

Bales of print, kegs and cases, burst boxes of canned provisions, bird cages, trade gin, some cases of cheap rifles destined for the King of Apaka, who was in revolt against German rule, and who was anxiously awaiting the consignment—these and twenty more varieties of things lay there festering in the sun, watched by the sea birds and blown upon by the wind.

"Good heavens," said Floyd, "what a spill!"

"It's just that," said Schumer, "and it's not good to see so much stuff gone to waste, especially when one's money has paid for it, or part paid for it. It wasn't all my venture. There's a man at Sydney who's my partner. Well, there's no use crying over spilled goods; let's try and do what we can. Now you are here we may be able to salve more of the stuff than I had hoped. First thing is to get some of the perishables under shade. The sun doesn't hurt rifles, but it doesn't improve prints and provisions."

"I'll help," said Floyd; "anything's better than doing nothing."

"Then come along, my son," replied Schumer. "Claw hold of the other end of this case, and you, Isbel, follow along with that mat of rice."

A few mats of rice had been among the cargo of the *Tonga*, and though here on the island there was evidence of an abundance of food, Schumer seemed to pay especial attention to the salving of provisions. Perhaps with that keen brain of his, which had carried him so far in life against tremendous odds, he foresaw the time when these same provisions would be more valuable as a trade asset than minted gold.

They worked for several hours, and then knocked off and came back to where the tent was pitched.

Schumer proceeded to light a fire, while Floyd and Isbel got together the things for supper.

Schumer the day before had managed to catch a small turtle, and he now set to to grill some of the flesh. He also boiled some water for coffee, and in half an hour Floyd found himself before the best supper he had ever sat down to.

"It's good for us there's water here," said Schumer, when they had finished. "You see, if this island had been a ring of coral hove up out of the sea there wouldn't have been any natural water here, but it's not. It's my belief it's more a ring of mountaintops just showing with coral bridging between; anyhow, there's lots of water—at least enough for us. Well, we'll take your boat out in the morning and have a good look at the lagoon, and see what we can find in those bays over there. I've got some fishing tackle and we can fish—shellfish makes good bait; there's no fishing of any account to be had on the shore edge, but there's big things to be done out in the lagoon."

He filled his pipe and lit it, and they smoked for a while in silence. The sun was setting, and from the great ring of coral came the sound of the surf, continuous, dreamy and less loud to the ears of Floyd than when he had first landed. In a little time he would not hear it; or, rather, he would not notice; it was one of the conditions of life here, a part of the strangeness of this strange place where perfect peace dwelt forever ringed around by the murmur of the sea.

"See here," said Schumer, after a few minutes' silence; "what about that money you said you had in the boat?"

"You mean the ship's money and papers?"

"Yes."

"Oh, they're in the boat still," said Floyd, rising up.

He went to the boat where she lay high and dry on the sand, and took out the tin box.

He brought it back to where Schumer and Isbel were sitting by the embers of the fire, and, taking his place on the sand beside them, opened the box and took out the bag of sovereigns.

He undid the string and poured the contents of the bag onto the hard sand of the beach.

There were two hundred and ten sovereigns—as they afterward counted—and the moon, which had just pushed up its face over the eastern reef edge, lit the pile which Floyd was now stirring with his finger, while Schumer, who had drawn himself closer on his elbow, looked on without a word. Isbel had drawn closer, too.

She had spoken very little as yet, and when she spoke it was a pleasure to listen.

To attempt the reproduction of Polynesian speech is fatal, and the authors who attempt it succeed in producing only a disgusting form of pidgin English. It is impossible to reproduce the inflections, the softness, the timbre, the soul of it. It is equally impossible to reproduce the infantile French of the West Indies.

Isbel's language was the human equivalent of the language of the soft-voiced birds; more than that, the missionary who had brought her up had guarded her from the vile "savvee" and "um" and "allee same" that foul the speech of the lower natives.

How much the missionary teaching had bent her mind to Eastern ideals or influenced her nature it would be impossible to say. There was a great deal of mystery about Isbel, centuries and centuries of the unknown and unrealized gazing from those eyes so dark and unfathomable.

"Well," said Schumer, breaking the silence at last, "that's a decent pile, and what are you going to do with it?"

"Well, it's Coxon's," said Floyd, "and now he's dead it will belong to his next of kin; he hadn't a wife and family, so he told me, but he's sure to have relations."

"Every man has who dies worth a cent," said Schumer. "Question is how are you to find them, and whether they'll thank you if you do find them, or swear that you've nailed half the boodle. You said the chap that fired the schooner was Coxon's brother-in-law; well, it 'pears to me you've suffered a good bit from his relations already, and deserve some recompense. If I were you I'd put those papers in the fire and the money in your pocket—however, that's your affair, not mine."

Floyd put papers and money back in the tin box.

"I'll put them in the tent for the present," said he; "there's lots of time to think over the matter, and little chance enough to act in it."

"Well," said Schumer, "you can do as you please when the time comes—and I wish it would come. I'm about sick of hanging here doing nothing. I'm going to turn in. I sleep in the tent, and there's room for you, too. Isbel has made a wigwam in the bush—the boat's all right; she's high above the level of the tide."

Half an hour later the great moon, swinging above the island, showed nothing but the embers of the fire, the trodden sand and the tent; the human beings whom the Fates had brought together on this lost and lonely spot had vanished, touched by sleep, just as men vanish from the world when touched by Death.

CHAPTER III
THE SECRET OF THE LAGOON

Floyd awoke shortly after sunup.

The gulls were shouting and flying against the blaze of the sunrise, fleeting like snowflakes across the blue sky beyond the reef opening, and fishing at the pierheads.

When the great lagoon was emptying or filling to the tide, the water at the pierheads went like a mill race; at slack water it lay gently flowing to the swell of the outside sea as now.

Floyd came from under the tent, glanced round him, stretched himself, and then crossed the reef to the outer beach, where the breakers were coming in—the eternal breakers of the Pacific, leisurely, monotonous, rhythmical, filling the air with their sound and spindrift, their ozone and life.

Nothing could be more extraordinary than the contrast between the inner beach and the outer beach of the island. You stood now facing a great lake, calm and colored with all the blues and greens of tropical water that varies in depth, and now, crossing the reef, you stood on the shore of a thunderous sea.

Floyd stripped himself of his clothes and went into the surf. When he had bathed and dried himself in the sun, he returned to the camp, where he found Schumer lighting the fire and Isbel preparing breakfast. They greeted him and he fell to to help.

He felt for the moment gay; the brightness, the sense of early morning, the sea breeze and the crying gulls all raised his spirits to the highest pitch.

Even Schumer, older and unenthusiastic to everything but trade, seemed more cheerful than usual.

"We'll take the boat now," said he, when breakfast was finished, "and prospect the lagoon. We want to get soundings, anyhow, in case a ship should come and may want anchorage inside. This island isn't charted—at least it's not on the British admiralty charts. I have the *Tonga* charts in the tent, and they make it all clear water from the spot where the hurricane took us to three hundred miles south, and we didn't run more than a hundred and fifty before we tripped over the reef.

"South of the three-hundred-mile limit there's a group of small islands, but they are not atolls. Now we're clear out of trade tracks and unknown, though you may be sure whalers have been here, for there's nowhere in the Pacific that whalers haven't pushed their noses, and whalers are useless to us. We don't want any blubber tanks showing their dirty hulls here; if they took us aboard they would drop us again at any decent port till after, maybe, a three years' cruise, and then they'd land us God knows where, crippled with work and tuppence in our pockets. No, sir, if any dirty whalers show their faces here they'll get bullets before they get us on board. Well, come on and help float the boat."

They got the boat off, and in a few minutes were out in the lagoon, Isbel forward, Floyd at the sculls, and Schumer in the stern sheets.

"There's breeze enough for the sail," said Schumer, when they were a hundred yards or so out. "Shove the mast up, and we'll take it easy. I want to have a full look at the floor of this lagoon, and take my time over it."

Floyd took in the sculls, and, helped by Isbel, who seemed to have a good knowledge of boat craft, got the mast stepped. Then they shook the sail out, and the boat scarcely heeling to the gentle breeze, they made straight across the stretch of water between them and the northernmost beach.

The floor of the lagoon was not of equal depth; near the break in the reef it was thirty-fathom water, shoaling swiftly to ten and five. The whole western half of the lagoon was three fathoms and under. At several places in this shallow zone the coral floor rose sharply and nearly reached the surface. It was necessary, indeed, to unstep the mast and take to the sculls, while Isbel, leaning over the bow, conned them.

The water was so clear that the shadow of the boat showed hard on the sand patches; looking down, the eye was held by a thousand things beautiful and strange. Color dwells like a wizard in tropical and subtropical waters; it seems inherent in those seas. Shells, fish, and coral all are gorgeous, and more than gorgeous—exquisite. Here seem to lie the remnants of a world more beautiful than any world we know—the ruins of a paradise.

Coral alone presents to us a whole world of art; its colors and its forms are infinite, and the artists of Paris or Tokyo make nothing more beautiful than the million art treasures eternally being formed in the depths and the shallows of the sea. Not only in the Pacific, but the Atlantic, not only in the Atlantic, but the Indian Ocean, from three-fathom water to a mile deep the construction of the beautiful is eternally in progress, unviewed and almost unknown.

Floyd, resting on his oars now and then, looked over into the luminous depths where flights of painted fish passed, their shadows following them over the sand patches and brain coral.

Here and there were streaks of dead and rotten coral of a seaweed brown, and here and there veritable gardens of color. Great shells moved about on the sand patches, crabs scurried hither and thither, globe-shaped jellyfish passed clear as glass, showing up for the moment by reflected light, and then vanishing like ghosts. Schumer, his battered old panama tilted back to protect his neck from the sun, seemed absorbed in the things below; he spoke scarcely a word, unless to give direction to the rower; Isbel, heedless of the sun, was equally absorbed. Always on the lookout for the shoal water, she said nothing except to give the direction "To the right," "To the left," and on the heaving of a sudden rock up through the brilliant water, "Ah, stop hard!"

The whole of this western part of the lagoon was very difficult water; unless buoyed it would be utterly unnavigable by a ship even of small tonnage.

Schumer, having explored the northernmost part of this zone, gave directions to Floyd to pull farther south.

They had scarcely entered this area when Floyd's attention became attracted to his companion. Schumer, leaning over the side and holding the thwart with his left hand, suddenly became rigid. The muscles of his neck stood out stiff, and his hand seemed trying to crush the wood of the thwart.

Then he turned with a great cry:

"Shell! Acres of shell—pearls! We've struck it!" Floyd, as excited as Schumer, drew in his sculls and looked over.

Fortune wears many cloaks, but her ugliest is formed of oysters. As far as Floyd could see, to right, to left, ahead, and astern, the floor of the lagoon was an oyster bed; all beauty of coral had vanished, and the water seemed deserted even by the colored fish that haunted the deeper parts of the lagoon.

"Row on," said Schumer; "let's see how far it stretches. It is the biggest find I ever expected to strike. I fancied there might be shell, I was on the lookout for shell, but it was only an idea of mine, and now it's here, a fortune right in our hands."

Floyd got out the sculls and the boat moved south.

Schumer was right when he had said "acres of shell." An hour's prospecting gave them the fact that the whole southern area of this the western portion of the lagoon was shell. There were three main beds with coral between, millions and millions of oysters, tons upon tons of shell, and no man could say the possibilities in the way of pearls.

When they had finished prospecting they beached the boat, and taking shelter from the sun under the shade of a little grove of artus and pura trees, set to on the provisions they had brought with them.

Right across the lagoon from where they sat they could see their camping place and the tent, the wreck, and the opening in the reef all in the blue weather, and beyond the opening in the reef a glimpse of the great Pacific and the fringe of pearl-white clouds on the horizon.

"Well," said Schumer, as they finished their meal, "the stuff is there right enough, and it only comes now to the question of lifting it. We have no labor, or none to speak of. Of course, we'll dredge and dive so as to get as much samples as we can, but we want twenty men on the work, and I don't see how we're to do it without letting others into the secret. It's this way: Some time or another a vessel is sure to happen along here and take us off; well, if it does we must keep mum. Our object will be to get to Frisco or Sydney, and there get hold of some chap with money and form a little syndicate. That'll water the profits considerable; he'll want half at least. But there you are—what's to be done?"

"Nothing," said Floyd; "we can't move without labor, and even that's no use without a ship. To rig an expedition up at Frisco or Sydney will cost a lot, and you may be sure any speculator who puts his money into the thing will want to gobble most of the profits."

"Before we'd let him into the know we'd make him sign a paper," said Schumer, "stating his acceptance of our terms, and then we'd make him keep his bond with a pistol to his head. I don't trust the law alone, but the law backed by a derringer makes a pretty good security."

As Schumer spoke, Floyd, who was watching his profile cut hard against the sky, noticed for the first time the flatness of the cheek bones and the relationship between the nose and chin.

Schumer was a very quiet man in his speech and manner, yet there was about him an assured confidence speaking of great reserves of energy; and now for the first time, as though the thought of being robbed of his treasure had revealed it, there peeped out a new man; something of the bird of prey showed in that profile, something of the desperado found echo in his voice.

"Well," said Floyd, "there's no use in making plans till we have something to go on. Let's settle on our immediate business; we'll have to get oysters up and rot them in the sun to see if there's any show of pearls, and it seems to me that we are very well placed for that. Suppose a ship comes into the lagoon; well, she can't come within a mile of this beach on account of the shoal water, and she won't be able to see our work. I propose we stick to our old camp by the wreck, and come here every day to work. We can leave Isbel on guard at the camp, and if she sights a ship she can light a fire to give us warning."

"That's sense," replied Schumer, who had become himself again. "We can rot the oysters on the weather side of the reef, and we'll set to work on the business to-morrow morning. Let's get back now to the camp. I'm going to fix up a dredge. Did I tell you I was a bit of an engineer? I've had to be a bit of everything this time or that. I once edited a paper and wrote it mostly, from the poetry column to the produce. I guess I'd have written books if my lines had been cast in quiet waters. Trade has always kept me going, and here where there's palm trees and blue water enough trade turns up in oysters."

His eyes were fixed across the lagoon on the palms near the wreck; the hawk-like look had vanished, and he murmured half to himself the verse of Scheffel:

> *"Zwölf Palmen ragten am Meeresstrand*
> *Um eine alte Cisterne."*

It was *"Dun Tode Nah"* he was repeating, and Floyd, who did not know the verse, knew the language.

"You speak German?" said he.

"My father was a German," replied Schumer. "I speak four languages and half a dozen Polynesian dialects. One has to. Well, shall we get back? There is nothing more to be done here for the present."

CHAPTER IV
SCHUMER'S STORY

They rowed back across the lagoon to the camp, and there Schumer set to on the construction of his dredge.

Floyd had suddenly found an object of interest on the island almost as absorbing as the oyster bed, and that object was Schumer.

Schumer had seemed to him at first a simple trader bound up in trade, one of a class that swarms in the Pacific. Bound up in trade he undoubtedly was, but there was all the difference in the world between him and the others of his class that Floyd had come across in his wanderings.

Perhaps the hardest thing in the world to put one's finger on is personality, or the power that tells in a man's appearance, actions, and speech. Its essence lies in complexity, and is born of all the multitudinous attributes that form spirit.

Floyd watched Schumer working on the dredge, and wondered at his ingenuity and power over metal and wood. He had but little material to his hand—cask hoops and old ironwork from the wreck, and so on—yet he made the most of it, and did not grumble. He explained the mechanism of the thing when he had finished. He had set Isbel to work stitching the canvas bag which was part of the dredge, and she sat mysterious as a sphinx, working and listening to him as he talked.

Then, later on, as they smoked after supper and watched the stars break out over the lagoon, Schumer went on talking, now of trade and the wild work he had seen here and there in the Pacific.

He was vague, rarely giving the names of islands or places, contenting himself with such wide terms as "It was an island south of the Marshalls," or "It was down in the Solomons." It was down in the Solomons that he had got the scar on his arm which he showed to Floyd.

"That's fifteen years old," said he; "it missed the artery or I wouldn't be here now. I was only twenty then and new to the islands, new to the sea also. I'd taken passage in a big schooner; two hundred and fifty tons she was, captained by a Yankee skipper, and manned by the biggest crowd of rascals that ever sailed out of Frisco to meet perdition.

"We put in at a big island southeast of Manahiki. I went ashore with the old man, the first mate, and two of the hands that could be trusted. We were all well armed, and lucky for us we were.

"It was the bos'n who started the trouble—a big, black-bearded chap, half Irish, quarter Scotch, with a tar brush somewhere in his family. Not a good mixture by any means.

"We hadn't been ashore ten minutes when this chap took the schooner. There were no preliminaries. She had a big brass swivel gun, and he turned it on the beach and let fly. He'd loaded her with a bag of bullets, and the first shot smashed the boat we'd landed in, smashed the only canoes in the place, and tore up the sand as if it had been plowed. Fortunately we had seen his game and scattered, but two natives were killed, and the rest took to the bush.

"So did we, and under cover of the leaves we watched what was going on in the schooner.

"They seemed pretty satisfied with themselves. They were sure against attack; they had smashed our boat and the canoes, and they were pretty certain we wouldn't try to board them by swimming, for the lagoon was full of sharks. They brought up grog and took to dancing on deck. Their object, of course, was to get away with the schooner and all the trade on board, change her name, and make for some port on the South American coast, and sell schooner and cargo and all. There was money aboard, too—the ship's money and some coin of the old man's, and fifty British sovereigns of my own hid in my bunk, though the beggars did not guess that.

"Yes, they should have knocked the shackle off the anchor chain and got to sea at once; they chose instead to drink and dance, celebrating their victory. You see they did not know whom they were dealing with.

"From where we lay we could have picked them off like crows with our rifles. Of course, that would have meant they would have gone below and hid, and then at dark they'd have gone away. It would have sobered them, too, and I did not want that.

"So we let them be, putting our trust in the bottle, and we set to and made a raft with the help of some of the natives who were hiding in the bush with us.

"There was a little creek hidden from the schooner by a cape of coconut and pandanus trees, and we made the raft there, and a rotten raft it was; but it served our purpose, and when dark came down we shoved off, us four and two natives.

"The tide was with us; it was running out of the lagoon. The natives had canoe paddles, but they scarcely used them. Not a soul was on deck; they were all in the saloon drinking, and the noise was worse than a tavern on the Barbary Coast of a Saturday night. They wouldn't have heard us coming alongside if we had come blowing trumpets—which we didn't."

Schumer paused to refill and light his pipe. The lagoon was now a sheet of stars, and not a sound came but the murmur of the reef and the splash of a fish jumping in the lagoon.

"We came alongside, and in a minute we were over the rail—she had a low freeboard—every man of us. We didn't trouble about the raft, and she went out to sea on the tide.

"The saloon hatch was off, and there they were all crowded like bees in a bottle fighting and playing cards and drinking and smoking, and there as they sat we began to plug them with our Winchesters. We got six before the smoke of the firing hid them, and then we fired into the smoke and stood by to down them as they came up the companionway. They were plucky, but mad with drink, and they had no arms to speak of. One of them had a bottle in his hand, the only thing he could find to fight with; when he tumbled over into the lee scuppers he still held it unbroken, and I guess he went before his Maker with it like that.

"We settled them all with the exception of the bos'n. He skulked below, and I went down to find him. The saloon was clear of smoke and the swinging lamp was burning; dead men were lying everywhere, but no bos'n. He'd taken refuge in the old man's cabin and had barricaded the door, so that I couldn't kick it in—only managed to crack the paneling; so I began firing through it with my revolver, and then out he came with two bullets in him and a sheath knife in his hand.

"He gave me this cut before we had done with one another.

"The upshot was that every man of them was given his dose, and we took the schooner out of the lagoon, us four, with four Kanakas who joined the ship, and we had good luck all the rest of the voyage, though my arm inflamed so that I nearly lost it.

"So you see a trader's life out here is not all trading; one has to fight sometimes for what one gets, and to keep what one gets."

Floyd could not help thinking that Schumer's part in the recapture of the schooner had been more than he had stated.

"What's made you take to trading out here?" he asked. "You're a sailor, aren't you? At least I made the guess yesterday that you were a sailor first and a trader after."

"Yes, I began as a sailor. I served my two years before these new topsail yards made reefing child's work. I served in a Hamburg ship. What made me a trader? Well, I suppose it was the common sense that made me give up sailoring. I do not like hard manual labor. As I told you before, it was on the cards that I might have cast my lines in the newspaper world. Books interest me, written books; the world interested me, and I might have been the correspondent of newspapers. I am a fair linguist, and I can write simple English and picture fairly well what I see in words; yet I am a trader. I do not know why I am a trader in the least. It is the way of life that has come to me."

He ceased, and they sat in silence for a moment.

Floyd, looking round, saw that Isbel had vanished; she had slipped off to bed somewhere in the bush—slipped off like an animal. It was her characteristic that she was one of the shipwrecked party, yet remained apart. She helped in cooking and boat sailing and in other ways; but she lived her own life as an animal lives it, thinking her own thoughts, keeping her own counsel, speaking little. There was nothing about her of the childish and the light-hearted that stamps so many Polynesians, which is not to say that she was gloomy or too old for her years. She was just a creature apart, and had always the air of a looker-on at a game in which she helped, but which did not particularly interest her.

"The girl's gone," said Floyd.

Schumer looked round.

"Crept off to sleep; she'll sleep anywhere—in a tree or in the bush. I can't make out Kanakas. I've read a lot of stuff written about them, but there's always something behind that no one can get at. They are right down good in a lot of ways, and right down bad in others. Missionaries civilize them and varnish them over, but there's always the Kanaka underneath; they make Christians of them, but it's only on the outside. Look at that girl—she's only a child, of course, but a missionary has had the handling of her, and in the time we've been here she has turned right in on herself and gone back to her people, so to speak. She's not bad, but she's a savage, and nothing will make a savage anything else than a savage, except, maybe, on the outside."

"She seems pretty faithful and helps us all she can," said Floyd.

"Oh, she's not bad," yawned Schumer; "and she's a good deal of use in her way, and she's company of a sort, same as a dog or a cat. Well, I'm going to turn in."

He rose up and stretched himself, and looked at the starlit lagoon.

"It's funny to think there's maybe a fortune in pearls under all that," said he, "no knowing—but it will take some getting."

"We'll get it if it's there," said Floyd.

CHAPTER V
DREDGING

They were up at dawn, and the fire was crackling and the coffee heating before the sun had fully shown itself over the eastern reef line.

Schumer had been able to salve cooking utensils and some unbroken crockery ware from the *Tonga*, to say nothing of knives and forks and spoons.

It seems a small matter, but a knife and a fork make all the difference when one comes to food, even on an island of the Pacific—a plate, too.

Condemned to eat with one's fingers and to share a knife in common, one feeds, but one does not eat.

There was condensed milk for the coffee, ship's bread and salt pork fried over the fire. Isbel had collected some plantains; they went into the frying pan to help the pork. She had also gathered some drupes from a pandanus tree growing near the wreck, and served them on a big leaf.

"There's a whole lot of seeds aboard somewhere," said Schumer, as they breakfasted; "onions and carrots and so on; I must hunt for them, and when we have time I'll see how they grow here. You can grow anything on these islands. The soil's the best in the world; maybe because of the gull guano. We'll want all the native-grown food we can get here, if things turn out as I expect, for we'll have to feed the labor we bring, and natives aren't happy without the stuff they are used to. Corned beef and spuds are all very well in their way, but it's breadfruit and taro and plantains that are the stand-by. Fortunately there seems lots. You see all that dark-green stuff growing over there straight across the lagoon—that's breadfruit; big trees, too, and the coconuts aren't bad.

"When we get the labor we'll have a main camp over by the fishing ground. I've been thinking it all out. There's no natural water there, but I noticed yesterday a big rain pond in the coral; it must have been cut out by natives some time or another. The funny thing about these ponds is that the water is saltish at high tides, but gets fresh with the ebb. In some of the islands the natives stock them with fish, salt-water fish swimming in fresh.

"Then we have the fishing to fall back on, and the lagoon is full. Yes, we are not badly placed as things go."

They placed the dredge on board the boat and some food for the midday meal, and pushed off, leaving Isbel behind to look after the camp and keep an eye out for ships. At the sight of a sail anywhere on the sea she was to light the fire and make a smoke with green wood, and she had a splendid lookout post, for the deck of the *Tonga*, onto which she could easily climb, gave a complete view of the horizon from all directions.

Then they rowed off, leaving her watching them, a solitary figure on the beach.

"Seems she'll be a bit lonely," said Floyd.

"Not she," replied Schumer; "she'll be happy enough alone, and she has lots to do between washing up and keeping a lookout. Kanakas are never lonely; it's a disease of civilization."

"You look upon these people as if they were animals," said Floyd.

"Which they are," replied Schumer—"animals dressed in human skin."

Floyd said nothing. He was not a psychologist or a philosopher, but a man of action; yet he gauged something of the strange make-up of Schumer's mind. Here was a man of keen intelligence, a quoter of Scheffel, an appreciator of beauty, apparently a kindly individual, but in some respects apparently hard beyond belief, and in others apparently blind.

Floyd had some knowledge of the Polynesian natives, he was gaining some knowledge of Schumer, and he was to gain more knowledge of both—of the civilized man and the savage and their respective worth.

They got to work in two-fathom water on the northern edge of the great bed. They stripped for the business. Both men were good swimmers and expert divers, and the dredge did its work fairly well. They agreed to take the diving business in half-hour tricks, one remaining in the boat with a view to possible sharks, though sharks were scarcely to be feared in that part of the lagoon, and to keep the boat moving when the dredge was in operation.

Floyd was the first to go down. At a depth of twelve feet it was as bright almost as at the surface. The water seemed to hold light in solution; glancing up, the white-painted boat floating like a balloon above him showed a tinge of rose; passing scraps of focus were all spangled and sparkled over as though powdered with jewel dust; his arm, newly immersed, was diamonded by tiny beads of air. In this silent, brilliant world of crystal and color one only wanted gills to find life in perfection and fairyland in material form.

There were few fish here, but occasionally a colored phantom would slow up, pause, and whisk off, fry would pass like a flight of silver needles, and great jellyfish quartered like melons and absolutely invisible till glimpsed by reflected light.

All these things he noticed in his first submersion; after that the labor of the business prevented him from noticing anything much except the work on hand, cruel and murderously hard work to the man unused to it. The dredge was almost useless at first; it had to be taken up and altered, then, as it was dragged along, he followed it, helping it, picking up loose oysters and putting them in the bag. He could only work for less than half a minute at a time, coming up for a two minutes' breathing spell, and as he worked he could feel now and then what seemed a warm wind trying to blow him aside as the wind blows thistledown. It was the swell of the incoming tide.

They had arranged to work in half-hour tricks, but they found this absolutely impossible; before the end of the first twenty minutes Floyd confessed himself beaten and Schumer took his place.

An hour before noon they knocked off. They had taken a large quantity of oysters, despite the limited means at their disposal, enough to sink the boat a strake or two and give them an hour's work in unloading and spreading their catch on the coral on the windward side of the reef.

Then they took three hours' rest under the shade of the trees. At sundown they had completed their day's work, and they felt as though they had been laboring for fifty years.

They had overdone it.

Though they had dived as little as possible during the second half of the day's work, using the dredge as much as they could, the work had nearly broken them, owing to the sudden and tremendous strain put on their lungs.

Schumer recognized the reason of their exhaustion.

"We should have broken ourselves to it by degrees," said he—"done a couple of hours' work instead of a whole day's. We are fools. We didn't want to strip the lagoon; we were only after a sample, and could have taken a week over it. Well, we can take things easy to-morrow."

They rowed back to the camp and found Isbel waiting for them, and supper.

They had come back in low spirits, but after supper and a cup of coffee the surprising thing happened—their spirits jumped up as though under the influence of alcohol. Prolonged strain in diving produces these results—the tissues that have been starved or partly starved of oxygen reabsorb it with renewed vigor.

They lay on the sand and smoked and talked, and Floyd built castles and furnished them with his prospective fortune.

"Suppose," said he, "we strike it rich—very rich—what may we net out of this?"

"It all depends," said Schumer, "if this is a real pearl lagoon; anything up to a hundred thousand, and maybe more. Pearls are a disease, and the disease is more prevalent in some waters than others. I don't know why, no one does. It may be the temperature or the stuff the water holds in solution, it may be the breed of the oyster; but there you have it. Every oyster under the sun is a pearl oyster, at least may be capable of growing pearls. I found a pearl once in an oyster which I was eating in a restaurant in Hamburg. It wasn't a big pearl, but it was a pearl. I sold it for thirty marks. But one thing is sure, it's only in tropical and subtropical waters that you find pearls of any account or to any account. It's only in the tropics and subtropics you find color and stuff that's rich and worth having. The north—pah! What does it give us? Iron and tin, wood, copper. It's the south where the gold is, where the pearls are. Why, the very earth in the south hides color and riches! Where are the diamond mines? In Africa and Brazil. The ruby and emerald mines? In Burma and Brazil and India. The gold? California and Africa. The silver? Peru. Look at the birds; there's not a colored bird in the north that hasn't come from the south; look at the shells and the corals, and the flowers and the people; look at the sun. No, the south holds everything worth having or seeing. You ask me what I would do if I were rich? Well, I would not go north, or only for a while. I'd stay in the south, fix my home somewhere not too close to the equator, take an island in these seas, and have it for my own."

"Can you buy islands?"

"You can buy land; one might buy a small island from some of the governments, or rent it; but I'd sooner have the most land in a big island than the whole of a little one. Once you have got your grip on land you have power. Nothing else gives you so much power; funny, that, isn't it? Money, you would say, gives power. It only gives the power to buy or to meddle in other people's affairs through paid agents. If you have got your grip on the earth, and the things that come out of it, and the people who live on it, you have power; and power is the only thing worth having in the world."

"Good Lord!" said Floyd. "There's a lot of things I'd sooner have."

"And what things may those be?"

"Well, I want to have a good time and see other people having a good time. I want to travel, not as the mate of an old hooker like the *Cormorant*, but as a man with money in his pocket and time to look around him. I want to be able to buy things. I want to dress decently and to marry some time or another and settle down. I'm fond of horses, though I've never had the chance to own one; and I'm fond of cricket, though I've never touched a bat for years. I'm fond of a jolly good dinner, and I'm fond of a good cigar. To get all those things one wants money."

"And all those things come to you if you have power," said Schumer. "It implies everything material, and much more. It's the sense of it, the feeling 'I am the stronger man,' that gives the mind freedom and ease to enjoy what money can bring. You are entirely English; you want enjoyment and luxury without foundation of strength."

"Oh, good heavens!" said Floyd, "I think we have a pretty solid foundation of strength; we own half the earth, and we hold it—why? Simply because we live and let live. We don't try to grind people down with what you call power. We give them power, liberty, whatever you like to call it. Now you are a man who has traveled, and so am I. Can you tell me any spot on earth that a man may be really free in that's not under the Union Jack or the Stars and Stripes? Take the German colonies, the Dutch; haven't you always some pesky official shoving his nose into your affairs? Take the very port officers and customs, and it's the same all through the country as well as on the coast. You can't breathe in these places the same as you can where there's a decent English or American administration. I've heard foreigners wondering how it is we hold India—all those hundreds of millions of natives under the rule of a few thousand white men. As a matter of fact, we don't hold it at all; it holds itself. A native in Bombay is as free as a duke in Piccadilly; that's our secret."

Schumer laughed.

"And at any moment," said he, "those very free natives are ready to rise in their hundreds of millions and cut your throats."

"I don't think so," said Floyd. "Men don't cut the throats of their best friends."

Schumer yawned.

To argue with Schumer was like pressing against India rubber—the pressure left no impression.

They talked for a while longer on indifferent subjects, and then turned in under the shelter of the tent.

The night was almost windless, and the great southern stars stood out like jewels crusting the whole dome of the sky from sea edge to sea edge.

The Milky Way, like a vast band of white smoke cut by the terrific pit of a coal sack, Canopus, and the Cross, filled the world with the mystery of starlight.

Away out on the weather side of the reef near the wreck, and clear in the starlight against the coral, was seated a figure. It was Isbel. She had not yet turned into whatever haunt she had in the bush, and with her knees drawn up and clasped by her hands she was watching the regular fall of the breakers.

The child seemed under the spell of the vast sea, an atom in face of the infinite.

CHAPTER VI
RISK OF WAR

"You can't get pearls from oysters till the oysters are rotten," said Schumer next morning, as they sat after breakfast consulting on the day's work. "Of course, you could take every individual fresh oyster and hunt under its beard; but you know how an oyster sticks to its shell even after it is opened, and you can fancy the work it would be. Once they are decayed they are mushy, and the work is easy though it's not pleasant. But it's surprising how quick you get used to it. We worked pretty hard yesterday, and I propose to take it easy this morning, and then a bit later on I want to have a regular overhaul of the saloon and trade room of the old *Tonga*. We have cleared the way pretty well, but I've been so busy catching stores in the bush that I've never had time for an overhaul. You see there was only Isbel and me to do the job. I expect the oysters we laid out yesterday will be fit to work on to-morrow."

"You've done this pearl business before," said Floyd.

Schumer laughed.

"I have helped in pearling, if that's what you mean, but I have never had any luck. I once had my hand on a fortune in pearls, but it did not come off.

"There was a French island in these seas, no matter where—it wasn't a thousand miles from the Marquesas. It was a double lagoon island, shaped like an hourglass; no use to look at, not enough trees to give any amount of copra. It had done a little business in sandalwood in the old days, but that was all gone. But the place wasn't deserted. There was an old Frenchman in charge; he had rented it under the French government, and he lived there with his two sons, and seemed happy enough, though doing next to no trade.

"I was in the outer lagoon twice as supercargo of a trading schooner; once we put in for water, and the second time we called on the chance of picking up a little copra. Lefarge was the old man's name, and he was a great fisherman; said he lived there mostly for the fishing and to have an easy life.

"Yet somehow he struck me as a man who would not be content to spend his time fishing and sitting in the sun, and his two boys struck me the same.

"When I wanted to explore the island and get round by the reef to the main lagoon he said that was forbidden, the natives held it taboo to white men, and so on.

"Then I began to suspect, and the only one thing I could suspect was shell, and maybe pearls.

"The more I thought of it the more sure I was; but, of course, I could do nothing; the place was his, and whatever it held, and we were peaceful traders, not pirates. So, when we had loaded with all the copra he could give us, out we put, wishing him good health and good luck in his fishing.

"Two days from the island we met a mail brigantine, and she signaled us that war had been declared between France and Germany, and our captain—Max Schuster was his name—began to swear, for we were bound for the Marquesas, which are French, and we'd have to alter our course and lose consignments and trade, and he sat down on a mooring bit, and cursed war and the French till I took him by the arm and led him down the saloon and explained what was in my mind.

"I told him of my suspicions about the island, and he pricked up his ears. Then, when I had been talking to him about ten minutes and explaining and arguing, he suddenly took fire.

"It's surprising how a dull man will refuse to be convinced—*won't* see, till all at once, when he does see, he'll rush at what you show him harder than the best.

"Schuster, when he saw fully the advantage of his position, little risk, and everything to gain, rushed up on deck. In less than five minutes the schooner was showing her tail to the Marquesas and making a long board for the island.

"Our crew were mostly Swedes, Kanakas, and an Irishman, and when they heard the news that Schuster had to tell them they were his to a man. The French were not much in favor just then; they had Noumea tacked on to their name, and the ordinary sailor loves a bit of a fight or any break in the monotony of sea life. We had plenty of trade rifles, Albinis—not the best sort of rifle, but good enough for us—and plenty of ammunition.

"We lifted the island at dawn on the second day, and were anchored in the lagoon a few hours later.

"Old Lefarge was on the beach tinkering a canoe. He didn't seem surprised to see us come in with the German flag flying at the peak, nor did his sons, who came out of the frame house set back among the bushes. They thought we had sickness or something on board, for they made no offer to put out to us. We lowered a boat on the port side, which was the side away from the beach, and got our men in and the rifles, and then rowed ashore.

"When they saw us landing they took fright, but our men covered them with their rifles, and Schuster and I came up to the old man and his sons and told them that war was declared, and that they were prisoners.

"They could do nothing, and they just gave in. We had them taken on board the schooner, and then we went to the frame house, and there, sure enough, in a big safe, were the pearls. We had searched the prisoners and taken their keys from them. The key of the safe was among them, and we opened it easily. There were twenty thousand pounds' worth of pearls, so we judged.

"Schuster was a man who always held tight by the law. I pointed out to him that since we were at war with France all French property belonged to us by rights, and that the best thing we could do was to land the prisoners and take the pearls. We did not want prisoners. I pointed out to him, also, that we were acting in the nature of privateers, but without a letter of marque, and that consequently our prize would go to the government, and we would get nothing.

"I pointed out that since this was French property it would be much better just to take it and be thankful, and say nothing. He said that would be piracy."

"So it would," said Floyd.

"Well, maybe it would; but what is war if not piracy legalized? You have a letter of marque and you are a privateer, you have none and you are a pirate."

"But even privateering has ceased," objected Floyd.

"Well," said Schumer, "if it has it ought to be renewed in war time; it breeds fine men, as you English ought to know, and it's every bit as legitimate as fighting behind naval guns. However, Schuster thought different about our case. He said he would take the whole lot, prisoners and pearls, to the nearest German island, and claim a share of the proceeds, and be within the law.

"So off we set, and it took us nearly three weeks to reach the island we were in search of, between head winds and calms. When we got there it was getting on for night, so we held off and on till morning, and when the pilot came aboard we gave him news of the war, and several canoes that had put out shot back to land with it; so that when we entered the harbor the place was decked with flags, and we were cheered right from the harbor mouth to the quay."

Schumer paused for a light, and went on:

"We landed our prisoners and the pearls, and the governor had laid a big spread for us, baked pig and lager beer, and so on, and Schuster was in the middle of a speech when the sound of a gun brought us all out on the beach, and there, entering the harbor, was the German cruiser of the station.

"The captain landed and asked us what we were doing with the flags, and when we explained he told us that there was no war, only a lying rumor. He had the latest European news from San Francisco, and he gave it to us.

"It was worth going through the whole of that business to see Schuster's face. He said nothing, and the governor said nothing, and it was fortunate they held their tongues, for the cruiser only waited four hours to water and put off again.

"When she had gone the governor bundled old Lefarge and his sons on board our schooner and the pearls, and he gave us orders to take them back to their island and dump them there, and he sent an armed guard to see that it was done. He judged, and judged rightly, that Lefarge would make no trouble afterward, simply because he would not want to advertise the existence of his island. He made them a present of a few cases of California champagne and some cigars, and old Lefarge was so glad to be out of the business and get back his pearls that he insisted on opening the champagne, and Schuster brought out some trade gin, and they all got drunk.

"There was a big moon that night, and they enjoyed themselves, Lefarge singing 'Deutschland, Deutschland über alles,' and the governor the 'Marseillaise.'

"Then they started fighting, and then they got sick.

"Men are strange things, once they let themselves go, and they are all pretty much alike when they are drunk."

"You took them back to their island?" said Floyd.

"Yes, and then we had to return and bring back the armed guard. Schuster lost nearly two months over the business, to say nothing of the provisions and loss of trade. He said he wanted to sink the mail brigantine that had given us the lie; but you can't sink a ship by wanting to. Well, let's get to work."

They rose up and crossed the coral to the wreck. She was lying at a slant that made it just possible to walk her decks without holding on to anything; her copper was already dull green, and the barnacles, long dead, showed up like bosses on the copper green like it, as though the verdigris had invaded them. The sun had boiled out the pitch of the planking, and the decks were warping, the planks bursting up from the dowels.

The great "dunch" she had received from the coral in beaching had shaken everything loose; the bowsprit had sprung up from the knightheads; all forward of the great breach in her side the planking was loosened from the ribs, and only wanted another storm to break away and give the sea a clean sweep of the interior of the hull.

But leaving aside the ravages of the sea, the work of ruin was going steadily on under the influence of weather and sun. A ship out of water is dead, and death means corruption. On the reefs and beaches of the ocean you will see wrecks, carcasses of ships, skeletons with the blue sky showing through their ribs. They have been eaten by the weather more than by the sea.

They reached the deck of the *Tonga,* and made their way down the companionway to the main cabin.

There was plenty of light through the broken sides of the vessel, and the sunshine from the outside world showed up the interior and was reflected by the varnished pine paneling and by a strip of mirror still absolutely intact. The table in the center was still standing, and above it the swinging lamp all askew, an empty bird cage lay in one corner, and all sorts of raffle littered the floor.

The captain and chief mate's cabin lay aft, and Schumer, opening the doors and fixing them so, began a thorough overhaul of the contents. He had already salved the ship's money and papers, the nautical instruments, charts, and books; what remained was mostly private property, and there was not very much of it. Some clothes, underwear, and boots and shoes made up the pile, together with native curios, cheap novels, some writing materials, and two revolvers with ammunition.

"It'll all come in handy some time or another," said Schumer, "and I propose that we stuff the lot back into the old man's cabin; they'll be as safe there as anywhere, unless another big storm comes and makes a clean sweep of everything. Now let's have another go at the cargo."

They had no need to enter the hold by the main hatch. The damaged side gave them ample means of entry. The confusion was appalling.

Schumer had already salved a quantity of canned stuff. Unable to move the boxes and crates, he had broken them open with an ax and removed the contents piecemeal; but, having only Isbel to help, and no very urgent incentive to the work, he had done comparatively little. Now, with the prospect of remaining on the island and the necessity of feeding possible labor when the time came for working the lagoon, it was a different matter.

Floyd, however, did not see it in the same light as Schumer, and when, after an hour's work carrying stuff across the coral, they knocked off for a rest, he put his ideas before the other.

"Look here," said he, "it's all very well breaking our backs over this business, but we haven't got the labor to feed yet; we'll have to go to Sydney or 'Frisco to get the money raised, and it may be six months after we are taken from here before we can get back, maybe longer. Then the chap that finances this business will do the provisioning of the expedition. I don't see the point in harvesting this stuff under the trees, especially as it's safe enough in the wreck."

"Now, see here," said Schumer, "if you are not prepared for everything in this world you never get anywhere. You say the stuff is safe enough on the wreck; I say it isn't. First, there's the heat of the sun, which doesn't improve it. Secondly, there's the chance of a hurricane making a clean sweep of everything. The tail end of a big storm landed her where she is; the front end of another may finish her. You say that it may take us six months or more before we can start on our business—who knows? Who knows that a likely ship may not call here with some man in charge of her who would join us in the venture? I would sooner have a decent shipowner in it than some American or Australian financier. You never know what may occur, and here is a lot of stuff that may save the situation when the time comes. No, we have got to get it safe, and get it safe we will, not only provisions, but as much of the trade as we can manage. It's all money, and you can do nothing without money, either in these seas or in Europe. So we'll just stick to this business, and we'll cover the cached lots over with sailcloth—we have lots of that. We had better stick to it for a week right on and get it over. I've been thinking about it ever since this morning, and something tells me that we'd be fools to bother about the lagoon, which is safe as a bank, while the stuff that will help to raid that bank is in danger."

"Suppose there are no pearls in those oysters of any account?"

"There's always the shell," replied Schumer, "and there are sure to be pearls. You are of the disbelieving sort."

"Not a bit—only—well, perhaps you are right. I'm not going to shirk any work that may be useful—and when do you propose to examine those oysters we fetched up yesterday?"

"I'll leave them a week," said Schumer; "the longer they are left the more rotten they'll be, and the easier to work. Besides, if we found no pearls, it would take the heart out of us, and, more than that, the hope of finding pearls when we do go will put the heart into us. Nothing is better to make one work than a pleasant prospect not quite assured in front of one. It's the gambling instinct—a big instinct."

Floyd laughed. There was something about the man Schumer that held him more and more and compelled belief and the admiration that all men have for strength and foresight. Schumer did a lot of thinking as well as working. He had said nothing up to this moment of abandoning the oyster business for a week and putting all their energies into the salving of provisions and trade—he had been thinking out the whole plan in silence. He disliked the labor of the salvage business as much as Floyd, but he imposed it on himself as means to a distant end, and Floyd, though he did not see the end in the same light as his companion, was not the man to hold back when another was working.

"I am with you," said he. "It will give us exercise, anyhow, and it's better than diving. Come on and let's get at it."

He revenged himself by outvying Schumer in energy. They worked stripped to the waist.

They had set themselves a herculean task. It was not only a question of conveying small goods piecemeal in extemporized baskets; it was a business also of carrying heavy stuff, bolts of cotton, and so forth that could not be divided up.

There was not only the conveying to be done, but the storing. In this nature helped them. The reef, or, rather, the island that formed this part of the atoll had a big sink in it amid the grove at the back of their encampment. Schumer thought that in ancient days natives must have made this hollow by artificial means for some reason or other, possibly as a big rain pond, though that supposition seemed negatived by the existence of the natural well that lay in the western border of the grove. However, it had been formed there. It was almost a pit, a hundred yards long, shelving toward the ends and densely protected by trees to seaward. Schumer calculated that owing to this density of vegetation and the fact of the ends having drainage into the lagoon, this trench would not fill up, let the rain come heavy as it might. On the fact that the waves from the heaviest sea could not reach it he was assured by the configuration of the outside reef.

He had fixed on a week's work, and at the end of that time, though they had done much, they had not done all; still, he seemed satisfied, as well he might be.

They had cached all the provisions, they had salved a fair portion of the perishable trade, and covered this portion of the salvage with sailcloth, and of all their work this was the most laborious and trying. They had removed the rifles, fifty in number, from their cases, and stored them with the ammunition in a separate cache; they had four navy revolvers of the Colt type, and these with the ammunition for them they kept in the tent. Last, but not least, there was the liquor—cases of trade gin, and a few cases of wine.

Schumer did not bother to cache these—he dealt with them in another fashion.

"It's waste of money," said he, "but I have been thinking it out. This square face is no use to man or brute; it's only good to sell, and we have no customers for it, and don't want them. It's dangerous stuff to have about. The wine is different; there's not much of it, and it may turn in useful, but the gin has to go."

He opened the cases, and they smashed the bottles, heaving them on to the raw coral beyond the wreck, so that the glass might not be in the way. The air stank with the fumes of the filthy stuff while the smashing went on. Isbel helped, the instinct for destruction that lies in human nature, and especially in children, seemed to have wakened up in her to its full.

She laughed over the work. Floyd had never seen her laugh before, and as he looked at her shining eyes and flashing teeth it seemed to him that despite all the labors of the missionary here was an atom of fighting and destructive force, useful for good or evil, and only waiting on events for its development.

CHAPTER VII
THE BLACK PEARL

The next morning they started for the oyster ground. There had been strong winds blowing for the last week and big seas tumbling along the reef, the spray finding the oysters that they had put out on the coral, otherwise they might not only have rotted, but dried up. As it was, they were just in the prime of their horribleness.

"Good heavens!" said Floyd, as they set to work. "This is worse than salving cargo—a jolly sight worse even than diving."

"You'll get used to it," said Schumer, "and if it's any comfort to you to know it's worse for me than you, for I have an olfactory sense more acute than ordinary. Get more to windward of your work. You ought to know that as a sailor."

"Upon my word!" said Floyd, "these things must have half stunned me; they are enough to make one forget one's instincts, even. Go ahead, I won't complain."

He got to windward, and the stiff breeze helped matters considerably. Schumer had brought a piece of sailcloth, also a canvas bucket, which they filled as required from a reef pool near by.

Every shell was searched and washed over the canvas, Schumer, with the eye and hand of an expert, doing the manipulation while Floyd poured the water in trickles as required.

Dozen by dozen the shells were explored, drained of their mushy contents, and flung away. Not a pearl showed.

Floyd forgot everything in the excitement of the moment. He had no longer a sense of smell, and then, as the heap of shells steadily grew without sign or symptom of what they were in search of, his spirits fell.

"Pour away," said Schumer; "this is only the beginning of the business; there's no knowing what is to come. Ah, here's something!"

He stood up, poured some water into the palm of his hand, examined what was in his palm, and then held out his dripping hand to Floyd.

In the palm lay a small black stone about the size of a pea.

"What is it?" asked Floyd.

Schumer laughed.

"Only a black pearl, worth maybe a hundred dollars. But it's fortune, all the same. We have struck it! A hundred dollars for half an hour's work for two men. It's good!"

He sat down on the coral, while Floyd, now deeply excited, took his seat beside him. The gulls cried and wheeled overhead, and the sun burned on the blue sea and the foam of the reef, and the wind blew the spray in their faces as they sat handing their treasure from one to the other, examining it and gloating over it.

Washed and dried now, its luster appeared. It was a perfect black pearl, not large, but of splendid quality, globular and slightly flattened on one side.

"It's worth more even than I thought at first," said Schumer. "It's a beauty. Well, we mustn't chuckle too soon; it may be the only pearl in the lagoon, though I don't think so. And the shell is of fine quality; all the indications are good."

"I thought all pearls were white," said Floyd. "Of course, I know nothing about them, and the only ones I have seen were in shop windows."

"And most likely false, at that," said Schumer. "No. Pearls are not all white. I don't know what makes the color in them, but there it is. Some are black like this, and a few are pink, and I've seen some gray—they aren't much good. Pink are the rarest, then come black, then white. Well, I'll put this fellow in my match box, and now let's get to work again."

He put the pearl in the match box and the box in the pocket of his coat, which he had taken off. Then, having placed a lump of coral on the coat to prevent any chance of the wind blowing it about, they returned to work.

They worked right through the whole take of shell, and the sun was setting when they had finished. The result was triumphant.

Twelve pearls was the harvest, including the black. Four of these were quite inconsiderable, but of good quality; four more, though larger, were not of good shape or quality, but there were three white beauties. The largest, Schumer estimated at a thousand dollars and over, the next largest at less than a thousand, and the third at five hundred.

There were also some seed pearls, tiny things like nits' eggs.

"If the whole lagoon pays up like that," said Floyd, "we'll be rich ten times over."

Schumer shook his head.

"We can't tell. Nothing is more uncertain than pearling. We are sure to find blank streaks, and it's possible we may have just struck the richest corner. In a lagoon like this a lot depends on the different temperatures, the depth, and the rush of the currents. But we've done well, and a lot better than I expected."

They set off back across the lagoon to their camping place, and the day's take was placed in the box with the ship's money. Schumer had suggested to Floyd that the money of the *Cormorant* should be placed with that of the *Tonga* in the same box, and Floyd had agreed, seeing the wisdom of centralizing their treasure so that in eventualities it might be more easily protected.

Together with the pearls the hoard made now a very respectable show, though Floyd had pointed out that the *Cormorant* money, being Coxon's, must not be counted in their mutual assets. Schumer had agreed, though evidently with reservations. The money of the *Tonga* was a different matter; he seemed to look on it as his own. Never once did he refer to it in other terms, nor had he told Floyd the name of the *Tonga's* skipper.

Floyd did not press the point—it was a matter entirely to do with Schumer.

CHAPTER VIII
THE LAST OF THE WRECK

That night, as they sat by the camp fire they noticed a great confusion among the gulls.

They seemed quarreling all along the western side of the reef. The voice of the gulls was one of the familiar sounds of the island, but not after dark. To-night they were clamorous.

They broke out again before dawn, and Floyd, listening, noticed a new note in their voices. They seemed not quarreling one with another, but against some common enemy. Then the sound died away little by little, and when he came out of the tent there was not a gull to be seen near the reef opening, where as a rule they congregated in numbers.

The sunrise was clouded, and the sun did not strike the sea till half an hour later than his ordinary time. The wind that had been blowing so strongly yesterday had died away, yet the boom of the surf on the reef was louder than on the day before.

Floyd crossed the reef close to the wreck and looked seaward.

A glacial calm held the sea, a calm underrun by a tremendous swell. A long, tremendous swell, an infinite heaving of the very depths of the ocean finding expression here in acre-wide undulations, solemn, slow to the eye, rhythmical and sonorous.

The beating of the breakers seemed ruled by a metronome.

There was no little wave and big wave, no hesitation of the sea. The breakers were equidistant and equal in volume, and their pace was set to the same funeral march.

Schumer came out of the tent, and, catching sight of Floyd, walked toward him.

"There must be a lot of damp or electricity or something in the air," said he. "I feel like a rag."

"Look at the sea," said Floyd; "there has been a big storm somewhere, if I am not greatly mistaken."

Schumer stood looking at the sea.

The sun seemed bright as ever, yet the water did not respond to his light; it had at once a surface brilliancy and a dullness in its depths. Toward the shore it was bottle green, and even the blue far out had a trace of tourmaline.

Schumer said nothing, and turned away to the camping place, where Isbel was making the fire.

"Shall we go on with the diving to-day?" asked Floyd, as they breakfasted.

"I don't feel like work," said Schumer; "besides, I doubt if it would be any use. There's a huge, big storm coming, if I am not mistaken. I feel it in my skin, and I feel it in my nerves. I suppose it's the electricity in the air, but I believe I'd spark if you touched me with a bit of metal. Listen! There go the gulls again."

Away on the reef beyond the fishing ground, so far away that their voices came indistinctly on the windless air, the gulls were crying again, and, standing up, Floyd could see them in wild flight about the reef like scraps of blown white paper.

Then they rose higher, continued their argument, and began to recede.

"They are off," said Floyd; "going out seaward, the whole lot of them. By Jove, that looks like business!"

"They know what's coming," said Schumer, "and they are clearing out of the track. Wonder what tells them. Instinct, I suppose."

He set off to examine the cache, taking Floyd with him. He had covered the perishable stuff with sailcloth, and he now set to make the lashings more secure. They worked an hour, and when they came out again the sun had lost his brilliancy—a vague mist hid the horizon on every side.

In the northwest this thickness seemed more dense, and the sea, still glassing in and breaking in rhythmical thunder on the reef, had turned to the color of lead.

But for the noise of the surf the silence was now absolute and complete.

It held so till noon, when a wind began to stir the palm tops; a wind that seemed to come from nowhere, rocking them and tossing them hither and thither, making cat's-paws on the lagoon, and flicking at the tent canvas like a worrying hand.

Schumer took down the tent.

He had already placed the valuables in a place of safety. He had dug out a hole beneath one of the trees and buried the cash box containing the money and pearls.

"You never know," he said, "if it's a cyclone that's coming. Nothing is safe above ground. A cyclone would lift an anvil; anyhow, this will be safe enough."

An hour after noon the great storm showed itself.

Away above the northwestern horizon a black line appeared, hard and distinct as the outline of a country.

It did not seem to advance—it rose. Till now it assumed the appearance of a wall. As it rose, it lightened to a dark copper color, and as it rose it lengthened, so that now it occupied the whole horizon from east to west.

The rapidity of this development was appalling, and the sun, as if shrinking before the coming attack, paled still more, dimmed as by a partial eclipse.

Now the wind came steady and strong, whipping the lagoon and bending the foliage, and then all at once dying away again into absolute stillness.

It was in this great pause that they heard a sound never to be forgotten; less a sound than a vibration—deep and almost musical, like the vibration of a great glass rubbed by a wet finger.

Isbel, who had remained on the reef near the wreck while the two men had gone for a moment toward the lagoon edge, called out suddenly, and they turned and came toward her.

Even as they turned, the first blast of the wind struck them, and, battling against it, they reached where the girl was crouching, pointing to the sea.

The sea beyond the limit of a mile or so was flat as a board, beaten to a dead level by the coming wind and white as frosted silver.

They did not wait to see more; turning, crouching, running as swiftly as possible, and nearly lifted from their feet, they made for the shelter of the grove. They heard the coconuts torn from the palms striking the sand, and Floyd had a momentary vision of nuts hitting the lagoon like round shot fired by artillery, and then the whole solid world seemed to smash like a ball of glass, as the blaze of lightning and the concussion of the first peal of thunder shook the island as a drum skin is shaken by the stroke of the stick.

Floyd felt Isbel nestling close to him like a frightened animal, and he put his arm round her to protect her. He heard Schumer calling out something, but what he could not tell. The wind had now followed on the thunder in its fullest force, and it yelled.

No earthly sound could be compared to that ceaseless, mad, devilish yell that seemed the expression of all the ferocity of all the ferocious things that had ever inhabited the earth.

It was enmity made vocal. The enmity of the infinite and eternal.

And there was no rain. For a moment Floyd thought that there was no rain; then, lying on his stomach and crawling a bit forward, he saw the rain.

It was not falling, it was driving across the lagoon in a great sheet upheld by the wind, and the lightning when it struck again showed through a roof of water.

Then, the first rush of the wind slackening, the rain, upheld no longer, came down with a roar.

"It's not a cyclone," Schumer shouted to Floyd; "it's just a storm—the grandfather of all storms!"

His voice was cut off by the voice of the sea, that had now added itself to the wind and the thunder.

The sea, no longer beaten flat, had risen in its might, and was raiding the reef. The sound was like the roar of a railway train in a tunnel. Something of the vibration reached them through the ground they were lying on.

They were wet through, but safe. The grove had weathered many a storm; the position of the trees and their relationship to the reef rendered this spot an impregnable stronghold.

Away on the opposite side of the lagoon breadfruit trees were being broken down, but here not a tree went, though the palms were bending like tandem whips and the leaves being torn from the artus.

As time passed, the sea began to rise more and more, while the face of the wind lost its first edge.

Toward evening the waves were making a clean breach of the reef by the wreck, and when dark set in, though the wind had lessened still more, the sea had risen in an inverse proportion, and they guessed the reason. The tide was flooding.

Then came new sounds. The wreck was going. The bones of the *Tonga* were being crunched by the wolves of the sea. They heard the noise of the tearing of timber from timber, the roll and rumble of balks awash on the coral, and then, worn out and huddled together under a piece of canvas which they dragged from the cache covering, they fell asleep, sure that the worst of the business was over.

When they awoke, the sun was shining, but the wind was still blowing half a gale. The fury of the storm had been in its first impact, but the fury of the sea was now even greater than during the night.

The waves were mountainous, and the reef where the wreck had lain was unapproachable, but the sun made up for everything.

They crawled out and sat on the sand, drying themselves in the sunshine, stiff and chill from the damp, and feeling like people recovering from an illness.

"That storm has been traveling a great distance," said Schumer, "and we got only the butt end of it That's what made it blow out so soon. A storm is like a man—it has only a certain length of life, and the farther it travels the more it loses in size. It doesn't seem to lose in force, only in *size*.

"This big sea shows that a big track of the Pacific has been stirred up. This sea will travel right down to the Horn, and it will last for days here. Look at the lagoon!"

The lagoon was strewn with wreckage, spars and planking and ribs floated near the shore, moving as if gently stirred by some giant's finger in the wind-whipped water; the reef, as far as they could see, was washed free of any trace of the wreck that had lain there the day before.

"It's a good business we salved the stuff out of her," said Floyd. "Your business, too, that was, for if I had been left to myself I wouldn't have troubled."

"I'll go and look at the stuff presently," said Schumer. "I believe it won't have been hurt by the rain—at least, the perishable stuff—I was too careful about the packing; and the drainage is all right—people rarely think of that. It doesn't do stuff any harm to be rained on if it is properly covered; what does matter is soaking. Yes, it's just as well we moved in time. Now let us get to work."

A fire was impossible, as there was not a dry stick to be found anywhere, so they breakfasted on canned meat and biscuit, and then set to work to examine the cache.

There was two feet of water in the cache, all the rest had run off to the lagoon by the drainage afforded at the two ends. Schumer had packed the perishable goods on top—they were quite unharmed. Having satisfied themselves on this point, they returned to the beach and the sea.

The wind had fallen still more, but the sea was still furious.

"It will be less over there on the reef by the fishing ground," said Schumer, "and we can begin again with the diving work to-morrow!"

CHAPTER IX
A WEEK'S WORK

Next day, though the sea still held, the wind had fallen completely, and the lagoon, protected by the reef, was calm, though heaving slightly to the impetus from without.

All the water close to the reef opening was wreck strewn, a section of deck floated like a raft, and they had to exercise care in navigating the boat.

"If we had hands enough," said Schumer, "all that stuff might come in useful to build a house with, or some sort of shanty that would give more protection than the tent. We'll want something in the rainy season. But there is no use in bothering, we haven't the hands."

When they arrived at the fishing ground they landed and found the heap of shells they had left scattered and almost vanished.

"That will teach us in future," said Schumer. "We must find some means of protecting the stuff in case of storms; those old rain pools would do if we could only drain them, but we can't without labor. It's always want of labor that has stopped us. Well, we'll get it some day."

Though no real business could be done on the fishery till more help was obtainable, the temptation to work was irresistible.

Those first pearls were always in their minds. It was humanly impossible to rest content with that sample, and refrain from the attempt to get more, even in face of the exhausting labor of diving and dredging.

But they worked less ambitiously now, and so carefully that the day's take of shell did not amount to half the take on the first day. As a result they were fresh when they knocked off, instead of being worn out.

They left the oysters to rot, and so it went on day by day, till at the end of the week they knocked off the diving one evening and contemplated their handiwork. Each day's take had been placed separately, and the first day's was now "ripe," to use Schumer's expression.

"We'll start on it to-morrow," said he, "and go through it slowly so that there may be no chance of anything escaping; the dredge wants mending, too—we'd better do that to-night after supper. Isbel can make another pocket for it. I wish we had diving dresses and an air pump, and when we get the business properly fixed we may be able to obtain them; but there's no use in thinking of that now."

They got into the boat, and Floyd sculled her back, Schumer sitting in the stern and conning them clear of the floating wreckage near the camping place. It grieved Schumer's heart to see all that stuff waste and ungetable. He was one of the men who can make use of anything almost to further or maintain his set purpose.

CHAPTER X
THE SCHOONER

They started for the fishing ground next morning immediately after breakfast, and set to work at once. They had bad luck for the first hour, and then, as if popped into their hands by the hand of luck, came a beauty, a perfect white pearl, twice the size of a marrow-fat pea, maybe even a little bigger, worth five thousand dollars if a penny—so Schumer said.

They sat down to congratulate themselves and feel their luck. You cannot feel your luck standing. Schumer lit a pipe and Floyd followed his example. They put a bit of seaweed on a shell and the pearl on the seaweed, and with it in front of them began to speculate and talk. They felt now that time was theirs, and Schumer knew, though Floyd was still to learn, that the flower of success blooms only on the youngest shoots, that the joy of striking it rich lives only in perfection during the first early days of the stroke, that the fever of life and the enchantment of triumph both die down and fade, that the fully grasped is nothing to the half grasped.

To be given a pearl lagoon by luck and to work it as a hog works a wood for truffles would be to act like a hog.

The stuff was all there; this and the success of the first day's work was ample confirmation of the riches lying under that green water, and Schumer expatiated on the matter.

"You wouldn't believe it," said he, "but the value of a single pearl grows in proportion as you can match it with others exactly like it. It takes eighty or a hundred pearls to make a woman's necklace. Eighty or a hundred pearls like that one would each be worth two or three times what each pearl is worth alone. Even twenty pearls exactly alike would be worth much more than if they were different, for they would form the basis for a collection. You would never dream of the work that goes on in the world matching these things. There are men at it all the time in Paris and London and Amsterdam. A perfect necklace of pearls once formed is always held together; it becomes an individual, so to speak, and is known to the trade by a name. The women belonging to the royal families of Europe hold a number of these collections, but there are lots of private ones, and every great collection is known and tabulated. So you see it won't pay us to peddle our stuff out little by little—we must hold all the pearls we get and match them."

"Look here," said Floyd, "one thing we have never settled—our shares in this business. There's Isbel, too; she has done her bit."

Schumer laughed.

"What's the use of money to a Kanaka?" said he. "We'll give her something, of course, but we need not take her seriously into our calculations. Our shares—well, don't you think it's a bit early to come to that? All this is a dream in the air at present; it may never go farther."

"Well, it's this way," said Floyd, "I always think it's well to start out knowing exactly where you are going to, and what you are to get. When you sign on in a ship you know your pay, and you know the latitudes you have got to work in, and you know the time you are to be on the job. I think it would be better here and now to settle up this business, and I think we ought to go half shares."

"Half shares?" said Schumer meditatively.

"I have been figuring it out in my head," said Floyd. "What have we each contributed to the business? I have brought my work and a boat; now, without a boat we'd have been done completely, because you can't reach here by the reef, and we couldn't have discovered the beds without a boat. Then there's my work. You have brought your knowledge of pearling, and, what is more, all that trade stuff and provisions from the wreck, your energy and enterprise and your work. When I said half shares I did not mean that all the trade and provisions of the *Tonga* should not be taken into consideration. I would suggest that when we settle up I should pay you for all that out of my share. Then there is the money of the *Tonga* and the *Cormorant*. While I hold that Coxon's money belongs by right to his next of kin, I think what I have suffered through his relative, Harrod, permits me to use that money to further our speculation, paying it back with interest to the next of kin when all is through. So I would be nearly equal to you in ready cash, and the question resolves itself into my boat and work against your work and knowledge of pearling."

"I must point out to you," said Schumer, "that I discovered the beds."

"That is true, but without the boat where would you have been? If a ship had come along and you had borrowed a boat to explore the lagoon, the whole affair would have been given away. I am not arguing to make a profit out of the business at your expense, only to give my full views on the matter."

Schumer sat silent for a minute, and Floyd again noticed that profile, daring and predominant, hard and predatory. It was as though the spirit of a hawk were gazing over the sea through the mask of a man.

"It seems to me," said Schumer, "that the boat belonged to Coxon."

"And the *Tonga*?" said Floyd.

Schumer shifted uneasily; then he laughed.

"Well, let it be so," said he; "half shares, and you pay for the trade and provisions; it's early to talk of dividing what we have not got. Still, as you wish it, I agree."

He spoke without enthusiasm. Then he rose up. They had been sitting on the weather side of the reef, with their backs to the lagoon and their faces to the sea; the wind had almost died away, and now as they turned they saw, away across the lagoon, a thin column of black smoke rising from the camping place through the almost windless air.

"It's the signal!" said Floyd.

"A ship!" cried Schumer.

He sheltered his eyes, and Floyd, doing the same, saw the figure of Isbel moving about near the fire. She was putting fresh brushwood on the flames, and even as they looked the smoke increased.

Schumer picked up the pearl that was still lying in the shell and put it in his pocket. He glanced at the heaps of shell still untouched. There was no time to cast all that back in the lagoon or hide the evidence of their work; it was necessary to get back at once, and, returning to the boat, which was beached on the sand, they shoved off, Floyd taking the sculls.

When they reached the beach, Isbel was there, and helped to run the boat up.

"A ship," said she. "Schooner, I think, away over there."

She pointed across the reef toward the outer sea.

The deck of the *Tonga* had always given them a vantage point and a lookout station; even without it now, just by standing on the reef where the wreck had been they could see the sail, and Schumer, after a brief glance, went off to the tent, which they had reëstablished by the grove, and fetched a pair of glasses.

Through them she leaped into view, a topsail schooner, with all sail set, making a long board for the island.

"She's coming here, sure," said Schumer; "a hundred and fifty or maybe a hundred and eighty tons I reckon her to be; but it is deceitful at this distance. Wonder what she is? Wonder what she's doing down here? She may have been blown out of her course by that storm; but she hasn't lost any sticks. Well, we'll soon see."

They watched the sail as she grew white as a pearl against the sky. The sea had lost all trace of the late storm, and there remained only the undying swell of the Pacific.

"I don't know what's the matter with her," said Floyd, as he took a spell with the glasses; "but she seems to be handled by lubbers. Either they have not enough men to work the sails, or the officers are fools."

Schumer took the glasses and watched her, but said nothing.

One of the coconut trees at the entrance end of the grove stood apart from its fellows; it had been stripped of nuts and pretty well stripped of leaves by the storm. At the suggestion of Schumer, Floyd, with a flag tied round his neck like a huge muffler, and with a hammer and some nails in his pocket, swarmed up the tree and nailed the flag to the wood. The wind was strong enough to make it flutter, and with a glass aboard the schooner it would be easily visible.

It evidently remained unseen, for no answer showed.

"She's blind, as well as stupid," said Floyd.

"There's something wrong with her," said Schumer, "and if she comes blundering into the lagoon she may hit that reef we noticed the other day on the left of the entrance. We had better get the boat out and show her the way in when she gets a bit closer."

The schooner was two miles from the reef when they began launching the boat. They rowed out through the break in the reef, and then hoisted the sail.

"She sees us now," said Floyd.

A flag had been run up to the peak; it was the Stars and Stripes. Then it was run down again, then again hoisted.

"Crew of lunatics," said Schumer, as the American flag went down again and was replaced by the Union Jack. "What are they at now?"

"They seem to be a mixed nationality," said Floyd, "and rather confused in their mind. Look, she's heaving to!"

The wind shivered out the canvas and the topsails flattened.

She was, as Schumer had guessed, a schooner of some hundred and fifty tons, and well found, to judge by her general appearance, her canvas, and what they could judge of her sticks.

As they came alongside they saw that her decks were crowded with men, all natives; not a white face showed, and as they boarded her a hubbub rose such as Floyd had never heard before.

Forty Kanakas, mad with excitement and all trying to explain themselves, some in broken English and some in native, produced more impression than understanding.

Schumer took hold of affairs by seizing on a big man whom he judged with unerring eye to be in some position of authority. Then he held up his fist and yelled: "Silence!"

The row ceased in a second, and only Schumer's voice was heard:

"You talk English?"

"Me talk allee right," replied the big man. "Me savvee English me——"

"Shut up and answer my questions! What schooner is this, and where from?"

"She de *Sudden Cross*."

"The *Southern Cross*; where from?"

"Sydney long time 'go; lass po't in de Sol'mons. Capen, off'cers, all gone; fish p'ison."

"Fish poisoning, was it? What was your captain's name?"

"Capen Watters."

"Walters, most like," said Schumer. "Well, what are all these men—they aren't the crew?"

"Some de crew; some labor picked up down de Sol'mons, an' islan's away dere."

"And your cargo?"

"Copra, most."

While Schumer was talking, Floyd was looking about him at the men on deck. There were a dozen Solomon Islanders, some wearing nothing but G strings, nearly all with shell rings through their nostrils, and some with tobacco pipes stuck in their perforated ear lobes.

He thought he had never seen a harder lot of natives than these. The others were milder looking.

Schumer, meanwhile, went on with his inquiries. The name of the big man was Mountain Joe; he was bos'n. The schooner, since the loss of her officers, had been in a hopeless state, as not a soul on board knew anything of navigation. There had been four white men—the captain, two mates, and a third man, evidently a trader or labor recruiter—and the fish that had done the mischief had been canned salmon; evidently ptomaine poisoning in its most virulent form had attacked the only people who had partaken of it.

When Schumer had received all this intelligence, he ordered the boat to be streamed astern on a line, and took command of the schooner.

Without with your leave or by your leave, he gave his orders no less to Floyd than to Mountain Joe.

The Solomon Islanders and the other natives who had no part in the working of the vessel fell apart from the crew, who sprang to the braces at the order of their new skipper, the sails took the wind, and the *Southern Cross* began to forge ahead.

The wind was favorable for the lagoon opening, and as they neared it Schumer ordered Floyd forward to con the ship while he himself took the wheel.

As he steered, he gave his orders to Mountain Joe to get ready with the anchor. The *Southern Cross* responded to her helm as a sensitive horse to the bit, and like a great white cloud she glided over the swell at the reef opening, and like a great white swan she floated into the lagoon.

Then the wind shook out the sails, and the rumble-tumble of the anchor chain sounded over the water as she came to in five fathoms, and within a pistol shot of the camping place.

Isbel was standing on the beach sheltering her eyes with her hand, and some of the Kanaka crew, recognizing her as a native, waved and shouted to her. She waved her hand in reply.

The schooner now swinging safely at her anchor, Schumer continued to give orders till all of the remaining sail was stowed.

Then he turned to Floyd.

"Now, we have her safe and sound," said he, "I propose we go down and have a look at the manifest, and so forth."

"You aren't going to land any of these people yet?" asked Floyd, following him down the companionway to the saloon.

"Not yet," said Schumer; "and when I do land them it won't be at our camping ground. Hello, you nigger!" this to Mountain Joe, who had followed them down; "what you doing here? Get on deck or I'll boot you up the ladder—cheek!"

Mountain Joe vanished.

"Look here," said Floyd, as he shut the door of the saloon, "do you believe that yarn of the fish poisoning?"

"I don't," said Schumer; "I believe the white men were done up. They were a hard lot, most likely, and they met their match. There was fighting on deck, for there was a bullet mark on the wheel, one of the spokes was injured; not only that, I could tell from the manner of those fellows that the big Kanaka was lying. Ah, what's this?"

He went to one of the panels of the saloon by the door. It was split by a bullet.

"Look at that!" said he.

"It's clear enough," replied Floyd, "there has been fighting down here, too. Devils!"

"Oh, well," said Schumer, "we haven't heard their side of the story yet. Come on, let us search and see what we can find."

They entered the biggest cabin opening off the saloon. It was evidently the captain's. Here things were in order, the bunk undisturbed, and a suit of pajamas neatly folded on the quilt.

"Bunk hasn't even been lain on," said Schumer, "and where would a sick man lie but on his bunk or in it? These Kanakas are fools—soft heads; they can't put two and two together, or imagine other people doing it. Now, let's look for the ship's papers."

They hunted, but though they discovered the box which evidently had contained the papers, sign of papers or money there was none. Neither was there sign of the log.

"They have done away with them," said Floyd.

"Looks so," replied Schumer. "Unless the old man swallowed them before he died. Ah, here's a coat of his!"

A coat hanging from a peg by the bunk attracted his attention.

He examined the pockets, and discovered a number of letters, an American dollar, a tobacco pouch, and a pipe. He returned the pipe and the pouch, and placed the letters in his pocket.

"We'll examine them later on," said he; "they may give us some news. Now let's look at this chest and see what it holds."

He raised the lid of a sea chest standing opposite the bunk, and began to explore the contents. It contained mostly clothes, boots, some island curios, and down in one corner another packet of letters, which Schumer took possession of.

On the inside of the lid was nailed the portrait of a stout woman—the unfortunate man's wife, perhaps.

To Floyd there was something mournful in the sight of these few possessions—all that was left on earth of a man living a few weeks ago, or maybe a few days ago, and now vanished utterly; done to death, most probably, by the savages on deck. But Schumer did not seem at all disturbed by any reflections on the matter. With speed but no hurry he went through the business, closed the lid, and rose up.

"Let's get on deck," said he; "we can overhaul the other cabins later on. I have seen what I wanted to see, and there's no use in leaving those fellows on deck too long without attention. I'll have another talk with the big Kanaka, and then we'll go ashore and have a council of war."

"Shall we let any of these chaps land?" asked Floyd.

"Not yet; and when we do we'll land them at the reef by the fishing ground. Looks like Providence, doesn't it? We wanted labor, and it seems we've got it."

"They seem a tough crowd," said Floyd, as he followed his companion up the saloon stairs.

"They are," said Schumer grimly; "but they'll be softer when I have done with them."

On deck, the crew and the Solomon Islanders were scattered about, mostly smoking. Some were seated on the deck; others, leaning over the bulwark rails, were staring at the shore. There was no sign of disorder or danger; the unfortunates were too glad to be in a place of safety, after their experience of driving about the Pacific without a navigator.

The open sea is a terrific place to the Pacific islander when he does not know in what part of it he is, and when he is left to his own resources. Schumer's prompt action in bringing them into the lagoon, the way he handled the ship, and the manner in which he had given his orders at once raised him to the position of the man in authority.

He ordered the boat, which was still streaming astern, with the rope held taut by the outgoing tide, to be hauled alongside, then he told Mountain Joe to get in, and, following him with Floyd, they pushed off for the shore.

When they landed, Schumer called to Isbel, who came out of the bushes. He told her to look after the big Kanaka and give him some refreshment, and then, taking Floyd by the arm, he led him over to the windward side of the reef, and at a point protected by trees from the lagoon they sat down.

Said Schumer:

"When you are starting out on any business everything depends on whether you have got a plan to go on *at the start*. A lot of darned fools blunder along in the businesses they take up without even a plan. If they have a plan, it's one that turns up by accident.

"Now, here's our position: Luck has sent us a schooner and a certain quantity of labor. Good management and foresight has given us a lot of trade, provisions, and arms; all that will be useless if we don't act at once on a plan.

"If we let those fellows land here, and if they discover the position of the cache, it's quite on the cards they might try to rush us. They mustn't touch the ground here; they must be segregated over there at the fishing ground. We have a splendid strategical position, with a section of the reef impassable, or next to impassable, for if they tried to come along it they'd have to go so slow we could pick them off with our Winchesters.

"But that's all meeting trouble halfway. Our policy is to keep them happy after putting the fear of God into them.

"I shall land them to-night over there, but first of all I am going to show them exactly how things stand, and what they may expect if they make trouble.

"Now come back, and we will have a talk with Mr. Mountain Joe."

They came back to the tent, where the dusky bos'n was wiping his mouth with the back of his hand.

Isbel, who had been giving him refreshments, was standing by. When she saw Floyd and Schumer approaching, she went off toward the tent, and the three men found themselves alone.

Out in the lagoon lay the schooner, the crowd on her deck leaning on the bulwark rails, and evidently speculating on what might be going on ashore.

Joe, who had been seated, rose up, and Schumer, taking his seat on the sand beside Floyd, ordered the Kanaka to stand before him.

Schumer, taking a tobacco pouch from his pocket and a book of cigarette papers, proceeded to roll a cigarette. As he ran the tip of his tongue along the gummed edge of the paper he looked up at Joe.

"What made you tell that lie," said he, "about the fish poisoning?"

Joe started as though some one had made an attempt to strike him.

"What fish p'isonin', sah?"

"Now, don't you try any games with me," said Schumer, who had lighted his cigarette. "I know all about the affair, and I am going to see justice done. Your captain was killed, the mates were killed, and the other white man was done away with and hove overboard. I take it he was not a trader, but a labor recruiter. Don't open your mouth to lie, or I'll put a bullet in it!"

He put his hand in his pocket and drew out a revolver, which he placed on his thigh.

"You just hear me through, for I am going to tell you things. To begin with, I doubt if you had any hand in the killing. I judge you by your face. Had you any hand in it? You may speak."

The man's lips were dry; his tongue could scarcely form the words:

"No, sah, it was not me."

"It was some of those Solomon Islanders?"

"Yes, sah."

"Which was the one that did it? There's always one that takes the lead."

Joe was silent.

"Which was the one that did it?" asked Schumer again, without the least change in his voice, but with his hand now on the butt of the revolver.

"De big one, sah, wid de woolly head an' eyes so."

He tried to squint.

"Ah, that chap! I noticed him, and I took his measure."

Then, little by little, he drew out the whole story. It had been a bad voyage for the *Southern Cross*. They had been recruiting down in the Solomon Islands, and the recruiter, Markham by name, had been nearly cut off.

He had adopted the usual methods, landing on the beach with a box of trade goods and without any weapons, while a covering boat hung offshore to protect him in case of attack.

The natives had seemed friendly, but all at once they had drawn off, scattering toward the bush, from where next moment had come a flight of their deadly spears, one of which had pierced Markham's arm. With the spear still in his arm, he had managed to get off, and under protection of the fire from the covering boat had succeeded in reaching the schooner. The spear had been cut out, or, rather, cut off at the barb and drawn out, but the wound had bothered him a lot.

The thirty natives he had managed to secure before the business suffered a good bit at his hand in return for it. The captain and the mates had not been behindhand; some of the crew had run away, and the schooner was shorthanded; that did not add to their good temper. They tried to make the Solomon Islanders help in the working of the vessel, but these gentry had not engaged themselves for ship work, but plantation work, and they said so. The captain had booted some of them and threatened to shoot others, and generally the schooner seemed to have been a hard ship. There seemed the distinct evidence of a trail of drink over the whole business, and the upshot was death for the afterguard.

Death dealt with belaying pins and an ax wielded by the woolly-headed individual with the squint.

Two natives had been shot dead on the spot, one had been wounded, and had died of his wounds. Then the decks had been swabbed, and the precious crew, without a navigating officer or the faintest notion of their exact position, had made sail, or, rather, made a fair wind that was blowing, trusting to chance to take them somewhere.

They had touched the skirt of the big storm, but they managed to weather it, and, seeing the island in sight, had made for it.

"Well," said Schumer, "I believe you have been telling me the truth. I am here to do justice, and justice shall be done."

He rose up, and drawing Floyd aside, walked a few paces with him along the beach.

"That fellow with the squint was evidently the leader in this business," said he. "I am not thinking so much of the trouble on board the schooner, for it's pretty evident that the old man and the mates and the recruiter deserved their gruel. What I am thinking of is the time before us. I am going to make these chaps work the fishery, and I don't want a potential murder leader among them. That wouldn't do at all. Besides, they must be shown at once their position in the scheme of things, and that position is laborers working for decent pay, but under a strong hand. Besides, all these fellows have murder on their conscience—or the thing, whatever it is, that serves for their conscience. That will always make them nervous and distrustful of white men. I can't clear their consciences, but I can clear their minds of the fear of consequences, and I am going to do it now.

"You have your revolver in your pocket; get your rifle, also, and come with me. We may have to fight; there's no knowing."

"I shouldn't mind if we have," said Floyd; "rotten murderers!"

"Oh, they are all right! They are only savages, doing according to their lights. They only require firmness to do according to the lights of civilization."

He went to the tent with Floyd, and they got their rifles and some extra ammunition. Then, with the help of Joe, they pushed the boat off.

The fellows on board watched the coming of the boat, evidently suspecting nothing, though they must have seen the rifles.

Schumer was the first to come on board, followed by Floyd.

They walked aft, and Joe, when he had finished securing the boat, followed them.

Schumer sent him below for two deck chairs which he had seen in the saloon; they were placed close to the wheel, and the white men, taking their seats, and with the rifles across their knees, Schumer threw his old panama hat on the deck about fifteen paces away from where he was sitting, and ordered all hands aft for a palaver.

No man was to take a step beyond the hat.

They came up, some of them still smoking, some chewing, and all evidently wondering what was up, and what the bearded white man with the fixed, determined face had to say to them.

Though he could speak in the dialect of the Solomons, he made Joe his interpreter.

He asked the labor hands first what wages the recruiter had promised them for plantation work.

They were very explicit on this point. They were each to receive in trade goods, tobacco, knives, and so forth what would be the equivalent of about seven pounds a year. They were, of course, to be fed and looked after.

Schumer, taking a pencil and a piece of paper from his pocket, made calculations. Then he addressed them through Joe. He said that he and Floyd were owners of this island, which was a very pleasant place, as they could see for themselves, with plenty of food, both grown here and brought to them regularly by a ship, which they also owned.

To allow this to sink into their intelligence, he proceeded to roll a cigarette; when he had lit it, he went on.

He would offer them work here, and a happy life, and a return home at the end of a year, if they desired to return. The work was very easy, and play, compared to plantation work; it was simply diving for shellfish. They could all dive?

A flashing of white teeth answered this question in the affirmative.

He would pay them exactly the same wages as that offered for plantation work; each man would have to collect so much shell—the amount would be fixed later—and for all shell collected over and above the stipulated amount, a bonus would be paid in tobacco or whatever they liked.

The bonus business had to be explained to them, and the idea took hold upon their imaginations at once.

They agreed to everything. The island pleased them; there was evidence of what Schumer had stated all round—plenty of trees, fruit, and in the lagoon fish. It seemed to them that they had dropped on their feet at last. They broke up into little groups and chattered over the business while Schumer sat watching them with a brooding eye.

Any other man, one might fancy, would have been more than satisfied by the success which had apparently met his offer. In reality, he had only begun what he had set out to do.

When they had talked together long enough, he gave orders to Joe, and they were lined up again. Asked if they agreed to the terms offered to them, they replied, "Yes."

Then Schumer, throwing the end of his cigarette away, crossing his knees, and nursing the rifle lying across his lap, began speaking to them in their own dialect without the aid of Joe.

He talked to the Solomon Islanders, but the others quite understood his words.

He pointed out that from what he had seen below stairs, he knew for a fact that the captain of the *Southern Cross* and the other white men had not died from fish poisoning, but from blows. He told them that an English man-of-war was cruising in the neighborhood of the island, and that if she caught them they would undoubtedly be hanged to a man; he gave them a pantomime with his hand at his throat to help their imaginations, and, seeing the effect produced, at once started on a new line.

They had nothing to fear if they trusted in him and in the white man beside him, but justice must be done. It was impossible for white men to allow other white men to be murdered or killed without bringing the murderers to book.

He did not believe that they were all implicated, but he did believe that there was one among their number who had led them to this act.

Dead silence among the audience, whose faces laughing a moment ago, were now a picture representing all the emotions that range between furtiveness and fright.

No one spoke.

"Very well," said Schumer, still speaking in the native, "if you will not speak it will be the worse for you. I am not your enemy. I am your friend, and am able to protect you all from the consequences of what has been done; but I will not do so unless I can punish the man who was chief in this business. You will not show him to me; well, then, I will find him for myself, for I have been born with the means of knowing men, and I can see their thoughts, just as you can see the fish that swim in the lagoon."

He rose from his seat and walked toward where they were standing. The line bent back for a moment, as though they were going to break away and run, then they stood their ground; every eye was fixed on him as he went from one to the other, lifting this one's chin with his finger, resting his hand on that one's head.

Floyd, still seated, had his rifle ready in case of accidents, but it was not needed. The diplomacy of Schumer had made the crowd afraid, not of him, but of the consequences of their act, and to cap that, they were held by the fascination of this business and the curiosity to see what was about to happen.

When Schumer reached the squint-eyed individual he placed his hand on his head. Then he snatched it away, as though something had stung him, and looked at the palm.

"You are the man," said he. "Look!"

He held up his palm for a second; there was nothing in it, but every man in that crowd saw something, according to his imagination.

CHAPTER XI
THE PUNISHMENT

Floyd's finger went to the trigger of the rifle across his knees. He expected a sudden attack by the criminal on his accuser, but the man did nothing.

A murmur went up from the crowd, the sort of murmur that would have followed the exhibition of a conjuring trick, while Schumer, taking his man by the arm, led him apart from the rest and made him stand with his back to the port bulwarks.

"Is what I say true?" he asked, turning to Joe.

He had calculated on everything, and he knew that Joe the informer would never, never reveal to the others that his—Schumer's—magic gift of seeing the truth through men's skulls was a trick based on information.

For a moment Joe, between the devil and the deep sea, gazed wildly round him, then he bent his head in assent.

"So," said Schumer, then he turned to Floyd. "You are one of the judges of this man. I am the other, but I am president of this court, and I have the casting vote—pronounce your sentence."

"He deserves death," said Floyd; "but——"

"But what?"

"I would prefer to isolate him on some part of the island and hand him over to the first ship."

Schumer turned to Joe, and, pointing to a whaleboat hanging at the davits, ordered it to be lowered.

When it was afloat he gave orders for the whole of the labor men to get into it, telling them that all was clear now that the chief offender was to be punished, and that no more would be said on the matter, that their work would be paid for on the terms he had named, and that their future lot would be happiness, good pay, good food, and plenty of it.

They crowded down into the boat. There were thirty of them, and they filled it nearly. Then, leaving Floyd on board with Joe and the Kanaka crew and the criminal, he got into the boat and took his place at the tiller.

The Solomanders rowed villainously, but they made the whaleboat move, and Floyd, with one eye on the murderer, who had now taken his seat on the deck, watched Schumer steering them for the fishing ground and landing them on the beach.

He landed them, and seemed to be explaining things. Floyd caught glimpses of him waving his arm about almost as though he were pointing out the view.

Then with two of them for oarsmen he came back.

Floyd, as Schumer came on deck, felt sick at heart. He hated the crime, and he hated the sight of the criminal, but he hated even more the idea of death, and he knew that the man now crouched on the deck was surely going to die.

Schumer, as he came on deck, seemed Fate itself—calm, cold, passionless Fate. The judge, the hangman, and the rope all in one.

The Kanakas seemed to guess it; the very brightness of the day seemed grown paler. Floyd walked to the bulwark rail and looked over at the boat where the two rowers were seated looking up at the vessel. His lips were dry. He could do nothing; whatever was going to happen was deserved, but it was horrible.

He heard Schumer giving his orders for signal halyard line and a block. The *Southern Cross* carried a brass cannonade for saluting purposes, and now he heard Schumer giving orders for it to be loaded.

I have said that the *Southern Cross* was a topsail schooner, and at this moment the crowd of laborers away out at the fishing ground had their attention drawn by the movement going on upon the rigging of the foremast; men were swarming up, and a fellow was out on the yard—he looked at that distance like a fly against the blue. He came down, as did the others, and he had scarcely reached the deck when a white jet of smoke shot like a plume from the bow of the *Southern Cross*, and the noise of a gun came on the wind.

Something black and struggling, and just like a spider running up a thread, went from the deck of the *Southern Cross* to the yardarm, touched it, and then sank some half dozen feet, and swung dangling against the sky. It was the murderer.

CHAPTER XII
THE POWER OF SCHUMER

During it all Floyd had kept his eyes turned away. When the men had come running aft with the halyard line they had knocked against him, making him shift his position, and now, with the dead man swinging aloft, he walked over to the weather side, seemingly an impassive figure, with his rifle under his arm keeping guard.

As he stood looking over the water to the camping place he saw Isbel. She had come out on the sands and she was standing with her hand shading her eyes. She must have been a witness of the whole tragedy, and she stood, motionless as a figure carved from stone—for a moment. Then she turned, and just as though something were in pursuit of her, she ran, making for the grove, into which she disappeared.

Floyd swore under his breath. That the girl should have been allowed to see such a thing struck him as a monstrous fact. Gentle, kindly, and willing she had been, almost unknown to himself, the one bright spot in his life on the island. The one human thing to keep life warm. Schumer had been a companion who had never grown into anything more than an acquaintance; Isbel, though he had talked to her as little as he would have talked to a dog, had been a friend. He did not understand her at all; she had lived her own life, thought her own thoughts, and said little; a child living in a child's world of which he knew nothing, but she had somehow kept his heart warm, and now she had been allowed to see *this*, the doing to death of one of her own people in the broad light of day.

What could she know of the justice of the case? He turned to Schumer, who had come toward him now that everything was finished, and, taking him by the arm, led him to the weather rail; they leaned over the rail as they talked.

"Do you know," said Floyd, "that child has seen the whole of this business?"

"What child?"

"Isbel."

"Well, what of that?"

"What of that? She stood there watching it all, and then she ran off as if some one were going to kill her. It was brutal to let her see it; goodness knows she has stuck to us and done everything for us a mortal could do, and now we repay her by letting her see us hanging one of her own people."

Schumer seemed disturbed and irritated by this news.

"One cannot think of everything," said he; "you speak as though you were accusing me. Am I to do all the thinking? Well, she has seen what she has seen, and it cannot be helped, though I would not have had it for a good deal. That girl may be very useful to us yet, and we do not want to make an enemy of her. She will brood over this and say nothing, and then maybe let us have it in the back some time. Well, we cannot help it; we must remedy it somehow. There is no use in talking about it with the business we have to do before us. First we must bring stores and some canvas to make tents for those labor men. Come, we will get the stuff together now and take it to them in the whaleboat; we will take two of the crew with us to help to row."

They rousted out some spare canvas from the sail room of the schooner, and had it sent into the whaleboat, which was still alongside, with the two Solomon Islanders who had rowed her out sitting on the thwarts and staring up at the form dangling overhead.

It seemed to fill them with curiosity, nothing more; yet Floyd noticed that when Schumer spoke to them they jumped to attention as though they had been addressed by some powerful chief. The crew also ran about at his least sign, hauled with all their energy, and hung on his words.

Schumer did not go to the cache for provisions; he opened the schooner's lazaret. She was well supplied. Though the mutineers had killed their officers they had not sacked the provision room and broached the liquor as they would have done had they been Europeans.

"They were helpless, you see, like a duck with a broken wing," said Schumer. "Didn't know where they were; didn't know who would catch them. Kanakas will drink, but they don't fly to drink like our chaps; it's not grained in them."

They made a selection of tins and had them brought on deck and hoisted into the boat. Schumer added some sticks of tobacco, and they pushed off and rowed for the fishing ground.

The laborers waiting on the beach helped them to land. They were a very subdued lot indeed; the sight of the hanging seemed to have put them under a spell as far as the white men were concerned, and they worked at the unlading of the stores without a word, yet with all their energy.

When the stuff was landed, Schumer began to talk to them. He asked them to choose a foreman, and, having consulted together for a few minutes, they picked out one of their number—a man with a huge shell ring through his nostrils, split ear lobes, and scar marks on his chest and all down his left arm.

Sru was the name of this individual, and Schumer, as he watched him step out from the ranks, regretted the choice. He suspected that they had chosen him, not because he was a favorite, but because he was feared. This is always bad, because in dealing with a mass of natives—and the same holds good for Europeans—authority has most to fear from the individual. It is the one man who makes the bother, and the man who is feared, if he is placed in a position of supremacy, is more likely to make trouble than the man who is loved.

However, they had chosen a foreman at Schumer's request, and it was not for him to interfere with their choice. He set to and gave them directions as to how they were to make their camp, placed the provisions and tobacco under charge of the foreman, ordered them to be ready for work next morning at sunup, and then returned to the schooner, leaving the two laborers behind with the others.

On board he gave an order for the body to be lowered and cast in the lagoon, where the sharks were patiently waiting for their prey; then with Floyd he returned to the camping ground, rowing themselves across in the ship's dinghy.

They had left on board the whole native crew with Joe to supervise them.

They beached the dinghy by the quarter boat, and walked up to the tent. Isbel was nowhere to be seen.

Schumer looked round for her, called, received no answer, and then, with his own hands, prepared to light the fire and make the supper.

The sun was now low down over the western roof, and the lagoon was filling with gold; the schooner, freed from the horror dangling at her yardarm, lay with her anchor chain taut, and the golden ripples of the incoming tide racing past her sides. She made a beautiful picture with the sunset light upon her masts and spars, the gulls flying and flitting about her, crying as they wheeled.

It was the time of the full moon, and she rose with the dark. Schumer had gone to the tent, where he had placed the letters and papers taken from the captain's coat on board the *Southern Cross*. He returned with them in his hand, and, taking his seat by the embers of the fire, he began to examine them.

He did not require a lamp; one could have read the smallest print by the moonlight now flooding the world.

It was a poor enough find. There were half a dozen letters in a woman's handwriting, mostly referring to remittances received or expected. The addresses at the head of them told nothing. "One hundred and two North Street" was the invariable heading, and for date Monday or Tuesday, without hint of the month in which they were written. "My dear Joe," they began, and the ending was always the same, "Your loving Mary." There were no envelopes to give a clew to the town they came from or the country.

"His loving Mary seemed to have a keen eye for the boodle," said Schumer. "Ah—what's this?" He had opened a letter with the printed heading: "Hakluyt & Son, Market Street, Sydney." The letter ran:

> Dear Captain Walters: Owing to Captain Dennison's illness we are prepared to offer you the *Southern Cross*, which is now lying in harbor. If you will call upon us to-morrow at ten-thirty sharp we will be happy to talk over the matter with you and make all arrangements.
>
> J. B. for Hakluyt & Son.

"That was written four months ago," said Schumer, looking at the date on the envelope. "They are the owners, and I believe I know Hakluyt & Son; pair of rogues, as all shipowners are, but they are rich, if they are the people I take them for; anyhow it's a good find. We know the owners. You see, a schooner is not a thing you can pick up like a purse and put in your pocket. Unless you run her into a port where there is no law and sell her for the price of old truck what are you to do with her? Change her name? Well, what about your papers and your log, and how are you going to muzzle your crew, even if they are Kanakas? You have boards of trade and port officers everywhere. It's one of the troubles of civilization, but it has to be faced. Now, on the other hand, knowing the owners, we have the law not against us but on our side. The schooner is practically derelict; if we bring her into port we can claim compensation. I see a lot of clear sky ahead in this business if it is properly worked, and we must remember this: the fish-poisoning business holds good; there's no use in having government inquiries, though I don't even dread those; we tried our man fairly and we hanged him as an example to the others who seemed mutinous."

"Look here," said Floyd. "I want to say something about that business. I don't deny that fellow got what he deserved, but there were others in the business, and there is no doubt at all that they had a lot of provocation. But you hanged that man less for what he had done than for what he might do in the future."

"Exactly; and to show the others what they might expect, and to show them that they have got masters over them."

"You hanged him as a matter of policy."

"Just so. As a matter of policy first, and as a matter of punishment second."

"Well, that's where I'm against you."

"How?"

"Killing for policy's sake. I may be wrong, but it's against my nature to hang a chap so as to strike terror into others. However, he is hanged and done with, and there's no use saying any more on the matter."

"Not a bit," said Schumer, going on with the examination of the papers. There was nothing else of importance; some receipted bills, some old letters from chums dated four years back, an envelope with a theater program in it, and another envelope with a faded photograph of a woman in a low-necked dress, evidently the photograph of some actress that had struck Captain Walters' fancy.

"It's funny what you find among a man's belongings," said Schumer. "I've come across a Bible and a pious letter from his mother in the leavings of one of the biggest blackguards in the world, and I met a man who told me he had gone through the gear of a parson who was laid out on a smallpox ship and found books and pictures that weren't holy. This Walters had an eye for a pretty girl, and sent his wife remittances pretty often; that's all his remains say of him. I reckon he was a poor sort, sentimental, with a taste for the bottle and with no hold on his crew."

They put the papers away, and Schumer retired to bed, while Floyd, relighting his pipe, strolled over to the ocean side of the reef. At night, and especially when the moon was full, this was a place of terrific loneliness. One heard the voice of the wastes of the sea. He sat down on a lump of coral and watched the rollers coming in and the bursting of the foam under the moonlight.

The events of the day had depressed him, yet nothing could have shown better results, as regards their plans, than the day's work just finished. They wanted labor for the fishery, and labor had appeared on the island as though summoned by a genie. They wanted a ship that would make no trouble, and here was a schooner floating in the lagoon, a vessel well found and seaworthy and without eyes or ears to spy on their doings.

Fortune had turned her face toward them and held out her hand, and had Floyd been listening to the story of himself and Schumer told as a yarn his commentary would have been "Lucky beggars!"

The reality was different, and it disclosed the brutality which attends success, especially the successful attempt to lift treasure that is in Nature's keeping.

Nothing could be more fascinating than the idea of raiding one of Nature's great banks where she stores her pearls, her diamonds, or her gold, nothing more trying to all the endurance and good in man than the prosecution of that great burglary.

The hanging business had hit Floyd a hard blow; more than that, the thought of Schumer was now beginning to threaten his peace like a phantom.

The running away of Isbel at the sight of the hanging had suddenly cast a new light upon Schumer and incidentally upon himself.

It was as though Innocence had spoken, condemning them both. And yet the man had deserved his fate. Floyd told himself this again and again; it was the knowledge of this that had prevented him from interfering. He told himself that, even as a matter of policy and to protect their own lives against another outbreak headed by the same leader, the action was justified.

And yet the phantom remained to disturb his thoughts. Schumer, the man who had bound himself up so closely in his life, the man whom he did not understand in the least, the man whose personality was so powerful, whose wishes always made themselves good, and whose word was practically law on that island.

Schumer was always right; that was part of the origin of his power; he had the genius to foresee everything that was coming and the head to prepare for eventualities. His suggestions were commands based on reason; his orders were worded so as to seem suggestions; his personality suffused everything, dominated all things, and made Floyd feel at times as though he were an automaton worked by strings instead of a living man moved by will.

Yet never had Schumer stirred resentment in him.

That is the most magical power in a great and dominating personality. It does not irritate; it lulls. Your little strong man gets his will—if he gets it—by setting everybody by the ears. Your big strong man works without friction; his men become part of him, his motives part of them; when they are free to think they may vaguely wonder at their own subservience and even resent it in a way, yet they come under again to the will that bends them as surely as the wheat stalks come under to the wind when it blows.

Floyd, having smoked for a while, tapped the ashes out of his pipe and rose up. As he was returning to the tent he caught the glimmer of something white among the outer trees of the grove and came toward it. It passed among the trees, and he followed it, pushing branches of the hibiscus aside and trampling down the fern that grew here in profusion.

He was following Isbel, and there, in a little glade amid the ferns, with her back to an artus tree, crouched in the moonlight, he brought her to bay.

There was something feline in her attitude, as though she were about to spring, and her eyes were fixed on him steadfastly as though watching for his next move.

"Isbel," he said, speaking loud enough for her to hear, yet not loud enough to attract the possible attention of Schumer in the tent near by, "what is the matter with you? Come, I am not going to hurt you. Don't you know me?"

He held out his hand, with the finger-tips pressed together, as one holds out one's hand to an animal; then he took a step toward her.

She turned and whisked away round the tree, and he heard her movements among the bushes as she vanished from sight.

He came out of the grove and went back to the tent.

Next morning when he came out of the tent the first thing that struck his eye was Isbel. She had returned, and was setting the sticks for the fire as though nothing had occurred. But when her business was done she vanished again, reappearing only in time to help in the preparation of the evening meal.

CHAPTER XIII
THE HOUSE

It would be impossible to bring home to your mind, unless you had experienced it, the vast change which the presence of the *Southern Cross* made in the picture of the lagoon. Not on the retinal picture, but on the mental.

Her presence altered everything. The place became a harbor. Those spars fretting the sky, that hull making green water beneath its copper brought civilization up hand over fist from a thousand leagues down under.

Loneliness had vanished, the crying of the gulls lost its melancholy, and the sound of the surf on the reef, when one noticed it, no longer spoke of desolation.

And, just as the schooner altered the lagoon, so did the presence of her crew and the labor men alter the life on the island.

In a moment life had become all hurry and work.

Isbel reappeared regularly to help in the preparation of their food; she would be on hand when wanted for any light job, but she never sat by them now when they talked; she avoided saying a word unless absolutely obliged to, and when she spoke she no longer looked Floyd in the eyes.

"She is frightened to death of us and she loathes us," he thought. "Me just as much as him. I don't wonder, either."

Schumer said nothing on the matter; perhaps he was too busy to notice the change in the girl. He certainly had his work cut out for him. On the first day he had to deal with the labor men, showing them their job. They knew nothing of pearls or the shell business, but they were like otters in the water, and they picked up the small technicalities of the labor at once.

Sru especially seemed to take to the work as though born to it, and Schumer left them under his foremanship and returned to the schooner, where he had work for the crew.

He wanted a house. He had already picked out the site for it in a little clearing of the grove well protected by the trees from possible storms. The wood was ready to his hand in the wreckage of the *Tonga*, which the lagoon currents had driven into the shoal water of the southern beach right opposite to the camping place.

Of course he could have cut down trees for his building material, but every tree in the grove by the camping place was a valuable asset as a shelter against the weather. To have used any of the timber from the other groves of the island would have meant not only the labor of felling and trimming trees, but of floating them off and towing across the water.

He made Mountain Joe foreman of the new industry, explaining to him carefully and minutely the whole business. All planking had to be collected, made into small rafts, and towed across the lagoon. The whaleboat was used for the purpose, and Schumer accompanied it himself on the first trip to show exactly what he wanted.

It took two days' hard work before sufficient planking had been got together, and then began the business of securing and towing across the heavy timbers to be used for posts and beams. The whole of this business from the start of the time when the wood was lying on the sand near the tent took over a week, during which time the fishery work was progressing, though in a leisurely manner.

"There we have thirty chaps at work," said Schumer on the night when the last of the timber was salved, "and you'd have imagined that they would have done fifteen times as much work as you and I per day. They haven't done more than three times as much. They play about in the water; they are a bone-lazy lot—well, it doesn't matter. If we had half a dozen dependable overseers to superintend the business when it comes to searching for the pearls it would be different, but there is only you and me. So it's no earthly use getting huge quantities of shell of which we can't oversee the working properly. Funny thing it is, but a business has to slow down unless it is perfect in all parts. Here we have the getters of the raw stuff, and I could speed them up four times their present rate and we'd skin the lagoon four times as quick if I had even three more men like you and me to supervise the getting of the real stuff—which is pearls. Yet if I had those three men they would want a partnership and so we'd lose in profits. It's as broad as it's long."

They were sitting by the fire, and Schumer as he talked was putting finishing touches to a drawing he was making on a leaf of his pocketbook.

It was the plan for the house.

He had made the sketch more as an exercise for his restless fingers than anything else.

Nothing could be more simple or rudimentary in the way of a house plan. The drawing provided for two rooms only, a big room and a little room. The main door opened on to the big room.

"It won't be much of a house," said the architect, as he showed the drawing, "but still it will be a house, and a house is a most important thing for us. Shelter! I'd just as soon shelter in the tent; sooner, but it's not a question of shelter so much as prestige. It's like wearing a clean shirt. You see, if we live the same as our men they'll get to think of us as the same, whereas if we live in a house and keep them under canvas, or in any old huts they are able to make, they think of us accordingly. The house gets on their mind. It is the symbol of authority and power. It becomes the government building. There's a whole lot in that—more than you would think. Then, besides, we want a secure place for the pearls. It won't do to keep them under canvas or in a hole in the ground. I'm going to build as strong as I can and make the door to match. We will have loopholes to fire through, in case of eventualities, though I don't think they'll be needed.

"The man who has to depend on defending his position by resisting attack in his own house is a pretty bad administrator.

"Still one never knows what may happen, and it is as well to be prepared."

CHAPTER XIV
MOSTLY ABOUT PEARLS

It took them a fortnight to get the main posts up and the planking started.

Joe proved himself an invaluable worker, with initiative enough to oversee the others, so that both Schumer and Floyd could leave him and give their attention to the fishery and the pearl getting. Sru, despite his looks and his scars, was shaping well also as an overseer, and the pearls were showing in a satisfactory manner. The pearls taken hitherto by Schumer and Floyd working alone were all free pearls contained in the substance of the oyster or lying loose under the mantle; now began to come in pearls attached to the shell and shells presenting blisters.

It was well that Schumer had some practical knowledge of pearling, or these blistered shells might have been cast with the others.

Now a blister on a pearl shell looks exactly like the bleb raised by a blister on the human skin. It is caused by some foreign body getting into the oyster, causing irritation, and a consequent extra secretion of nacre which covers the foreign body over. But it must never be forgotten also that a pearl lying in the shell may cause sufficient irritation to stimulate this extra secretion of nacre, and that, as a result, a blister when opened may be found to contain a pearl.

At the end of a month, when the house was nearly finished, they had on their hands two dozen of these blistered shells and a hundred and four pearls as the result of the month's fishing, besides eighteen shells to which pearls were adhering.

On paper that would seem to make a good show, but the practical results were not so rosy, though fair enough in all conscience, considering the cheap price of labor.

To arrive at a true estimate of the take one must disregard Schumer's rough statement as to values for something more precise.

The most valuable of all pearls are those that are *perfectly round*.

A perfect pearl must have this shape, and it must have four other qualities. It must be either pure white or pink; it must be partly transparent;

it must be free from all specks or blemishes, and it must have the true pearl luster.

Next to the perfect comes the Bouton pearl, flat on one side and convex on the other; lastly comes the drop or pear-shaped pearl.

All these belong to the first class, and if they conform to the four cardinal rules as to transparency, *et cetera*, they are valuable, the value of each depending upon the weight in grains.

Then come the second class, consisting of imperfectly shaped pearls of good luster and quality and perfectly shaped pearls of imperfect luster and quality.

Lastly we have the baroque pearls.

These are sometimes of very large size, but of extraordinary and irregular shape. They are really masses of nacre that have been formed around large, rough foreign bodies that have got into the oyster. They are sometimes hollow, and then they are known to jewelers under the French name *coq de perle*.

Now of the hundred and four free pearls taken in the month's fishing only six were absolutely perfect and only two of these of large size. Yet these two alone well repaid the labor of getting them. Of the other ninety-eight there were twenty baroques of small value, and of the remaining seventy-eight, twenty were estimated by Schumer to be worthless, the last fifty-eight varying in value from half a sovereign to four pounds.

Taken altogether, the catch was good, especially when the blistered shells were split, for in two of the twenty-four blisters a pearl was found of fair quality. The cavities of the remaining "blisters" revealed nothing but some discolored water that smelled horribly.

Beside the pearls taken the value of the shell had also to be reckoned. The shell was that known to commerce as golden-edged, and its value might have been anything from fifty to a hundred pounds a ton.

When I spoke of twenty of the pearls being worthless I referred less to the pearls than the remains of pearls; every healthy pearl is of some value, even down to the tiny seed pearl, but the pearl, no matter how large, that loses its beauty by disease is worthless.

It is the grief of pearl fishing to come across things that a year ago may have been worth anything from a couple of hundred to a thousand pounds and that to-day are worthless. Things as ugly as dead cod's eyes that, a year ago, were fit to be the symbols of beauty, and it is impossible to say exactly what causes this decay. There may be several causes, diseases that attack the pearl as well as the oyster; but the result is there as a proof of the vandalism of nature.

Among the trade of the *Tonga* had been some parcels of surgeons' cotton wool. Schumer rooted a parcel of this out, and, turning the gold and papers from the cash box, lined it with a sheet of the wool. He placed the baroque and lesser-valued pearls on this sheet and covered them with a single layer of wool; on this layer he placed the pearls of the second order. All those of the first class he kept apart in a small wooden box, each pearl packed separately in its own nest of wool.

The few shells with pearls attached to them he placed in a cocoa box, each shell in a jacket of wool.

"We can't cut the pearls off those shells," said he. "It's jeweler's work, and we are only carpenters at the business. They'll keep till we get them to Europe."

A fortnight later the roof was on the house, a roof thatched with palm leaves bound down with coconut sennit, and the pearls and all their other valuables were placed in the smaller of the two rooms.

The indefatigable Schumer, immediately the main door was in its place, set his men to work making a table. The two deck chairs were brought from the *Southern Cross*, also a spare saloon lamp and some drums of paraffin oil. Otherwise the schooner was left intact.

"Those Hakluyts would be sure to make a disturbance if we touched any of the saloon furniture," said Schumer. "They'd swear, maybe, we had looted the ship, and it's my ambition to bring her into Sydney harbor with everything standing and without a scratch on her that a Jew could swear to."

"Schumer," said Floyd, "I've been thinking of that. When do you intend that we should take her to Sydney?"

"Well," said the other, "now we have things fixed the sooner we make a move the better. At first glance one might say keep her here till we have finished with the lagoon and then shin off in her with all the pearls we can get. That's what a fool would say, and that's what a fool would do. Where lies the folly? This way.

"To keep her like that would mean to steal her, and, as I said before, you can't steal a ship these days without being caught. Suppose, even, we were to give all the ports in the world good-by and wreck her, where would we be with our pearls on some desolate shore, or if on a civilized shore, where would be the customs officers?

"No. Pearls aren't worth two cents without a market for them, and we must get to Sydney, not only to claim salvage on the schooner and maybe to get the Hakluyts to let us rent her, but to make the beginning of a market for our stuff. We'll *have* to bring some one else into the affair. I wish we hadn't. I've been figuring on every means of getting out of it, but I can't find a way."

"How are we to leave the fishery here to itself while we go to Sydney?"

"We can't do that; one of us must stay to look after things."

"Well," said Floyd, "if that is so I know which is the one that will have to stay—and that is myself."

"It's a strange thing," said Schumer rather grimly, "but I had come to the same conclusion. I don't undervalue you in the least, as you very well know. I try to attach the right values to all things and people. It's the only way to arrive at success—but your value as a negotiator of this business is negligible simply because you have no knowledge of trade, and—if you will excuse me for saying so—no stomach for it. If Hakluyt is the man I imagine him to be he'd turn you inside out, pearls and all, inside two minutes, gobble the pearls and throw away the skin. No, I must go and deal with him personally, and you must stay here and look after the fishing, but I don't propose to start yet, till we have the thing more fully in hand."

"Look here," said Floyd, "why not take the schooner back to Sydney, sell what pearls we have got there, and then, with the money they bring and the money we have already, charter another schooner for our work. In that way we would keep the matter in our own hands."

"One would think," said Schumer, "from the way you talk, that pearls were to be sold as easy as dairy produce. Sydney is the last place I would sell pearls openly in, and the very last place I would try to sell them secretly in. Paris is the market for pearls, or London. Besides, you must remember that Sydney is a sort of center for pearling in the Australian Pacific, and if wind got about of our island, we would be dogged to a certainty.

"No, we simply have to get help, and it's better to have one man with money as our partner than half a dozen interlopers crying: 'Share up, or we'll give the business away.' Of course," finished Schumer meditatively, "we could use our guns against them, but those sorts don't go unarmed, and we are only two, for the natives don't count. As like as not, they'd turn against us from the first, and they'd certainly do so if they saw us being beaten."

They had been sitting under a tree as they talked, close to the nearly completed house, and, as Schumer finished, Floyd saw Isbel coming across the lagoon from the fishing grounds in the schooner's dinghy.

The dinghy of the *Southern Cross* was a tiny affair, even for a boat of this type. It held two at a pinch, and its lines were the lines of a walnut shell. It was a dainty little boat, and had evidently belonged to a yacht at some time or another, to judge by its fittings, or what was left of them. Isbel was standing up and sculling with a single oar from the stern.

"I say," said Schumer, "what has that girl been doing over at the fishing ground?"

"I don't know," said Floyd, shading his eyes; "didn't know she had gone there. She must have gone to the schooner and taken the dinghy."

"Well," said Schumer, "that won't do. I don't want her palling up with those labor hands; they are her own people, and she knows a lot too much about us and our affairs to let her get thick with them. She knows where all the trade is cached, for one thing. Besides, she hasn't been the same for a long while. I can't get a word out of her."

"She has been different ever since you hanged that chap," said Floyd.

"Well, she'll have to change her tune, or she'll see the rough side of me," replied the other. "I'm not going to stand any Kanaka tricks, and I've shown them that already."

"Seems to me," said Floyd, "that all you have done by that hanging business is to turn Isbel against us."

Schumer did not reply. He was walking down to the lagoon edge at the point where the little boat was preparing to beach.

"Hi," cried he, "what have you been doing in that boat?"

"Been to the fishing grounds," replied the girl, as the dinghy took the sand and she stepped out into a foot of water and helped Schumer to haul the boat up; "been to see the men; they are my people."

"Oh, they are your people, are they?" said Schumer. "Well, you mustn't go to them; we want you here. And it seems to me we are your people, too. You have been with us long enough on the island to make you one of us, and yet you go off at the first chance to your people, as you call them."

She said nothing; she did not look in his face.

Floyd, standing by, watched her. She had brought the scull ashore; she was holding it in her hand, and, as she stood there in the scanty white cotton garment that fitted her with the grace that only comes from the wearer, he thought what a pretty picture she made against the blazing lagoon and far-off reef.

"Remember," went on Schumer, "that you are one of us, and belong to the island, that we have helped you just as you have helped us, and that though you have always been treated with kindness, I can punish those who disobey me."

Floyd, as he listened and watched, thought that he perceived the faintest curl of her lip at this latter clause, but he could not be sure; that inscrutable, yet childish, face was very difficult to read, and more especially now as she raised her eyes to those of Schumer.

"I will not use your boat again," said she; "it was only the little one. Do you want me any more now?"

"No," said Schumer, turning away. "I have nothing more to say."

She put the scull back in the boat, shaded her eyes, and looked over the lagoon toward the fishing ground, as though at some place where her heart was, but her body could not be.

Floyd, as he went off to superintend the house-builders, shook his head.

The three of them had been almost a little family before this had taken place. The pearls were dividing them already. Isbel had become a stranger to him, and to-morrow Schumer might be his enemy.

CHAPTER XV
PLANS

One evening, a fortnight later, Schumer, who had just come back from the fishing camp, found Floyd seated on the sand near the house and engaged in mending some tackle. He took his seat beside him, lit a pipe, and gave him news of the day's work.

"Everything is shipshape here now," finished he, "and it's time to strike for Sydney."

"When do you propose to start?"

"At once."

"At once?"

"Why not? There are stores enough on the *Southern Cross* for the trip, and it's only a question of getting the water on board; that will take us a day. The weather promises well, and I'd propose to start the day after to-morrow."

Floyd said nothing for a moment. The projected expedition that would leave him alone on the island had weighed on his mind for the last few days. Whatever Schumer might be, he was a companion, the only other white man in the place. To be left absolutely alone, with no one to talk to, was a dreary prospect, but it was for the good of the business, and he was not the man to grumble.

"Well," he said, "if it has to be, there is no use talking. We can't both leave the place, and since you are the best man for the trade end of the affair, I must stop, but it will be a pretty lonely business."

"Oh, you'll find lots to do," said Schumer, laughing. "I only hope you won't find too much. I have drilled these fellows into pretty fair discipline, and it's for you to keep it up. I warn you if you don't you'll have trouble. You mustn't let them come any of the funny business over you, and you must back your authority with your gun if need be. Your only danger is the cache. We give these fellows tobacco and so on, and the question hasn't begun to enter their thick heads as to where all the stores come from, but it may, and if they scent the cache, there will be trouble. You just remember that knives and trade goods are like minted gold to these chaps, and if they suspected a whole Bank of England of them here under the trees, they'd ten to one try to raid it. You mustn't ever let them land here."

"You bet I won't," said Floyd. "How long will you be gone?"

"Three weeks to get there and three to get back, makes six weeks, and allowing for a fortnight there—let's say nine weeks to give it a margin. You may expect me back in the lagoon in nine weeks. If I'm not back by then, you may begin to suspect I'm with the sharks."

"You will take the money with you?"

"Of course; and I'll take the best of the pearls, too, for several reasons. First to show our samples, second because I'm leaving you the lagoon. If I never come back, you'd have the lagoon, and if you bolted with the lagoon, I'd have the pearls.

"I won't take all the pearls, only a selection of the best."

"Oh, I don't mind," said Floyd. "I can trust you; and, even if I couldn't, you would not be such a fool as to leave a pearl lagoon for the sake, of a six weeks' take of pearls. Well, come on to supper; there's Isbel laying out the things; we can talk afterward."

Though the house was now finished, with the door on, and the table in, they always took their meals in the open. Isbel had laid the plates and knives and forks on a cloth before the door, and in the center of the cloth a kava bowl with some flowers in it.

Schumer was always very punctilious as to the service of meals, laying the cloth himself if no one else were there to do it. He had salved all the *Tonga* linen, and he would doubtless have insisted on napkins had the *Tonga* carried them; unable to go as far as napkins, he had contented himself with flowers. He believed in keeping up appearances, even if there were no one to observe these appearances but their two selves and Isbel, and he was right. Slackness is one of the rots of the world, and the least bit of ceremonial is the finest tonic in life.

Isbel, who never ate with them now by any chance, and who had voluntarily debased herself from the position of companion to the condition of servant, went off and left them to their food. The sun sank behind the reef, and in a sky of pansy blue the first vague sketch of the constellation began to show itself to the darkening sea. Then almost as though touched off by a taper, the stars blazed out, crusting with light the whole dome from the sea line to the zenith. It was the night before the new moon, and always on these nights when the whole lighting of the world was left to the stars a deeper peace seemed to pervade the island and the ocean and the sky. The voice of the reef seemed to sink lower, and the night wind to blow warmer, and the lagoon to hold in its depths a profounder calm.

The wind to-night brought faint odors of vanilla and frangipanni from the trees of the grove, and across the lagoon a trace of song from the camping place by the fishing ground. The natives were amusing themselves, and the light of their camp fire showed like a red spark across the starlit water.

The two men on the beach sat smoking and watching the schooner as she rode to her anchor, with a single light showing. The Kanaka crew, whom Schumer had always kept apart from the labor men, were on deck, and their forms could be seen indistinctly in the starlight as they lounged about, smoking and yarning. A fellow was fishing over the after rail, and now and then one could see a splash in the water and a streak of silver, as a groper was hauled up.

Faint and far away and coming, no doubt, from the fo'c'sle could be heard the strains of a concertina playing a thready and wandering air, while occasionally across the lagoon from the deep soundings came the splash of a great fish jumping, while the ring of it spread in a circle of silver on the water.

CHAPTER XVI
SCHUMER GOES AWAY

They got the water on board next day, and the day following they were up before dawn to catch the slack of the tide which was due an hour after sunrise. It would then be still water at the break in the reef.

Schumer had made all his last preparations the night before. He would breakfast on board the schooner when she was free of the lagoon, and as Floyd rowed him across in the dinghy, the sky over the eastern reef was paling, and the stars above, that had been leaping all night like hearts of fire, showed signs of the coming day.

When Schumer was on board, Floyd pushed off again, having wished him good luck, and then hung on his oars half a cable length away, watching the preparations for departure.

He could hear Schumer's voice giving orders, and the bare feet of the fellows on deck running forward to the capstan.

"Break down," came the order, and following it the chorus of the Kanakas mixed with the rasp of the anchor chain as the slack of it came in, till the order was given, "Vast leaving."

All sound now ceased, and at that moment, just as the first light of day was striking the palm fronds and the topmost spars of the *Southern Cross*, the schooner, riding at her taut anchor chain, seemed the ghost of a ship stricken suddenly into unreality by the profound silence that had suddenly fallen upon her. A moment passed, and then the voice of Schumer came again, ordering the hands to set the mainsail, and to haul on the throat and peak halyards.

There was scarcely a trace of morning bank in the east, and the light, now strengthening rapidly, showed the great trapezium of canvas slatting to the faint and favorable wind. Then the foresail took the breeze, dusky forms swarming on the jib boom were casting the gaskets off the jib, now the men on deck were hauling at the jib halyards, and just as a horse answers to the pull of the bit, the *Southern Cross* veered round to the pressure of the sail, while the voice of Schumer came again, ordering the anchor to be hove up.

As it left the water and rose to the cathead, the schooner, with way on already, began to steal toward the reef opening, the first rays of the sun turning her canvas to vague gold against the new-born blue of the sky.

The form of Schumer appeared for a moment at the after rail and waved a hand, then it vanished, and Floyd, having watched the *Southern Cross* make her first bow to the swell of the outside sea, returned to the shore.

He hauled the dinghy up, and then, climbing across the coral to the break in the reef, watched the dwindling sail, till the sun dazzle half blinded him. Then he turned away and sought the house.

The two men had used the main room of the house for sleeping in at night, a bunk mattress taken from the *Southern Cross* being placed in each corner, and removed in the daytime to the smaller room. Floyd, without waiting for Isbel's help, removed the mattresses, and then began to wash and shave. The trade room of the *Tonga* had supplied them with all toilet necessaries, even to scissors, and its saloon had given them a mirror; as Floyd's eyes fell now on the scissors he recalled the fact that Schumer had been his hair cutter, even as he had been Schumer's. Well, it would be nine weeks before he would have the chance of a haircut, unless he could press Sru into the business. The thought of this made him laugh as he left the house and came out on the beach.

Isbel had lit the fire and laid the breakfast things. She was turning away when he stopped her.

"Schumer is gone," said he; "he has taken the ship and gone away, but he will be back in a little time."

"He will be back——" She broke off the sentence and raised her eyes to his, and though she was gazing full at him, she did not seem to see him. She seemed looking at something a hundred miles away, and the sensation of being gazed through as though he were clear as glass, and absolutely negligible, gave Floyd a queer sensation—almost a shiver.

"In a while," said he. "What ails you, Isbel—what have I done to you that has altered you so? We used to be good friends. It was not my fault, that trouble with one of your people; he had killed a man. He had committed murder, and the man who commits murder must die."

Isbel listened to him just as though she were listening to the sound of the sea or the wind, with the same far-away look, the same air of abstraction. Then she said, speaking not in answer to him, but as though she were making a statement about some ordinary matter:

"I have no peace here. I wish to go to my own people. Schumer will come back, but he will not find me."

"Hello!" said Floyd. "What do you mean?"

But she would say nothing more; she would not even look him again in the face, and, irritated at last, he turned away and sat down to breakfast.

If Schumer were to come back and not find her, where on earth did she propose to go? What did she mean? For a moment the horrid idea occurred to him that she might intend suicide; then he dismissed it; Isbel was not the sort of person to commit self-murder without any appreciable cause; though mysterious enough, she was too healthy and sane for that folly. All the same, as he breakfasted, her words kept ringing in his head:

"Schumer will come back, but he will not find me."

"God knows," thought he, "it will be hard enough here all alone without her bolting off or doing something foolish—anyhow, there is nowhere for her to bolt to, unless she bolts into the lagoon—confound Schumer and his methods. If he had left that chap alone, she would not have taken this dead set against us."

When he had finished breakfast, he went to the pierhead at the break on the reef and swept the sea line with his eyes. Away, far away, like a flake of white spar, a sail showed against the sky. It was the *Southern Cross*, almost hull down on the horizon.

CHAPTER XVII
THE FIRST OF THE TWO PEARLS

He came back to the beach.

Schumer had left him two boats, the dinghy and the boat of the *Cormorant*. They were both on the beach, and as the dinghy was the easiest to launch single-handed, he used it and pushed off to the fishing ground.

The gulls started after him from the reef opening, and now their voices came singly, mewing and miauling, the very voice of desolation itself.

Looking back as he rowed, he could see the figure of Isbel; she was putting things straight about the house, and just at that moment, as if stirred by the loneliness and the voices of the gulls, his heart went out to her. She was the only live thing in all that place for him. There were living things—fish in the lagoon and Kanaka laborers on the reef—but Isbel was the only warm spot for his mind to cling to.

The child had differentiated herself from her surroundings. By some extraordinary magic she had, without effort and almost without speech, pushed the image of Schumer to one side, and the forms of the Kanakas to the other.

Schumer, despite his powerful personality, seemed a dead thing beside Isbel, and the Kanakas, powerful and brawny as they were, seemed puppets—things of mechanism—fantoccini. What was the magic property that gave her the ascendency in the mind of Floyd?

For one thing, Isbel, despite her silence, her self-isolation, and the other-world atmosphere with which she surrounded herself, had always proved herself sterling.

Never had she failed them in any least particular, every humble duty that had fallen to her she had carried out honestly, and no paid servant could have worked more industriously in their interests.

Like Schumer, she had a strong personality that spoke in her actions and her movements. Unlike Schumer, her personality remained with one even in her absence. She was a good memory and a living memory. Schumer, in his absence—despite his wonderful personality—was only the recollection of a strong man absent.

That is all the difference between the mechanical and the vital, between the grip of iron and the grip of flesh.

Then she was a woman, or at least the germ of a woman; she was graceful, she was pretty as a wild flower, and, above all, she was an unknown factor, a hint of strangeness, the suggestion of a being from another star.

As he rowed, widening the distance between himself and the camping place, he was considering Isbel in all her aspects; the absence of Schumer and the loneliness and isolation of his own position had thrown her, so to speak, into the arms of his mind. He was considering also the fatal effect that had followed on the sight of the hanging. She had never been the same since that. The deed had stricken division between them, had called up all the barriers of race which she had expressed in those memorable words: "I have no rest here. I wish to go back to my own people." When he reached the fishing ground, he found the work in full swing under the supervision of Sru.

That gentleman was seated on a coral lump, smoking, and the lagoon, close to the shore, was occupied by what might have seemed, at first sight, a bathing party.

They did not use a boat now; they had constructed a raft, and all round the raft bobbed the heads of the pearl fishers, while on the raft itself several more were stretched, sunning themselves and smoking. All were stark naked and seemed happy as children.

Sru alone was garbed, and his simple dress consisted of a G string.

Sru saluted Floyd as the boat approached, and left his seat to help in beaching her; then he stood by Floyd as the latter inspected the few shells that had been taken already that morning. Sru was the only one of the working party who could talk in English, and though his conversation was as scanty as his G string, he could make himself understood.

As Floyd conversed with this man, he experienced a new sensation. Schumer had done the overseeing of the overseer up to this; Floyd had never come closely in contact with the men, and now, as he stood on the burning beach, almost in touch with Sru, he felt as though he were standing in touch with some man of the stone age and the silurian beaches.

The whites of Sru's eyes had a yellow tinge, and the glint of his teeth as he raised his lip was like a gleam of ivory reflected from a million years ago, the scars on his breast and arms, seen close to like this, had a deep significance, and the smell of him, hot, gorse-like, and faintly goatlike, was the smell of all fierce and savage things, hinted at and vaguely expressed. The John Tan plug he was smoking lent its fierce perfume to the natural scent of him, and he spat between his teeth and grumbled in his throat when he was not talking.

Sru was a revelation when you found yourself close to him like this, under the sun on a desolate beach, and with civilization thousands of miles away.

After a while Floyd ordered the raft to be brought to the beach edge, and, getting on to it, pushed out to inspect the work of the divers.

Oysters do not lie flat at the bottom of the sea; they lean with mouths agape at an angle of twenty to twenty-five degrees with the sea floor. The great clams do likewise. Floyd, looking down, could see the men who had just dived groping along the bottom, skylarking as they worked. One fellow who was in the act of rising with a couple of shells which he had secured, was caught by the foot by a companion. He dropped the shells and retaliated, the pair coming to the surface, bursting with want of air and suppressed laughter.

As Schumer said, they were like children, and their work had a large element of play in it. Still, they worked after their fashion, wet hands continually seizing the raft edge and depositing the dripping shells on it.

Although the quickest way of dealing with oysters in the mass is by rotting them, the search for pearls can be conducted on oysters fresh from the sea, and Floyd, as he sat on the raft, amused himself by opening some of the shells with his pocketknife, choosing the largest for this purpose. He found no pearls, but plenty of surprises. Nearly every large oyster in the southern seas gives shelter to a "messmate." A little crab, a small lobster, a worm, or a shrimp, lives in the shell along with the host. In some fisheries, as down in Sooloo, lobsters are only found, but here, as Floyd opened shell after shell, there was always something new—now a crab, now a worm, now a harmless creature, half shrimp, half crawfish.

Tiring of the business at last, he put ashore and turned his attention to the heap of shell "ripe" and gaping, putrid from exposure to the air, and waiting to be searched for pearls. He had got so used to the business now that it was scarcely unpleasant. Sru and one of the hands assisted him, and the work went forward without result for an hour, not even a seed pearl appearing in all the slimy mess carefully washed out in the trough of the canvas.

Schumer seemed to have taken the luck away with him. They knocked off for a rest and a smoke, and then went at it again with, as a final result of their morning's labor, a baroque pearl about the size of a sixpence, and a pearl of indifferent luster and weighing about ten grains.

"No good," said Sru, with a grunt of dissatisfaction; "heap few, heap big work."

"Heap plenty, maybe soon," replied Floyd, turning away. He felt depressed without the least reason for being so. No one knew better than he the uncertainties of this work, and how much it approximates to gambling. It was, perhaps, the feeling that Schumer had taken the luck away with him that caused the depression. Want of success is never inspiriting; actual defeat is a better tonic for the mind. He placed the morning's catch in the box he carried for the purpose, and, getting in the boat, rowed back to the encampment.

Work was never carried on during the middle of the day, and it was not till three o'clock in the afternoon that he returned.

Isbel had prepared his midday meal for him, and he left her behind, putting things in order. He had scarcely spoken to her, judging that in her present humor it was better to say nothing and trust to time and the absence of Schumer to soothe her feelings. He knew little of the mentality of Isbel. Arrived at the fishing grounds, he set to with Sru on a heap of shells that lay awaiting treatment.

The size of the oysters to be dealt with varied considerably. Nothing, indeed, varies much more than the size of the pearl oysters as taken in the different fisheries of the world. In some places the oysters are so small that from three to four thousand go to make a ton; in others they are so large that a ton weight of them only runs to four or five hundred. Occasionally gigantic specimens are obtained, weighing from fourteen to sixteen pounds, bare shells.

The largest of these oysters being handled by Floyd and Sru would have scaled a thousand to the ton, perhaps, and the medium size about fifteen hundred.

The afternoon work was scarcely more fruitful than the morning. It began with the capture of two small, but almost perfect, pearls, globular in shape, but weighing, perhaps, less than fifteen grains. These were taken in the first fifteen minutes, and then for the next three hours nothing showed but slush and slime.

The oysters one after the other were cleared out into the canvas trough with a sweep of the finger. Each pair of shells were then examined for adhering pearls or blisters, and flung aside if showing neither. Then, when sufficient putrefying matter had been collected in the troughs, it was carefully washed away and searched.

The shells cast aside were collected by two of the men and stored.

It was just at sunset, and at the washing of the last lot, that Floyd, groping in the seaweed-colored and viscous mass in the trough, felt his fingers closing upon a pebble. From the size of the object, he fancied for a second that it was a pebble. Instantly, and before he had brought it to light, he knew it to be a pearl.

It was. A perfectly round pearl, of enormous size, at least enormous in comparison with all the pearls he had hitherto seen. But it was not till he had cleansed it of slime in the bucket of water which Sru held for him that he saw what a prize he had obtained.

It was near sunset, and the golden light, mellow and tremulous, that was illuminating the sea and turning the west to flame, lit the treasure lying in the palm of his hand.

It was a pink pearl, exquisite, lustrous, and almost, one might say, luminous. It was the size of a marble. Not one of those enormous glass marbles with colored cores which we all remember as objects of worship, but an ordinary, practicable, play-with-able marble of full size.

"Good Lord!" said Floyd.

Sru grunted.

To Sru all this lust for pearls was an inexplicable business. If it had been a hunt for colored beads, he could have understood it, but pearls to him had no more beauty than cod's eyes, and far less beauty than colored shells. Coming from a district where pearling was unknown, he had no idea, either, of the value of these things.

But even to Sru the new find was pleasing, because of its color, the vague luminous pink, the luster, the semi-translucency, and the perfect shape of the thing pleased him.

But they did not excite him. He could not understand that the lump of colored nacre that weighed, perhaps, two hundred grains, and was worth, perhaps, five thousand pounds, was the equivalent of mountains of plug tobacco, shiploads of cotton stuff, knives, guns, and ammunition, oceans of gin.

Floyd, after his momentary exclamation, controlled himself, turned the thing over in his hand as though it were some ordinary object, and then put it in the pearl box, carefully covering it with the cotton wool. He put the box in the pocket of his coat, which lay near by, and turned again to the searching of the last remnants of stuff in the trough. Nothing more showed, and, having washed his hands in the canvas bucket which Sru held for him, he put on his coat, and, having given him some directions as to the storing of the shell, returned across the lagoon to the house.

He knew that what he had in his pocket was worth all the stuff they had taken from the lagoon. Schumer had educated him on the subject of pearls, but even Schumer, with all his knowledge, could not have fixed the value of this splendid find, perfect in all parts, and weighing at least a hundred grains.

After supper he took it out of its box and examined it by the light of the fire. It was even more beautiful by the glow of the burning sticks than by the glow of the sunset.

CHAPTER XVIII
THE VANISHING OF ISBEL

Next morning, when Floyd came out on the beach, he could not find Isbel.

He called to her, and there was no reply; then he started off to hunt for her in the grove, but she was not there.

He went to the seaward side of the reef; the breakers were falling and the gulls flying, but there was no sign of Isbel. She had vanished as completely as though she had never been. Floyd, in perplexity, shaded his eyes and gazed toward the sea line, as though he fancied some ship might have come and taken her off, but the sea line was as empty as the sea, and the only thing visible away out there was a frigate bird sailing on the wind.

The bird was passing the island with supreme indifference, traveling under the dominion of some steady purpose, and heading for some destination, perhaps half a thousand miles away. It dwindled in the blue, and Floyd, turning, took his way back to the beach.

The dinghy and quarter boat were still there, otherwise he might have fancied that she had gone to the fishing camp; the thing seemed inexplicable, and trying to put it from his mind, he set to on the preparations for breakfast. He lit the fire and put some water on to boil, opened some canned stuff, and then, having set a plate and knife and fork, made the coffee. He did all this automatically, working by instinct and habit, and almost heedless of what he was doing. A great desolation had fallen upon him, and a great fear, and in the midst of this desolation and fear something was calling out to him, a voice he had never heard before.

With the food untasted before him, he sat with his chin on his hands, gazing at the beach, white in the burning sunshine, and across the water of the lagoon, blue and ruffled by the morning wind.

Isbel, from the very first, had been for him a pleasing figure, quaint and with something of mystery about it. He did not know till now how much of his subconscious life she had occupied, nor how much he had really cared for her. She had grown on him till he had come to love her; that was the fact, and a fact that he recognized now in the pain and fear and desolation of his heart.

It was the strangest and rarest form of love, this love of his for Isbel. The love of a lonely man for a flower, or a child, and with just the hint of the love of a man for a woman.

She was the germ of a woman, and by just that extent did the bond of sex hold him to her.

His life had been very lonely. Right up from his boyhood he had lived pretty much uncared for. He had made friendships, but the wandering life of the sea breaks ties just as it casts away lives; he had no home, no family, and the men he had grown to care for, old chums and messmates, were like the gulls—once parted from and lost to sight, never to be found again.

As he sat like this, on the wind which was setting across the lagoon from the fishing ground, came a snatch of song from the fishermen who were at work.

He rose up, and, leaving the food still untasted, came down to the water's edge and, pushing the dinghy off, got into her and sculled across to the camp.

He had some thought of telling his trouble to Sru, and some vague idea of seeking help from him. Never for a moment had the idea come to him that Isbel might have joined the fishing camp.

It seemed impossible for her to have got there across the rough coral of the reef, and equally impossible across the lagoon. Yet when he landed, the first object that caught his eye was Isbel. She was seated in front of one of the tents engaged in shredding some coconut pulp into a bowl, and when she saw him she did not seem at all put out.

She had gone back to her own people, literally, and to look at her he might have fancied she had never parted from them. Floyd nodded to her. He could have laughed aloud in the relief of seeing her safe and sound; she nodded in return, and went on with her work. She did not seem in the least put out or ashamed of herself for having deserted him, and now that his fears about her were removed, he felt irritated at her coolness.

All the hard things that Schumer had said about Kanakas rose up in his mind—"animals dressed in human skin," "creatures without souls," and so forth.

But these sayings vanished from his mind almost immediately. They had no clutch in them, simply because they had no truth in them, and Isbel, as she sat at work before the tent, formed their last antidote.

Never had she looked prettier than this morning, seated there on a little mat, a fresh scarlet flower in her hair, her feet tucked away, and her brown hands busily at work.

Floyd came up to her.

"So there you are, Isbel," said he. "I did not think you would have gone off and left me like that."

Isbel made no reply; she continued her work without looking up; one might have fancied that she had not heard him.

"Of course," said Floyd, "if you had told me, I would not have tried to stop you. Why should I? You are perfectly free here to do as you please. I would even have brought you here myself in the boat. How did you get here?"

"Along the reef," said Isbel, without looking up.

"Along the reef—why, you must have cut your feet to pieces!"

For reply Isbel pushed a foot out from under her robe.

It was a perfect little foot, honey-colored, perfect in form, the toenails polished like agate. He had seen it often before, but it seemed to him that he saw it now for the first time. As he looked at it the toes spread apart, and it was flexed and extended, as if to show that it had sustained neither scratch nor injury. Then it vanished.

"Well, you are cleverer than I am," said Floyd. He would not stoop to question her as to how she had negotiated the reef. If she did not choose to tell, why, then let her keep silent. He turned on his heel and walked off to where Sru was waiting for him. Then, as they made for the place where the oysters were lying ready to be examined, he glanced back; she had vanished into the tent.

He said nothing to Sru on the matter, nor did the foreman make any comment about the girl. They set to on their task, working an hour without any result, and then knocking off for a rest and a smoke.

It was during the second spell, and Floyd had just turned to place the only take of the morning, a small and nearly valueless pearl, in the box, which he carried for the purpose, when their attention was drawn by shouts from the fellows who were working in the lagoon.

They had been shouting and splashing at their work, but these outcries had a new note that brought Floyd and Sru to their feet in a moment, and down to the lagoon edge.

The dinghy, in which Floyd had come over, was lying on the sand, with the incoming tide rippling up to her; they pushed her off, reached the raft, and found what was the matter.

One of the workers, Timau by name, while groping along the bottom of the lagoon, had stepped into a half-open clamshell, the shell had closed on his foot like a trap, and he was a prisoner.

This is one of the most terrible accidents that can happen to the pearl fisher. The great clam grows to an enormous size, and, like the oyster, he does not lie flat on the sea floor, but tilted at an angle of twenty-five degrees or more. The sand, if there be much sand where he lies, tends to silt round him and hide him, and so he lies, a veritable man-trap for the unwary.

The raft was crowded with men, all shouting, and not one of them, seemingly, with the vestige of an idea as to how they were to render assistance. Timau could be seen clearly; he had fallen on his back, with his right leg bent and the knee pointing upward; the right foot was held by the terrific shell, whose contracting muscles were powerful as iron bands.

Nothing could be more shocking than this seizure of a man by a shellfish, this quiet destruction of the highest form of life by the lowest form of intelligence.

The shark moves under the dominion of will, and the cuttlefish knows at least hunger, but the great clam is fed by the water that laves it, and its only expression of will is to grip and hold whatever dares to violate its sanctuary.

For a moment Floyd was as much at a loss as the others; then he saw on the raft the iron bar used for breaking down coral formations that were encroaching on the beds. It was about two-thirds of the thickness of an ordinary crowbar, and measured about three feet in length.

He scrambled on to the raft, seized the bar, and dived.

He was not wearing his coat, but otherwise he was fully dressed; in the moment between seizing the bar and diving he had thought out the whole plan of action. The great clam, inclined to an angle of twenty degrees, had to be pried open, and to do so the under shell had to be brought level with the lagoon floor, so as to obtain a purchase.

The watchers above saw him thrust the bar between the shells, an act easy enough to accomplish, as they were held four inches and more apart by the victim's leg. This done, he inserted his booted foot as if to tread down the under shell, while he levered up the top shell.

He had reckoned on his weight being sufficient to press down the shell, forgetting that a man weighed in sea water scales very much less than a man weighed in air. Yet, even so, he managed to reduce very considerably the angle, and with a tremendous effort managed to wrench the two shells apart.

He rose instantly, nearly bursting for want of air, and as he rose the fellows on the raft, courageous enough now, dived like one man to fetch up the body of Timau.

They brought it to the raft, where Floyd was resting, and hauled it on to the logs, while Floyd, on hands and knees, examined it.

Timau seemed a very dead man. The right foot and part of the leg was black and lacerated; there was neither movement of heart nor sign of respiration, and Sru, who had also bent down to examine him, rose up with a grunt.

"Heap dead," said Sru; "no more fishing for Timau."

Floyd ordered them to push the raft ashore. This having been done, he had the body laid out on the hot sand, and started to work at once with artificial respiration.

He had to do the business alone, for not one of the hands could understand what was required to be done, nor would they have helped had they understood. This was witch business; the man was dead and beyond recall; it was plainly against nature to try and bring him back.

However, back he came. Floyd had been working for some ten minutes when the first signs of returning life showed themselves. Ten minutes later Timau was leaning on his elbow, blinking at the world to which he had returned, hiccuping and endeavoring to speak.

Floyd had him carried up to the nearest tent and laid on a mat. Then, with the help of Isbel, who had suddenly appeared, he set to to dress the injured foot. The lower end of the fibula was fractured, all the skin over the lower part of the leg was lacerated and bruised, and there was a nasty cut on the instep. They laid wet cloths on the wounds, made a bandage over them of coconut sennit, and left him so far recovered that he was able to smoke a pipe.

CHAPTER XIX
THE MIRACLE

Timau made a good recovery. In a couple of days he was hobbling about with the aid of a stick, and in a week, but for the bandage on his foot and leg, he seemed a well man.

He was also a distinguished personage in a way; honored as a man returned from the grave, yet, at the same time, avoided as much as possible. In other words, he was feared, and he made the best of the situation by doing no work and drawing full allowances in food and tobacco.

He did not show the least outward gratitude toward Floyd for his rescue and restoration, and Floyd, in his turn, found himself somewhat in the same position as Timau.

Sru, while working just the same, showed considerable reserve in his dealings with his manager. A man who could bring a corpse back to life was not a person to be dealt with lightly, and the strange thing was, that Floyd's beneficent action did not seem to strike Sru in the light of beneficence. It was quite plainly evident that it was looked upon more as an act of evil than of good.

The other natives seemed of the same mind as Sru; they never laughed and tom-fooled now when Floyd was present—they worked better.

Isbel seemed quite unmoved. He saw her now nearly every day when he came to the fishing camp; she had quite settled down in her new home, and seemed always busy, yet somehow to Floyd's eyes she seemed changed. It was toward the first week of Schumer's absence that Floyd became fully alive to this change in her. She was no longer a child. Just as some tropical plants bloom in a night, so in the course of a few weeks she had changed, at least to his eyes. It was as though a new person had come upon the island.

But the miracle of the change in her had touched him, too.

The whole world seemed suddenly altered. Life, in a moment, had become a different thing. Life, in a moment, had become worth living, the sky and sea bluer, the sun more friendly, the island more beautiful.

Isbel had not changed the least in her manner toward him, but the magic of life that had touched her had touched him through her. She was always in his thoughts—when he returned at night to the house, and when he returned in the morning to the fishing ground, when he lay awake at night and when he worked with Sru by day.

He was in love, but he did not recognize the fact for a long time, and even then he formed no plans and dreamed no dreams after the fashion of lovers.

The idea of Isbel was enough, the sight of her, the memory of her.

Had she shown by the faintest sign that she was thinking of him, it would have been different. The will to possess her would have at once arisen. But she showed nothing, living and moving as remote from him as the moon that silvered the reef and shone upon the water.

One morning Floyd, who ever since the departure of Schumer had recorded the time by making a notch each morning on the doorpost, completed the forty-ninth notch. It was exactly seven weeks since Schumer's departure. He had lost all record of the day of the week. The *Cormorant* had been lost on a Wednesday, and on landing he could easily have reckoned the day by the time spent in the boat, but he had not troubled. Schumer had also lost the day of the week, but the loss affected them very little here, where even the hour of the day was of small account.

"He ought to be back in a fortnight," said Floyd to himself, as he sat down in the shadow of the house to smoke a pipe before starting for the fishing ground. "Wonder what luck he's had."

He sat smoking and reviewing the events that had happened since Schumer's departure and the take of pearls.

Since the capture of the pink pearl, luck had been very uneven. All told, the take had amounted to a hundred and five, leaving out seeds and worthless specimens. Of these only twenty were of any considerable size or value. There were also twenty-five blistered shells, which Floyd had put aside to be dealt with by Schumer.

The unevenness of the luck lay in the fact that during some weeks the catch would be quite negligible, during others quite good; some days would be blank, while on the other hand three of the best had been taken on the same day.

To-day was to prove lucky, for when he approached the fishing ground, Sru approached him with a large oyster in his hand.

The natives ate oysters sometimes, always cooking them first, a strange thing, considering the fact that they would eat fish not only raw, but living.

This was one of the oysters destined for food. It had been opened, and when Sru reached Floyd, he lifted the upper shell, and, putting his finger under the mantel, raised it, disclosing a loose pearl.

It was as big as the great pink pearl, but of a virginal white. Floyd had experienced many sensations in life, but none so vividly pleasant as now at the sight of this thing fresh from the lagoon, and in its strange home.

The pink pearl had been fished out of a mess of putrescence, but here was a gem handed to him as if by the dripping hand of the sea.

He took the oyster, carefully extracted the pearl, and held it in his palm, while Sru looked on, evidently pleased with himself, and the other hands stood around, glad of any opportunity to knock off work.

"Good," said Floyd; "you shall have two sticks of tobacco for this, and I will give the same to any one who finds another like it."

He put it in the box, trying to assume as careless a manner as possible, and then turned to the work of the day, ordering at the same time the idlers to get back to the lagoon.

When the day's work was over, Sru demanded his tobacco.

"To-morrow," said Floyd. "I will fetch it over in the morning when I come."

But Sru, who was very much of a child, despite his size and strength, was not to be put off till the morrow. He wanted his reward at once, and Floyd, irritated, yet amused at his persistency, ordered him to get into the dinghy and accompany him across the lagoon to the camping place.

Here he left him by the boat, while he went off to the cache for the tobacco.

He had to remove the tarpaulin to get at the case where it was; having finished this business, he turned to come back and, doing so, caught a glimpse of Sru.

Sru had left the boat and followed him unnoticed. He had been watching him through the trees, and must have seen the cache and its contents, the piles of boxes and bales of stuff, all half-glimpsed or hinted of under the tarpaulin.

A chill went to Floyd's heart. He remembered Schumer's words and his warning against letting any of the labor men land just here. Schumer had been so strict that even the Kanaka crew of the *Southern Cross*, who had helped to build the house, were never allowed to go beyond a certain point. And now Sru had seen everything.

The man was walking back to the lagoon edge when Floyd overtook him with the tobacco, and Floyd, furious though he was, could say nothing. Sru had broken no orders in following him, and to show any anger now would be the worst policy in the world.

He got into the dinghy, rowed over to the fishing camp, landed Sru, and returned. It seemed to Floyd that the capture of a big pearl always brought trouble. The finding of the pink pearl had been followed by the going off of Isbel, and now this had happened.

He lit the fire for supper, and then set to prepare the meal. When it was over, he sat smoking and watching the starlight on the water of the lagoon. Dark ripples were flowing up from the incoming tide, round points of light showed here and there, the result of eddies or the splash of jumping fish; away, seemingly miles away, the camp fires of the pearl fishers showed spark-like in the blue gloom of night.

The camp fires fascinated Floyd. Isbel was over there, and over there, also, was Sru. Sru, with his yellow-tinged eyes, the scars of old battles on his body, night in his heart, and the knowledge of the cache in his head.

What a fool he had been to disregard Schumer's advice; the wise Schumer, who foresaw everything, had even seen his—Floyd's—stupidity.

Well, there was no use in complaining; the thing now was to make preparation for whatever might happen. The house door was strong and the walls, without being loopholed, had convenient spaces—"ventilation holes" Schumer had called them—through which a rifle might be fired.

He rose up and, going to the house, lit the lamp and began to overhaul the arms and ammunition. This done, he retired to bed with a loaded rifle by his side.

CHAPTER XX
THE TROUBLE WITH SRU

When he came to the fishing ground next morning, he kept a keen lookout for any alteration in Sru.

Sru, however, seemed just the same, and the hands were working as usual. Timau, wholly recovered now, was working with them, but there was no sign of Isbel.

He asked Sru where she was, and Sru cast his yellow-whited eyes about as if in search of her. He opined she might be somewhere in the grove that lay to the right of the camping place, and indicated the place with his hand. But as Sru spoke with seeming indifference, Floyd noticed an expansion of his nostrils and a new light in his eye. It was as though something had suddenly irritated him.

That something could only be Isbel.

Floyd thought little of the matter. He knew Isbel's ways, and could easily imagine that her strange nature might give cause for friction between herself and her own people. He set to work and put the thought of her out of his mind—or fancied that he had done so.

As a matter of fact, she was never quite absent from his mind, and he had reached the stage now of anger with the Kanakas that she should be of their blood and living among them as one of them.

The strange psychological fact presented itself that though Isbel was a Kanaka, he was beginning to feel toward Kanakas some of that contempt, amounting to dislike, so evident in Schumer. That she who was so different to these people around him should be of the same blood was, so to speak, an insult against her.

Sru's savagery and scars, Timau's ugliness—for Timau was a most unbeautiful type, though, withal, having a certain honestness in his plainness, the monkey tricks of the others, and their general childishness and fatuity, all these things were a reflection on Isbel.

And she chose to live among them! She had discarded him for them. It only wanted that to complete his feelings on the matter.

Before he returned to the camping place that night he caught a glimpse of her. She was down by the lagoon edge, filling a bowl with sea water, and when he spoke to her she replied to him as usual, yet her manner was different. She seemed upset about something. He might have fancied that she was sulking, had he not known her so well by unconscious study of all her moods and expressions. This was not ill temper—as a matter of fact in all his experience she had never shown ill temper—but something else. She was unhappy. Something had occurred to disturb her or to frighten her. She seemed cowed, and as she went off with the full bowl, he was on the point of running after her to seek an explanation.

But he checked himself in time. He knew quite well it would be useless, and he dreaded to give her any cause of offense. Sru most likely had spoken harshly to her, or she had fallen out with some other member of the tribe. It was not for him to interfere in the domestic affairs of this strange company, and now for the first time fully he recognized the veil of difference that separated him from this race, alien to him as the people of some other star.

He got into the dinghy and returned to the house. It was the evening of the new moon, and even as he rowed across the lagoon she showed in the blue east like a reaper's sickle held up for the sun to look at before his setting.

Never had Floyd felt lonelier than this evening. Isbel seemed suddenly to have pushed still farther away from him, and the lonely beauty of the island under the sunset, and the sickle moon, seemed part of the new loneliness that had fallen upon his life.

Halfway across the lagoon he stopped rowing and put his hand to the pocket in which he carried the pearl box. He had left it behind on a ledge of coral by the working place. It contained the day's take, two small pearls of little value; still, it must be recovered.

He turned the boat and rowed back. The hands had all dispersed along the reef armed with fish spears, the tide was falling, and there were often big fish to be got in the rock pools at low tide. Not a soul was in sight, and, having found the box lying just where he had left it on the ledge of coral, he turned back toward the boat. He had nearly reached it when a cry from the grove which lay to the left of the camping place made him start.

It was Isbel's voice. In a moment he was away among the trees, and there he found Sru, Sru struggling with Isbel.

The thing seemed absurd, absurd as the idea of a child struggling with a tiger, and yet she was holding him off, with no breath now to cry out, one hand twisted in his long hair, and the other striking at his face.

Next moment Floyd had Sru by the throat, half strangling him with a powerful grip; then, releasing him, he struck out.

The blow landed right on the point of the chin, and Sru, felled like an ox under the poleax, crashed into an hibiscus bush and lay without kick or movement as if he were dead. Floyd turned to Isbel. She had fallen and half risen, supporting herself with one hand on the ground. She seemed dazed, like a person who had received a violent blow.

He bent down, picked her up, and, holding her in his arms, carried her down to the boat. He did not worry about Sru; his one thought was to get Isbel to a place of safety. If Sru were dead, there would be no more trouble over the matter. If, on the contrary, he was only suffering from the effects of a knock-out blow, he would certainly seek vengeance when he recovered. When he placed Isbel in the boat, he found that she had lost consciousness.

The sun had not set; it was at the moment of conflict between the starlight and the last rays of sunset, the pale sickle of the moon had grown to a brilliant orange gold, and the light was strong enough to brighten the lagoon water.

Arrived at the beach, he stepped out, and, lifting Isbel in his arms, carried her up to the house. She was no longer unconscious, and, as he carried her, he felt her arm clasped round his neck. It was as though she were accepting his protection and thanking him at the same time.

Arrived at the house, he placed her on the bunk mattress upon which he always slept, lit the lamp, and knelt down beside her. "You'll stay here now, Isbel," said he; "you will not run away from me any more, will you? I've been pretty lonely without you, but I did not mind so long as I thought you were happy with your own people. You see how they have treated you——"

She raised herself on her elbow and looked into his face, the lamplight struck her hair and forehead, while he saw nothing for the moment, and knew of nothing, but the brown depths of her eyes, so close to him, so mysterious, so luminous—yet so dark.

"I will stay," said she. "I did not know you before. I know you now."

He took her hand and she let him hold it for a moment. It was the first time that hand had been in his, a hand firm, yet soft, subtle, yet capable, warm as life itself. Then he released it and rose up. There was grim business to be attended to, and as he fetched the two rifles and their ammunition from the adjoining room, the feeling came to him that up to this he had never really lived, but had only existed as a spectator of life. Here was life raw and real, the battle for existence and love and everything worth having; the supreme moment which many of us never know.

He placed the rifles on the table and the ammunition beside them, and then went back and fetched the revolvers. When he returned, he found that Isbel had left the mattress and was standing by the table, with one hand resting on it, and her eyes fixed on him.

"These are for Sru if he comes with any of those fellows behind him," said Floyd. "It's as well to be prepared."

"Schumer showed me how," said she, "before you came here—long before. Look— —" She opened the breech of one of the Winchesters, extracted the cartridges, and put them back. "Then you fire—so." She put the rifle to her shoulder and took aim at some imaginary object, then, lowering it, she turned to him, and for the first time she smiled.

Her eyes lit with a new light, her little teeth shone, it was as though something bright and fierce, some unknown spirit, dwelling in her nature, had suddenly peeped out. He recalled the day when they had smashed the bottles on the reef, and she had assisted, laughing at the destruction. She had not smiled, she had laughed, little short laughs sharp as the thrusts of a stabbing spear.

"Ah," said Floyd, "you know how to use a gun. Well, that's all the better. If they come to make any trouble, we will be able to give them something they won't like, you and I."

"You and I," said Isbel, with the same smile. Then, suddenly, she pressed her little white teeth on her under lip.

She placed the rifle back on the table, and, turning, left the house by the open door.

Floyd looked after her, wondering what had happened now. He finished the examination of the rifles and revolvers, and then, leaving them upon the table, came outside.

Isbel was lighting the fire to prepare supper for him.

CHAPTER XXI
BEFORE THE ATTACK

That night he made her sleep in the house, while he took his place outside. He arranged to call her when half the night was over, so that she might keep watch while he slept, and as he sat with his back to the house wall, and a loaded rifle by his side, he tried to forecast the possibility of an attack and the upshot, should it occur.

The fact that Sru had seen the cache weighed with him as much as the occurrence of that evening. The two facts combined made the position very, very threatening. The labor men had no arms and ammunition, but they were thirty in number; they had no boat, but they had the raft, and though the reef was almost impassable, Isbel had got along it that night of her flight, and what she had done, these fellows could doubtless accomplish also.

He could see the sparks of the camp fires away across the lagoon, but though the wind was blowing from over there, it brought no sound on it. Usually one could catch stray snatches of song from across the water, or the fellows shouting as they speared fish in the rock pools by torchlight.

To-night the silence seemed ominous, and the light of the camp fires like threatening eyes. Now and again would come the splash of a fish, and now and again the wind breezing up for a moment would set the foliage moving in the grove, the breadfruit leaves clapping like great green hands, and the palm fronds rustling and cheeping.

The surf on the outer reef was low of sound to-night, yet, occasionally, over to the west, where the full trend of the swell was meeting the coral, it would speak louder and become angry like the sound of a train at full speed.

Even the stars had taken on the aspect of attention; they seemed watching and waiting to see something that would surely occur.

Floyd had to get up and pace the sands to break the spell. Then, after a while, he sat down again. The fires over at the fishing camp had died out, the wind had fallen to the merest breath, and the surf on the western reef no longer snarled.

Danger seemed to have drawn away from the island, leaving behind her the profoundest peace. Floyd, whose eyes were longing to close despite all his efforts to keep awake, felt a touch on his shoulder. It was Isbel come to relieve guard. When he came out next morning, the sun was up, and Isbel had lit the fire and was preparing breakfast.

They sat down to the meal together, and, when it was over, Floyd declared his intention of going, as usual, to the fishery.

"We must keep the work going, at all costs," said he. "If I did not, they would think I was afraid, and then they would be sure to attack us. Besides, there may be nothing to fear. Sru is the only one I care about, the others are pretty harmless, with no one to lead them, and Sru may be knocked out. He looked pretty dead when I left him."

Isbel shook her head.

"One blow would not kill Sru," said she. "Too strong. If you go, I go with you."

"You," said Floyd. "And suppose—suppose they attack us?"

"Suppose you go alone and get killed," said Isbel, "what become of me here alone? No, I go if you go. I can shoot. I stay in the boat to keep it safe, whiles you go to the fishing. If they come to take the boat, I kill them. If they strike at you, I kill them. You don't know me. I know myself. I have no fear at all."

"I believe you," said he. "Yes, we will go together; you are worth half a dozen men——Isbel, why did you run away from me that time?"

Isbel looked down.

"I went to find my own people," said she at last. "I was afraid."

"Afraid of me?"

"I don't know," said Isbel; "you and Schumer, and being alone with you made me afraid."

"And you are not afraid any longer?"

"With you I am not any more afraid," said Isbel, speaking with difficulty, and drawing a little pattern on the sand with her finger tip. Then, looking up: "Not even with Schumer, if you were there."

Floyd was about to take her hand, but he restrained himself.

"That is good," said he. "You need never have been afraid of me. I care for you too much to let any one hurt you, and that morning when I came out of the house and found you gone, when I searched in the grove and along the reef and could not see you and thought you might be drowned and that I would never see you again, the world seemed no use any longer."

He rose to his feet as if to check his words, and walked off to the house, leaving Isbel still seated on the sand, and still drawing the pattern with her finger.

He returned with one of the Winchester rifles under his arm, a revolver in his hand, and one in his pocket.

Isbel rose, and, going down to the lagoon edge, they pushed the dinghy off, got in, and started for the fishing camp. As they drew near they saw that the fishing was going on apparently as usual, and the first person to greet them on the beach was Sru.

There were all the elements for a strained situation, but Sru showed no sign of the incident of the day before, and when Floyd stepped out on the sand, nodded his head as usual, and grumbled something in his throat that seemed intended for a welcome. But his eye lit on the Winchester Isbel propped against the seat of the dinghy, and it doubtless took in, also, the revolver butt sticking from Floyd's coat pocket.

The seeming indifference of Sru to what had happened struck Floyd as almost uncanny; then, as they set to work, he let the matter drop from his mind. If it satisfied Sru to take a thrashing and say nothing, it satisfied Floyd's policy to let the matter drop. The man had been punished for his misdeed, and the incident was closed, for the present at least.

Now Schumer would undoubtedly have tried the man and shot him offhand, not only for the attack on Isbel, but to safeguard the little colony. Floyd, though just as courageous as Schumer at a pinch, and probably more so, was incapable of acting the part of executioner. He could not kill a man in cold blood.

So he worked side by side with the yellow-eyed one, and as the labor went on he forgot more and more the danger of the situation, but he might have noticed, had he turned, that Isbel, who had taken her seat on the sand by the boat, never left her position for a moment, and that position enabled her, if need arose, to stretch out her arm and seize the Winchester that was propped against the seat of the dinghy.

Neither would she have anything to say to the fellows who were diving. The raft came several times ashore to discharge shell, and some of the hands drew close to her, but she told them to clear off.

Floyd heard her voice once or twice hard and sharp, a quite new voice for her. He could not tell what she said, but he noticed that none of the fellows approached her.

Some of them, as far as he could judge, seemed deriding her just as schoolboys joke at one of their number who has made himself unpopular, but they kept their distance.

At the dinner hour shortly before noon, the whole crowd of the labor men, joined by Sru, drew off to a spot close to the tents, and, squatting in a ring, set to on their food.

Work was always knocked off in the middle of the day, Floyd returning to the house for a siesta. He came now toward Isbel, intending to help her to push the dinghy off, but instead of rising, she made him sit down beside her.

"See them," said she. "They sit all together and like that." She made a ring on the sand with her finger. "I go and hear what they say if you wait. It is no good when they sit like that all together and talk while they eat—— Wait!"

She rose up and walked along the beach edge, picking up shells. Then she drew close to the grove and vanished into it. Some of the tents were situated close up to the grove, and the hands were seated eating and talking close to the tent. They looked after Isbel as she was walking along the beach edge. When she disappeared, they seemed to forget her, and went on with their palaver. Floyd waited. Five minutes later he saw the form of the girl away out from among the trees. She walked right down to the edge of the lagoon, and then came along toward Floyd, still picking up an occasional shell.

When she reached him she showed him the shells.

"No good," said she. "But look at them so they may see."

Floyd handled the shells and pretended to admire them; then she placed them in the dinghy and they pushed her off.

It was not till they reached the middle of the lagoon that she told of what she had done, and what she had heard.

She had crept through the grove to the back of one of the tents, and listened to the chatter that had come clearly heard on the slight wind that was blowing toward the grove.

Something was afoot, and whatever they were going to do was to be done that night. From what Isbel gathered, an attack was to be made on them, and the attackers would cross the lagoon on the raft.

Floyd, who was rowing, pulled in his sculls.

"The raft," said he. "I never thought of that. They can get twenty chaps on to it. We must stop this. It is going to be war anyhow, so we may as well strike first."

He told Isbel the fear that had suddenly occurred to him, and she laughed. Then taking to the sculls again, he rowed on as hard as he could, till they reached their destination.

Leaving Isbel to look after the dinghy, he ran up to the house and came back with a hammer, a big nail, and a coil of rope. Then they pushed off again, making for the fishing camp. The raft, when not in use, was moored by a rope to a spur of coral jutting out from the sand.

As they approached, they could see the labor men still seated at their pow-wow. Heads were turned as the dinghy drew near to the raft, but not a man moved till Isbel, with a rifle in one hand and a knife in the other, cut the mooring rope.

Then a yell rose up, and the whole crowd, rising like one man, came racing down to the water's edge, picking up stones as they ran, while some of them, turning, made off for the fish spears in the tents.

While Isbel had been cutting the rope, Floyd, with three blows of the hammer, had driven the big nail into one of the logs, tied the rope to it, tied the other end of the rope to the rings in the stern of the dinghy, and was now sculling for his life. The heavy raft moved slowly, and the crowd on shore, held up for a moment by the water, were just taking to it when Isbel's rifle rang out, and the foremost of them, hit through the shoulder, sat down with a yell on the sand. The rush was broken for a moment, and Floyd, as he tugged at the sculls, saw a sight that would have made him laugh, had he been watching from a place of safety.

The balked ones literally danced on the sands. Fury drove them, but fright held them, and the dance was the result till the fellows with the fish spears made their appearance, racing down from the tents.

Floyd instantly put the dinghy alongside the raft, and, springing on to it, took the rifle from the girl, while she, getting into the dinghy, took the sculls and went on with the towing.

Floyd dropped the first spearman twenty paces from the water's edge, and he fell on his belly, while the spear slithered along the beach.

The second spearman, struck fair in the forehead, flung out his arms and fell on his back. The spear, striking the sand with its butt, stood upright and quivering, the point, still dark with fish blood, impotent and pointing to the sky.

It was enough for the others. They broke and ran, and, as they ran, Floyd fired on them, catching one fellow through the leg and knocking a tuft of hair off another's head.

In thirty seconds the beach was clear.

Floyd through it all had acted almost automatically and as if firing at a target. The whole business seemed strangely impersonal and unreal. That he should be standing there, killing men like flies, seemed part of the everyday business of life, and yet, at the back of his mind, something was crying out against it all, a voice small as though it had traveled from a thousand miles away, and without substance or sound or weight in effect on his mind.

He stood with the taste of the cartridge smoke in his mouth, staring at the beach, while from behind him he could hear the sound of the sculls in the rowlocks as Isbel strained at the oars.

They were now well out from the shore, and he took his place in the boat at the sculls, while Isbel got on the raft.

The beach they were leaving was all trodden up, and the bodies of the two dead men lay, one huddled up as though he were asleep, the other spread-eagled and looking like a brown starfish, the spear he had been carrying so valiantly standing beside him, barb pointing to the sky.

The light wind was blowing the dry sand in little eddies, and under the blazing sunlight the salt white beach and the emerald shallows of the lagoon made a dazzling picture. Nothing could seem farther removed from death or the thought of death than this brilliant scene, where the slain were lying unburied and Death himself was watching from the grove of trees that formed its background.

Isbel stood on the raft as he towed it, her hand shading her eyes, her gaze fixed on the shore.

Floyd, recalling her horror of the hanging and the effect it produced upon her, could not help wondering at her attitude now, till he remembered the difference between the cold-blooded execution of a man and the killing of a man in self-defense.

When they had reached the middle of the lagoon, she turned from gazing at the shore and sat down on the raft. They did not speak to one another till the dinghy was landed and the raft moored by a long rope which they tied to one of the seats of the quarter boat, which was lying high and dry on the sand.

"Well," said Floyd, when this was finished, "we are in for it now, Isbel, you and I. These fellows won't sit down and do nothing, or, if they do, I am greatly mistaken."

"No," said Isbel, "they will try to kill us." She said it quite simply, as though she were talking of some matter of little moment.

"And we'll try to stop them," said Floyd, with a laugh. It is the sign mark of the Anglo-Saxon and Celts and all breeds that spring from their mixture, that they go laughing into battle, die jesting, and carve their enemies with epigrams as well as swords; battle brings a levity of spirit that in its turn brings victory, and Floyd, now that war was declared, moved lightly and felt a liveliness at heart such as he had not experienced since boyhood.

He had destroyed the enemy's fleet, but he had not destroyed their land forces, and worse than all, he had not put their general out of action.

Sru was still alive, and he was more dangerous than all the others.

When the firing had begun, Sru had flung himself flat on his stomach on the sand, and from that position had yelled his orders. It was evident that he was the directing spirit of the whole business, and it was nearly certain that he would not take defeat lying down.

The weak position of the house as a defensive stronghold lay in its proximity to the grove and the fact that it did not command the approach to this bit of the island by way of the reef. The back of the building was close up to the trees, and, though there were chinks that made good loopholes for firing through, the trees, and especially their shadow by night, gave good cover for an attacking party.

Then there was the prospect of a siege. Floyd, taking his seat on the sand in the shade of the trees, called to Isbel to sit down beside him.

Then they held a council of war.

"How many fish spears have those fellows got, Isbel?" asked he.

"Many," replied Isbel. "They were making them a long time ago—too many for fishing."

"You mean they were made for the purpose of attacking us—I mean, of attacking me, for you were with them then?"

Isbel nodded.

"Yes, but I did not know. I thought then it was for the fishing. Now I know better. It was Sru who told them to make more spears, and they would all get together and talk. I had no feeling at all that it was wrong, else I would have listened. But now I see it all."

This cast even a darker light on Sru. He must have been plotting all along and from the first. Plotting to seize Isbel for himself, kill the only white man on the place, and seize all the valuables he could find. That was doubtless his plan of campaign. As to the far future, and how he was to escape from the island and from punishment, he was unlikely to have made any plan. The savage view is a short view, and is mainly occupied by immediate desires and the means of gratifying them. It is only the trained intelligence that forecasts and lays plans only to be carried out in the far future.

Sru wanted Isbel, and tobacco more than he could use, knives for which he had no use, firearms to glut his desire for lethal weapons, printed cotton, and the satisfaction of the lust to kill. He most likely promised himself Floyd served up roasted in plantain leaves, for he belonged to the man-eating order of Solomanders. So in his dark mind he had constructed a scheme for getting these things and satisfying these desires, and had carried out his scheme while working in amity with the man he intended to destroy.

His military genius had not proved itself on a par with his genius for villainy, but he had the numbers, while Floyd only had the rifles, for rifles, even though they be Winchesters, firing five shots apiece, are of limited use without men behind them.

From the edge of the grove bordering the rough coral of the reef a good lookout could be kept toward the fishing ground. From here the lagoon, exclusive of the segment, including the reef opening, could be watched.

One could see the fishing camp and the whole of the roof leading from it. Standing here, one could command with a rifle all that strip of rough and broken coral that made a natural defense, and along which an attacking force must come, if it wished to reach the house by land.

Floyd determined that this was the point where watch must be kept by night. The coral, though rough and sharp here and there as knives, was not impassable to a determined foe. Isbel had got along it that time she ran away, and these fellows, with foot soles like leather and nerves insensitive to cuts and falls, could do what she had done.

He posted Isbel now to keep watch, while, going back to the house, he made preparations for a possible siege.

Taking the tarpaulin from the cache, he made a collection of all the tinned food that came first to hand. There were two bags of ship's bread still left, and these, with the tins of bully beef, potatoes, and so forth, he carried to the house. Then he filled two of the water beakers at the well and placed them in the main room of the building.

Then he remembered the albini rifles. These, with their ammunition, were stored separately, and the conveyance of them would have meant a considerable amount of labor and time. He took only the ammunition which was made up in four large parcels. These he carted down to the dinghy, rowed her out into five fathom of water, and dumped the parcels in the lagoon.

The bottom of the lagoon where he dumped them was pretty rough coral, so they would not be shifted much by the tide, and could be fished up later on.

Having completed all these preparations, he rejoined Isbel at the lookout post.

It was late in the afternoon now, and neither of them had eaten anything since morning, so he sent Isbel to the house to get some food, and, taking his seat with his back to a tree, waited her return.

Alone like this, he sat with his eyes fixed on the enemy's country, on the lookout for any sign of movement on their part. He had brought the telescope with him, and used it now and then without effect. Through it he could see the fishing beach and the bodies still lying upon it, the spear, sticking upright from the sand, the trodden-up sand, and the deserted tents. That was all. There was no sign of the enemy, who were no doubt hiding in the grove behind the tents, or on the reef beyond the grove.

He argued that they must have been considerably scared to have effaced themselves in this fashion, yet he knew enough of savages to prevent him from building too much on moral effect. They might be scared now, but the effect would wear off, and the desire for revenge and blood and loot reassert itself. Even now, though they were in hiding, they were doubtless holding a powwow, with Sru as chairman.

The position was bad. The pearl fishing had ceased, the island was in a state of war, there could be no peace or parleying with the enemy simply because there could be no trust placed in them while Sru was alive and active. At best, they could hold their own only by a continuous watch and defensive until Schumer returned. But Schumer might be delayed; he might never come back, the *Southern Cross* might even now be lying at the bottom of the Pacific, or hove up on some reef a thousand miles away from the Island of Pearls. As this thought came to him, he cast his eyes across the great space of sea visible on the ocean side of the reef. The sea, in the late afternoon light, lay calm but for the gentle swell that heaved it shoreward, but he knew well the treachery of that sea, of all seas the most fair—and faithless.

He was aroused from his thoughts by Isbel, who had returned, bringing him some food. She had also brought with her a rifle and some more ammunition. As she stood with the gun in her hand, gazing over toward the fishing camp, Floyd watched her, wondering at the change in her and the difference between this figure and the Isbel he had known at first—the girl he had seen that day of his first landing on the island.

Even during the last couple of days she had changed. Nothing makes for the development of the best and the worst in us like war. The struggle for existence, brought to a flaming point, is the true fire assay for character. Not only does the human soul develop in this ordeal, but the human being ages. Isbel, since the morning of the day before, seemed a year older, and Floyd's boyish character had taken on a sternness and received a solidification that ten years of ordinary life might not have effected.

She sat down beside him, and they ate the food she had brought, talking little, and each ever on the watch for any movement of the enemy. There was nothing. Nothing but the gulls flying in the blue, and the waves breaking on the coral and the wind moving the foliage of the distant trees.

The island might have been deserted but for their presence and those brown spots lying on the sand of the distant beach.

CHAPTER XXII
THE GREAT FIGHT

No fires were lit on the fishing beach that evening, nor did the wind from across the lagoon bring any sound of singing from the fishermen.

Floyd remained at the lookout post while Isbel, returning to the house, put everything in order and gave a last touch to the defenses and a last look around. Then she returned and took her place beside him.

The moon, stronger to-night, yellow and brilliant, hung in the apple-green dusk of the eastern sky. It looked exactly like the quarter of a crystallized orange; then, as the sky steadily and swiftly darkened, it lost its yellow tinge and became a sickle of frosted silver.

The light was powerful enough to sparkle up the whole lagoon and show the reef like a curving gray road set on either side with the lagoon water and the foam of the sea.

The fishing beach showed clearly, and the grove, even the tents could be made out as gray flecks against the darkness of the trees, but sign of life there was none.

"I would like it better if we could see more of them," said Floyd. "They are a lot too quiet."

"They will come to-night, I think," said Isbel. "They are hiding now and talking. Sru will lead them."

Floyd laughed. "He led them finely on the beach over there this afternoon," said he, "lying on his stomach all the time!"

"That is why I fear him," said Isbel. "He is very clever; the others are not clever, but they are good to fight. Sru is the head; they are the hands. Sru is a devil."

"You did not know what Sru was that time you left me and went back to them," said he.

"No," replied Isbel; "I thought he was good then. He said to me: 'Why not come back to your own people?' The words he said to me grew in my mind like seeds in the ground. I did not know you then. I thought you were the same as Schumer."

"You know me now."

"Yes," replied Isbel, "I know you now."

He could see her profile against the stars and the line of her delicately shaped head. She was sitting with her hands about her knees, in just the same position as on the day when, drawing near the beach, Schumer had stood to receive him, and Isbel had sat watching, seemingly indifferent, gazing at him with those eyes whose gaze held so much of the unknown.

She wore a flower in her hair that day, and she wore a flower in her hair to-night, a perfumed blossom plucked as she was passing through the grove. The scent of it came to him with a trace of the hot, gorse-like perfume of her hair, and for a moment he forgot Sru, the island, the fight on the beach, and the whole desperate position. For a moment only. As they sat beneath the stars, watching the moonlight grow stronger upon the lagoon water and the reef, suddenly from away out there came a cry like the sudden clamoring of sea fowl. A sound fierce and sharp and with the ring of triumph in it. The invisibility of the enemy and the absolute silence they had maintained up till now lent the sound a weird significance.

"They are starting," said Floyd.

Isbel nodded. She said nothing; she was listening. Then she said: "They will have been talking, all sitting round as they were to-day. Sru will have been making plans to come here and kill us. Then when all their minds went together like men with spears they shouted like that and jumped to their feet and started."

She spoke like a person who was watching it all in some magic glass, slowly and in a dreamy manner and with a detachment as though what she were viewing had nothing to do with them.

"They'll start more before I have done with them," said Floyd viciously.

The events of the day, the tension of waiting, and that shout, cruel as a barbed spear coming out of the night, had raised the fierce fighting spirit of his race, a spirit all the more potent and terrible from the underlying sobriety that tempers its fierceness and levity.

"It's funny to think we may be knocked out before the sun rises again," said he. "What do you think happens to a man when he's dead, Isbel?"

"I don't know. It is, I think, all the same as before he is born. He doesn't know."

"That's what I have often thought myself," said he. "Look! What is that?"

Away toward the far end of the reef they saw moving points upon the coral. Huge insects seemed crawling here and there, aimlessly at first, and now approaching nearer.

"They are coming," said Floyd, seizing a rifle. "They are spreading themselves out, and that confounded coral gives them good sheltering places. We must stop them if possible."

He stood up, and, putting the rifle to his shoulder, aimed it at the nearest moving spot and fired. He continued blazing away till the chambers were empty. The movement ceased, but almost immediately it recommenced, and now they could see the brown figures crouching and crawling, spread out fanwise, taking cover at every projection, and always advancing closer.

It was almost impossible to fire effectively, owing to the uncertain light and the fact that at the first flash every figure fell flat or dodged behind cover.

Between the rough coral and the point where they stood lay forty yards or so of smooth ground, across which the final rush would be made.

"It seems we can't stop them," said Floyd as he emptied the contents of the second rifle, while the girl reloaded, "and once they get near the edge of that smooth bit they'll rush us. Get everything together when I give the word and make back for the house. Ah, I had one then!"

A shriek following the shot he had just fired told of a hit, but it did not stop the advance. On the contrary, the wretches had now reached the psychological point, the point where instinct told them collectively that a rush must surely succeed, and where optimism told them individually that it was the next man who would be hit.

They left cover boldly, and, heedless of the rough coral, of the pitfalls and sharp edges, leaped to the attack like bounding kangaroos.

Floyd bagged two of them with his two last shots; then calling to Isbel, who had also been firing, he led the way through the trees toward the house.

Isbel, with forethought, had lit the lamp in the main room, and the glow of it shining through the loopholes in the walls showed them their way. Once inside, they barred the door, placed the guns on the table, and began to reload.

They did not speak a word. Coolly and swiftly they shoved the cartridges in their places, and then, each with a rifle, stood at attention to the hell of voices from outside.

Never could Floyd have believed that human beings were capable of such sounds of ferocity and malevolence. Only in the long boo-hoo of the storm that had torn the bones of the *Tonga* to pieces had he heard anything like this outburst.

Fists and feet were thundering at the door, spear points poking through the openings in the walls, but all that was nothing to the uproar of the voices. The calling of monkeys and the shrieks of parrots seemed mixed with the howl of hyenas, and more terrible than these came an incessant, fierce whistling, harsh as the whistling of steam.

Floyd was less a philosopher than a man of action, yet even so, and though he had no time for philosophy in such a crisis, his mind for a moment was held by one stupendous fact—these fiends storming the house were not devils just let loose from the infernal regions; they were the "hands."

The men he had worked with and overseen, pleasant and childlike creatures full of fun and laughter, most of them. It is true that many of them had, when in repose, that hard, set expression which seems to have come from ages of watching across the sun blaze on the sea, but their faces could express good humor, one might say, fluently, and as they had always been well treated on the island they had never cause to express anything else.

When Floyd had seen them first on the day that he and Schumer had boarded the *Southern Cross* they had struck him as a very hard lot, and a good deal of that expression had come from the shell nose rings and the slit ear lobes distinguishing most of them; as he got to know them better that impression became less vivid. Yet it had been the right one. The shell nose rings and split ear lobes were surely "features" inasmuch as they spoke of ages and ages of savagery, blood, and darkness.

Yet the second impression had been right in its way. Despite all their savagery these people were human, had in them a certain bonhomie and sense of humor, and possessed many of those traits which we associate with the word "gentleman." The latter curious fact had been impressed on Floyd several times in his dealings with them. Sru, for instance, the worst of the lot, though he had probably dined off his enemy in his time, and though he had planned and plotted murder, would not have hurt your feelings for the world by word or gesture. Floyd, having reloaded, disregarding the door toward which the main attack seemed directed, chose loopholes near the ones through which the spear points were being thrust, and fired with effete, to judge by the sounds that followed the shots. Isbel, crawling and creeping close to the walls, seized on the spear shafts, and, using all her weight, broke them off.

She managed to break three like this, and then returned to the loading. Dark, cool, swift, and absolutely fearless, she seemed in these mad minutes the very spirit of destruction. They had ammunition in abundance, and when she was not engaged in reloading for Floyd she used one of the revolvers herself. The smoke of the firing blown back through the loopholes made a haze round the steadily burning lamp, near which, from the ceiling, a big spider was swinging from his thread, laying his nets utterly undisturbed by the sounds and fumes of the fight.

Then gradually the attack died down. The gentry outside had exhausted themselves mostly by yelling; they had done no damage and had received several injuries. Had they possessed a single firearm they might have made the position untenable, but they had nothing, and they had evidently come to recognize the fact that poking spears through loopholes was useless work, besides being dangerous.

Floyd wiped his brow with his coat sleeve.

"The fools have never thought of forcing the door," said he; "they might have done it with that crowbar. You remember the piece of iron I used to break open the big clamshell. They never thought of that. They came with spears only, and there is nothing over on this side they can use to force the door with. Let's hope they won't remember about it."

"Listen!" said Isbel.

Sounds were coming from the grove at the back of the house, sounds more of a jubilant than a warlike nature.

Floyd knitted his brow; then his face cleared.

"I know what it is," said he. "They have got at the cache."

The fragment of moon low down in the west lit the beach, and very soon Floyd's suspicion was justified. Peeping through the loopholes of the front wall, they saw the whole band of the enemy debouching on the sands away to the left, and every man laden with loot.

Some were carrying bolts of cloth, and others cases of provisions and boxes of tobacco.

They thought themselves beyond rifle range, and, like children, they wanted to examine their treasures. Floyd, assured that none of them had remained behind, opened the door, and, rifle in hand, stood watching them. Then he opened fire, and they scattered, leaving their treasures on the sand. Some ran along the lagoon edge, toward the reef opening; one dashed right into the water and swam in the same direction, while the main body made back for the shelter of the grove.

Not one of them was hit as far as he could see, and the men who had made toward the reef opening would return by the seaward side of the reef.

"I almost wish I had left them alone," said he. "It will only make them more vicious. The sight of that stuff lying there will keep them going. However, it is too late to bother now."

He turned back to the house and shut the door. He had been speaking to Isbel, and fancied her to be just behind him. She was not. She was at the table, quietly preparing some food. He noticed now for the first time that the flower was still in her hair. It looked dark purple in the lamplight. And now for a moment a strange sensation stole over him, as though the whole of the business were a fantastic dream, a sensation of unreality that infected even his own being. It passed, and, coming to the table where the food was now lying beside the rifles and ammunition, he drew one of the chairs up and sat down sideways to the board.

Isbel remained standing, and as they ate they talked, and what they said had little to do with the main business in hand. It was not a thing to be talked about. The situation was hopeless, if ever a situation was hopeless, and no plan had yet appeared to either of them by which their position could be bettered.

Ideas had come to Floyd only to be dismissed as useless, the idea, for instance, of making a dash from the house and taking to the dinghy, which they could easily push off. That would not help them in the least, since there was no place of safety to which the dinghy could take them. Their assailants would not expose themselves to rifle fire by day, and by night they would attack as they had done before.

The only spot where they could put up a defense for any time would be the pierhead at the break on the opposite side of the reef, and there they would be cut off from all food supplies.

"It's a good thing we have plenty of food here and water," said Floyd. "We have water enough for a week and food for a fortnight. I expect those fellows will get back to the fishing camp to-morrow and leave us alone."

He said it for the sake of saying something, but Isbel shook her head. She knew the men they had to deal with.

"They will never leave us till we kill them or they kill us," said she, clearing the things from the table. "Or," she finished, "till we kill Sru."

"Yes," said Floyd, "he's the center of the whole business. Well, we will do our best to nail him."

He rose up and went to one of the loopholes by the door. Peeping through, he could see the trade goods still lying on the sands, but not a sign of the enemy.

One of the most disturbing things in this fight was the manner in which the attackers would suddenly efface themselves, as after the first fight over on the fishing beach. They had vanished now as though annihilated, leaving neither outpost nor sign to hint of what plan they might be brewing.

The moon was very low down over the western reef. It was close to dawn, and soon the sun would be flooding the world with light. If another attack was in preparation it would not be long delayed, yet not a sound came to indicate an approach to the house.

"All the same they will come," said Isbel, "and they will come before day."

"You think so?" asked Floyd.

Isbel nodded. She had taken a seat on one of the chairs, and was sitting with her hands clasping her knees. Floyd, who had taken his seat at the table, was leaning his arms upon it and following with his eyes the graining of the wood.

The spider overhead, who had finished making, or maybe repairing, his net, had just fallen on luck; a long-legged fly that had been flitting about the rafters was his prisoner.

The fly, caught by a few strands of the infernal web, was making a fierce resistance. It was caught by one of its legs and by the body. The wings were free, and the buzz of their vibration made Floyd look up.

Then, for something to do, he rose and examined the thing more closely. Isbel rose, too.

The spider was quite patient about his work, and horribly scientific in his methods. The buzzing wings did not disturb him in the least. He ascended to the rafter which was his base, and then came down again, fixed a thread to one of his victim's legs, and reascended. He was binding the legs together, making everything absolutely secure before the final assault and the moment when he would bury his fangs in his prey and suck its blood.

Watching the little tragedy, Floyd and Isbel for a moment almost forgot their own position. Then Floyd, with a laugh, raised his finger and broke the strands of the web, releasing the fly.

"It was in about as bad a position as we are," said he. "Maybe it's an omen."

Isbel did not know what the word "omen" meant, nor did she ask, for at that moment, as they stood in silence watching the released one trying its wings again, a sound coming from the back of the house made them turn.

A soft, stealthy sound, as though people were creeping close to the wall, and now and then the sharp snap of some stick of the undergrowth trodden upon and broken.

Floyd, springing to the table, seized a revolver and began firing through the loophole of the back wall. He fired six shots at random; then he paused to listen.

The sound continued. The men outside were evidently crouching at whatever work they were on, and so were safe and below the level of the loopholes.

"Brutes!" said he. "There is no chance of reaching them, but what on earth can they be about?"

Isbel, who had been peeping through one of the chinks near the door, came toward him.

"The day has broken," said she.

CHAPTER XXIII
DAYBREAK

Even as she spoke the words, and as though in answer to the question he had asked, a faint smell of burning filled the air of the room, and through one of the chinks, like a little gray snake, a wreath of smoke coiled upward, clinging to the woodwork.

"So that's what they were doing!" cried Floyd. "They have fired the house."

Through every chink and crevice a curl of smoke was licking upward, and now came the sharp, crackling sound of brushwood burning and the snap and hiss of sticks blazing alight.

The air of the room was already turned to a gray haze of smoke, smoke that made the eyes smart, the smoke of burning hibiscus and poison oak and bay cedar bush, choking and suffocating fumes, followed now by flames as the wretches outside flung coconut shells on the fire, shells that blazed like flare lamps once ignited.

"The place will burn like a torch," said Floyd, "once the scantling gets alight. Listen! What's that above? They have got on the roof; they are lighting it. We must quit and make a dash for the dinghy. It's our only chance. Wait!"

He rushed into the smaller room, and returned with something in his hands. It was the tin box holding the pearls.

He opened it, emptied the contents wrapped in cotton wool, and filled his pockets.

"I'm not going to leave these behind," said he, speaking as if to himself. Then to Isbel: "Take a revolver and this package of ammunition. I'll take the other and a rifle. Unbar the door and run first. Don't stop to fire unless you can't help. Hark! What's that?"

A sound like a sharp clap of thunder shook the air and was followed by a yell from the grove behind the house and from the beach on either side.

"Open the door!" said Floyd.

Isbel undid the bars, and flung the door wide. Instantly the draft settling from the grove filled the place with volumes of smoke.

"Now," said Floyd, "run!"

They dashed out of the house, across the beach, running, half blind with the effects of the smoke. They had expected a flight of spears. They found instead an empty beach, full dawn, and a reef over which the last of their assailants were scrambling.

A great white cloud filled the break of the reef. It was the *Southern Cross* coming in with a fair wind and a flooding tide.

The first rays of the sun were on her topsails, which the wind scarcely filled. The water under her was still violet with night. White gulls, rose-colored gulls, golden gulls, as the sunrise took them, were flocking and screaming in the pale sapphire above her, schooner, gulls, lagoon, and sky making a picture more lovely than a dream.

As she cleared the reef entrance and rounded to her anchorage, the wind spilling out of her sails, a plume of smoke broke from her, and again the report of a gun shook the island.

As it died away the splash of the anchor was followed by a roar of the chain through the hawse pipe, and the *Southern Cross*, her long, long journey over, lay at her moorings swinging to the incoming tide.

Isbel turned to Floyd and clung to him, weeping. All her courage had suddenly vanished now that there was no need for it.

Floyd, holding her tight in his arms, kissed her black, perfumed hair. The flower had fallen, but a trace of its scent remained.

It was the moment of his life, and then she drew away from him, cast one dark glance obliquely up at him, and stood with her breast heaving and both hands shading her eyes.

She was looking over the water in the direction of the *Southern Cross*.

The schooner was lowering a boat. It was the whaleboat, and Floyd saw the men tumbling into her, followed by a white-clad figure—Schumer.

Even at that distance he recognized Schumer. Following Schumer came another white-clad figure, evidently a European.

Besides the two white men there were twelve hands in the boat, fourteen in all, and as she approached rapidly, urged by the long ash sweeps, Floyd saw the rifles with which the men were armed, the barrels showing as they rested, muzzle upward, by the seats.

As the boat came ashore Schumer, from his place in the stern sheets, waved his hand to Floyd. Then the fellows, jumping out, beached the boat, and Schumer, following them, set foot on the sand.

He did not waste words.

He had seen the whole business at a glance, and he had brought canvas buckets. Dense columns of smoke were rising from the back part of the house, but the roof had fortunately not caught alight. The crew had their orders, and in a moment they were filling the buckets and carrying them up to the grove while Schumer, Floyd, and the newcomer helped and superintended.

The mutineers had piled stacks of underwood, sticks, and all the rubbish they could find against the house wall. The stuff was burning with more smoke than flame, and the fire had fortunately taken no considerable hold on the building. They kicked the rubbish aside, flung water on the wall, and in twenty minutes or so the situation was saved.

Isbel had been posted by Schumer as a lookout in case the enemy should return. She had not contented herself by standing by as a watch, but had gone as far as the grove end, from where the reef could be seen up to the pierhead. She had seen nothing. The whole crowd of the enemy, in fact, had scattered back to the fishing camp by the road they had come the night before, and Schumer, standing now on the beach, could see them through his glass congregated about the tents.

Then he turned to Floyd. "Well," said he, "you seem to have had a lively time. What was the bother?"

Floyd explained in a few words, and, Isbel not being by, told of the trouble with Sru.

"He was plotting mischief all the time," said Floyd, "and this is the result."

"Well," said Schumer, "we will deal with the gentleman all in good time. What luck have you had with the pearls?"

Floyd told.

Taking off his coat, and laying it on the sands, he began to remove the pearls, in their casings of cotton wool, from the pockets. He explained why he had placed them there, and, as he went on with the work, Schumer and the stranger, standing by, looked on.

Schumer up to this had been too busy to introduce the newcomer. He did so now.

"This is Captain Hakluyt," said he. "He's in this venture, as I will explain to you afterward. His firm owns the *Southern Cross*."

Floyd looked up, and nodded to Hakluyt.

The new man's face was not a certificate of character. There are faces that repel at first sight, and Hakluyt's was one of them.

He had the appearance, not so much of a man who was ill, but of a man who never enjoyed good health. Anæmic looking despite his exposure to sun and wind, he seemed unable to bear either the full light of the sun or a full gaze. He was continually blinking, and to Floyd in that moment he suggested vividly the idea of a sick owl.

It was the curve of the nose and the blinking of the eyelids that produced this impression. The eyes themselves were not at all owllike, being small and set close together.

The whole figure of the man matched his face, slight and mean, with shoulders sloping like the shoulders of a champagne bottle. It was a figure that no tailor could improve.

His hands, as he stood with the thumbs in the armholes of his waistcoat, showed lean and clawlike, birdlike. Birdlike is the term best suited for the whole man; light, restless, peering, and without grace, for it is a fact that the animal and the bird translated into human terms lose both grace and nobility. Man standing or falling by his approach or recession to the type, man.

As Floyd looked up from his work he took in Hakluyt's appearance fully for the first time, and the idea that this man was the new partner in their concern filled him with repulsion and uneasiness.

He had been on the point of exposing the pearls triumphantly to view, but in a flash he altered his decision, and, asking them to wait for a moment, left his work and ran up to the house for the tin cash box from which he had taken them.

He placed it on the sand, and packing in the precious cotton-wool-covered parcels, closed the lid and handed it to Schumer.

"We can examine them afterward," said he. "Keep them for the present. They are not a bad lot, but they might be better."

"We'll put them in the house," replied Schumer. "I've got a safe on board; brought it from Sydney, but I can't get it ashore till to-morrow. Meanwhile they'll be all right in the house. Well, Hakluyt, what do you think of the island?"

Hakluyt looked about him as though taking stock of the place for the first time.

"It is not so bad," said he. "It is a fair bit of a lagoon, but it might be bigger."

"Oh, it will be big enough for us," replied Schumer, with a laugh. "Come up to the house with me, Floyd, till I put this stuff away. I want to have a talk with you."

They left Hakluyt, and walked up to the house.

"I say," said Floyd, "if that's our new man I don't like the look of him."

Schumer laughed.

"He's not a beauty," said he, "but he's the best I could find. He's Hakluyt & Son. He's the son; the father's dead. He's in a good way of business as a shipowner and ship's chandler in Sydney. He has got the money and the means to help us. I have drawn up a contract with him; he gets a third share."

"A third share. That means that the total profits will be divided into three parts. One for you, one for me, and one for Hakluyt."

"Just so," said Schumer, "and you pay me for the trade goods we salved from the *Tonga*."

"Of course," said Floyd, "but it seems to me that Hakluyt ought to stand in with me and pay something."

"I suggested that, but he refused. He would only come into the deal on condition that he got a third share of the profits without deduction."

Floyd felt inclined to grumble at this. Hakluyt would have the benefit of those goods or what was left of them, but he said nothing. He wanted explanation on another point.

"How about the *Southern Cross*?" said he.

"In what way?"

"Well, we salved her, didn't we, or as good as salved her? Hakluyt ought to pay for that."

"It was this way," replied Schumer. "Before coming into the venture he wanted half profits. He gave me to understand that our connection with the *Southern Cross* was in no way a salving job, since the crew were on board, and he said straight out that he would fight the matter in the courts. Now, as he has lots of money to fight with, and we have none, or next to none, I didn't see any sense in that. He said to me: 'I'll tell you what I'll do. In recognition of your trouble in bringing the schooner back to Sydney, I'll be content to take only a third of the profits in this pearling business. What's more, I will use the schooner for it free of charge and victual and man her.'

"Now, that seemed to me a fair proposition, and I agreed to it. What do you say?"

Floyd did not reply for a moment. He could come to no decision. The whole thing was so intricate and the values involved were such unknown qualities that at last he gave it up. If Schumer was satisfied it was doubtless all right. Schumer knew more of business affairs than he did, and it was better to leave it at that.

"Well," said he, "I suppose you couldn't do better, but it seems to me Hakluyt won't do badly out of the business. Wait till I show you something."

They had reached the house, and, taking the cash box from Schumer, Floyd placed it on the table and opened it.

He carefully removed some of the contents till he came to the package he was looking for; then, carefully removing the cotton wool from it, he exposed the pink pearl.

"Heavens, man!" said Schumer. "Why didn't you tell me of this?"

"Wait!" said Floyd.

He took another small ball of wool from the box, unrolled the wool, and held out the big white pearl.

Schumer laughed.

"Any more?" he asked.

"Not of that size," replied Floyd. "Well, what do you think of them?"

"Think of them? They are a fortune in themselves."

He carefully rolled them up again and replaced them in the box.

Meanwhile Floyd had been unpacking other specimens, which Schumer examined in their turn. He seemed well pleased with the take since his absence, as well he might be.

"I will have the safe brought ashore to-morrow," said he. "Meanwhile they will be all right here. Put them all back and come on. We have to tackle these scamps now and bring them to their senses. I don't want any fighting, if possible, for that would mean killing more of them, and we want them all for the fishery."

"Do you mean to say you are going to trust them to work again?"

"Of course I am. Why, man, it is nothing when one is working fellows like these to have revolts and rows. You shouldn't have let them get so much out of hand. I don't blame you, mind, for you are new to the business, but in the first instance you should have dealt properly with Sru. You should have shot him after that business about the girl. Martial law is the only law by which you can hold your own in a case like this. Well, we will see. Take your gun and come along."

They went out, and Schumer ordered the whaleboat to be manned.

Floyd for the first time recognized that the crew of the whaleboat were the same Kanakas who had formed the original crew of the *Southern Cross*. Mountain Joe was one of them. He saluted Floyd when he was recognized, and then took his place as stroke oar. Each man had a rifle and seemed to know how to use it, and they had all the stamp of men reliant and trained to arms.

They were not the same men—viewed as fighting men—that Schumer had taken away with him. He had done wonders with them in his absence, and the thought suddenly occurred to Floyd: Did Schumer expect that there would be trouble on the island during his absence? Did he train and arm the crew of the *Southern Cross* in view of this possible trouble?

It seemed so.

Then came another thought: Suppose you had been defeated and killed, would not Schumer have benefited? There would have been one partner the less, and ought he not to have warned you more especially as to the danger of a revolt?

Schumer had, in fact, warned him casually to be on the lookout, but his warning had chiefly to do with the cache and the necessity of preventing its locality and contents from becoming known. He had not dwelt on the matter of a possible revolt, nor had he prepared plans to meet it.

Did he hope to return and find a clear field and his partner put out of the way?

Floyd instantly dismissed the idea as unworthy of himself and Schumer. He had no tittle of real evidence to support such an idea—yet it had occurred to him.

There are some ideas that arise not from any concrete basis, but from vague suggestions. This was one of them.

As they approached the fishing beach they could see the enemy scuttering about in alarm. Fellows came out of the tents, shaded their eyes for a second, and then darted off into the grove. In less than a minute not a soul was in sight.

"There'll be no fighting," said Schumer as the boat came to the beach, and they sprang out. "Floyd, you stay here with the men and I'll take Mountain Joe up to the wood edge and have a palaver. I'll leave my gun with you so they may see we've come for peace, not war. They are sure to be peeping and spying from the trees."

He left the rifle, and, taking Joe with him, walked steadily up from the lagoon edge to the grove. Twenty paces from the trees he stopped and began to speak.

Floyd could hear his voice, and it was strange enough to see him standing there and seemingly addressing the trees.

Mountain Joe also put in a word now and then as if on his own account.

The effect was absolutely negative, and Floyd expected to see them turn and come back.

But Schumer knew the native mind and its ways, and he did not seem the least disconcerted at his failure. He paused in his oration, walked up and down a bit, and then began to talk again.

Presently, not from the trees before him, but from the trees at the left-hand side of the grove, a native appeared. He stood for a moment, now resting on one foot, now on the other. Then he said a few words, to which Schumer replied.

They kept this up for a minute or so, and then, from the wood, another native joined the first, then another and another.

"They are all right now," cried Schumer to Floyd. "Come up and help to jaw them. Leave your gun behind."

Floyd handed his rifle to one of the men and came right up to the group of natives before whom Schumer was now standing. He was talking to them, to use his own expression, like a Dutch uncle. Talking as only he knew how.

The Polynesian native, pick him up in most places, has a good deal of humor in his composition. He can both feel and use sarcasm. He has over and above this a certain bonhomie, a good spirit readily worked if one knows how.

Schumer knew how. He did not speak them fair by any means. He told them what was in his mind about them, told them they were pigs who would have dashed to their own destruction but for his arrival, yet told them it in a way that did not stir resentment.

These half-civilized creatures had been cast right back into savagery by some influence beyond their control. Sru had not been the influence, but he had worked it, just as a sorcerer might raise a devil.

Sru had not yet made his appearance. Schumer asked for him, and the reply came that he was dead and lying over somewhere in the grove near the house. One of the stray shots fired by Floyd while the brushwood was being placed against the house wall had found Sru and sent him to his last account.

"Well," said Schumer, "that's the best news we have had yet. It clears up everything. You don't want to punish these fellows, do you? Seems to me you have given them a pretty good grueling already, three dead and several wounded."

"I don't want to punish them," said Floyd. "You can tell them I call it quits. Sru was the man most to blame, and now he is dead. But there is one man I have a grudge against—Timau—and I don't see him here."

"Timau," said Schumer. "Which one is that?"

"He's a fellow whose life I saved at a great deal of risk and trouble. He stepped into one of those big clamshells and got seized, and I managed to free him, but he's not here."

Schumer turned to the natives and asked them where Timau was; then he translated to Floyd.

"It seems he wouldn't take part in the business because you had brought him back from the dead."

"So I did, with artificial respiration."

"Just so—and Sru bound him and put him in one of the tents. He's there now. We had better go and loose him."

They walked up to the tents, and there sure enough they found Timau lying on his side and chewing tobacco. He had managed to get one arm free and could have freed himself entirely had he taken the trouble. He had not. He just lay there, chewing and waiting on events. He was the laziest of the whole crowd employed on the fishery, and since his return from death he seemed to take everything as a fatalist.

But he had refused to join in the attack on Floyd.

Schumer undid his bonds, and he stood up, stretched himself, grunted, and walked off to join the others.

Schumer looked after him.

"He's a cool customer. Well, there's an end of the business. To-morrow they will all be working again, except the dead men. Now let's get back and bury Sru. We'll have to hunt for him in the grove. Then you can come on board and we will have something to eat. You haven't had breakfast?"

"Lord, no!" replied Floyd. "I had a sort of supper some time in the night, but what I want most is sleep. I'll lie down and have a snooze when we have finished up with Sru."

They came back to the house, and then started out to find what the grove had to reveal to them.

The cache had been half rifled, but most of the goods that had been taken were still lying on the sands and had not been injured.

Then they found Sru lying at the foot of an artus tree, a broken spear in his hand. He was lying on his face, and he would not trouble them any more.

Schumer buried him after a fashion of his own. He ordered two of the crew to carry the deceased to the pierhead at the break in the reef and cast him to the sharks.

"They'll look after him," said he.

CHAPTER XXIV
HAKLUYT

Next day work resumed as usual, Hakluyt assisting, or, at least, standing by to watch the proceedings.

The mutineers had destroyed nothing. All the shell that had been taken since the beginning of the work was intact, and the oysters that lay awaiting search when the revolt broke out were still there, lying where they had been left. As though fate wished to stimulate Hakluyt's interest in the business on this the first day of resumption of work the take proved to be exceptionally good. Three large pearls of good size and form came to hand besides several of less value.

"You mustn't reckon every day's take by this," said Schumer. "Often there's nothing much. In this business it's the take of a week or month that counts."

"All the same it is good," said Hakluyt. He spoke as though there were some obstruction in his nasal organ, and Floyd, listening to him and watching him, felt more than ever the aversion for him that had influenced him so powerfully on their first meeting.

Hakluyt watched all the proceedings just as a predatory bird watches its prey. He stood with his thumbs in the armholes of his waistcoat—his favorite attitude—a cigar in his mouth, and his panama hat tilted back.

He had a habit of thrusting his head forward, tortoise-like—one might have fancied that his neck was telescopic like the neck of a tortoise—and continually he kept drumming on his chest with his finger tips. On the middle finger of his left hand he wore a huge ring set with a diamond, an adornment that did not match with the shabby suit of white drill that flapped about him in the wind, showing to full disadvantage the thinness of his legs and arms and the protuberance of his stomach.

"That chap," thought Floyd to himself, "would do anything short of murder—and maybe wouldn't stop at that."

Isbel also did not seem to have much liking for Hakluyt.

With the return of Schumer, Isbel had gone right back to her previous position in the social scale of the island and also to her home in the grove. She helped in the cooking as before, and she kept watch for ships when

Floyd and his companions were over at the fishing grounds, but beyond that she had little to do with them.

From the moment of the landing of Schumer she had avoided Floyd. It was as though a veil had suddenly fallen between them after that moment when suddenly released from death she had clung to him as they stood watching the *Southern Cross* casting anchor. She had drawn away, and now it was as though nothing had ever been between them at all, as though they had never fought together and lived together and faced death together.

Floyd, simple soul, could not understand her in the least. At first he was perplexed, thought he had done something to offend her, and tried to imagine what it could be. Then he sulked—turned his head away when she drew near and avoided speaking to her.

One day, a week after the return of Schumer, he was on the windward side of the reef behind the grove and the house. Schumer and Hakluyt were over at the fishing camp. It was an hour before noon, and he had finished the work he had been upon and was seated on a lump of coral watching the breakers coming in, a wonderful vision of sunlit foam.

The breeze brought the spray almost to his feet, and a scent of ozone and seaweed and salt that seemed to come from the very heart of the sea.

As he sat like this a shadow fell on the coral before him, and, turning, he saw Isbel.

She sat down beside him.

He had been thinking of her, and nothing could have surprised him more than this action of hers in coming and sitting beside him. He moved slightly as though to make room for her, and then turned his face seaward again.

A frigate bird was approaching the island, moving without an effort on the wind. They watched it as it came along. Its shadow passed over them and vanished, and Floyd, turning his head to take a last look at the bird, found himself face to face with his companion.

Isbel had not spoken a word, but now, as their eyes met, her lips moved as though she were whispering something to herself impossible to say aloud. She seemed like a person in a trance, and her eyes, wide-pupiled and fixed on those of her companion, seemed trying to tell something impossible to tell by speech.

Next moment he had taken her in his arms. For a moment she resisted slightly, as though that soul, strange and free as the soul of the sea bird, were struggling feebly against the final capture of man.

Then she raised her lips to his.

CHAPTER XXV
ORDERED TO SYDNEY

Next morning Schumer took Floyd aside.

"Hakluyt is well pleased with the work here," said he. "He thinks the prospects even better than I made them out to him, and now he wants to go back."

"Does he?" said Floyd. The news came as a pleasant surprise.

"Yes, he has got his business in Sydney to attend to and he's keen on getting back at once. Of course he goes in the *Southern Cross*, but he can't go alone, for the schooner has to be brought back."

"To be sure."

"You must go with him," said Schumer. "There is no one else for the job."

"I!" exclaimed Floyd.

"Yes, there is no one else. I have been away too long. In fact I only got back in time to save the situation. You are a very good fellow, Floyd, but you aren't much use for working natives. It's not your business in life; it is mine."

"But see here," said the other, "why can't Hakluyt send the schooner back with another man in charge? There are lots of men in Sydney who could do the job."

"Yes, and what would that mean? Letting another man into our secrets. Surely you are not against doing your share of the work."

"I!" cried Floyd, flushing. "Have I ever refused to do all in my power to help? Of course I will go. Only, the thing has come on me as a surprise, and, I will say it frankly, an unpleasant surprise. You say Hakluyt wants to go back at once. Well, I think you might have told me of it some days ago. You must have known all along."

"I did not," said Schumer. "Of course I knew he wanted to go, but I did not know he wanted to go so soon. What does it matter? You have no preparations to make."

"How about the navigating on the way back?" asked Floyd, ignoring the last remark. "You had Hakluyt to help you coming, but if I am to come back single-handed it seems to me I will be in a bad way."

"You will have Mountain Joe," replied Schumer. "I have given special attention to that gentleman's education on the voyage to Sydney and back. You remember he could work out a dead reckoning even when I took him in hand. He was absolutely useless by himself, but under guidance he could be quite useful. Well, he knows a lot more now, and if I could get to Sydney with him as he was then, you can surely get back from Sydney with him as he is now."

"Oh, I suppose that will be all right," said Floyd. "And what am I to do in Sydney besides dumping Hakluyt there?"

"You will unlade the shell which I am sending and take in some more provisions. The *Southern Cross* wants an overhaul—that will take a week or ten days—she wants some new spars and a few barnacles scraped off her. We want a big lot of canned stuff, vegetables, and bully beef. I'll talk to you to-night about that. Hakluyt is in the way of getting it cheaper than we could if we were working alone."

"How long do you think we will have to stay in Sydney?"

"Oh, about three weeks or so."

"It will be over two months before I can get back."

"About that."

"And when exactly do you want me to start?"

"Oh, in a couple of days. It will take us that to get the shell aboard. I am going to start on the work this morning. I'll get all the hands on it, crew and fishermen both. We can get the stuff on board on the raft and with the help of the whaleboat."

"Very well," said Floyd, "I'll go."

He turned away and walked along the lagoon edge. Always when Fortune turned toward him she had something unpleasant to add to her gifts. The pink pearl had been followed by the running away of Isbel, and the great white pearl by the mutiny of the hands. Isbel had been given to him only yesterday, and now he had to leave her.

Since yesterday he had lived in a state of extraordinary happiness. Wonderland. To love and to find that you are loved. There is nothing else. No dream can come near this reality. And now he had to leave her.

He crossed the reef, and stood looking out to sea. The Pacific lay blazing beneath the morning light, blue beyond the sun dazzle and heaving shoreward to burst in foam at his feet. The breeze came fresh across it, vivid and full of life. Floyd loved the sea.

It had become part of his nature and part of his being. It was his second mother. But to-day he was looking at it with fresh eyes. It was no longer the sea; it was separation from all he cared for and all he loved. He would have to leave Isbel and leave her with Schumer.

When he had landed on the island first, Schumer had impressed him favorably, but little by little and by that slow process through which a complex and illusive personality makes its quality known to a simple and straightforward mind, he had come to the point of distrust as regards Schumer.

He had no fear at all that Schumer would harm Isbel. Isbel was a person who could well take care of herself, and Schumer, he distinctly felt, was not a man dangerous to women. The instinctive feeling of danger had to do with himself. He was a fifth wheel in Schumer's chariot, an absorber of profits, and though he refused the thought that Schumer might attempt to get rid of him, he could not refuse the instinct.

He felt suddenly surrounded by an atmosphere of danger none the less disturbing from the fact that he could not tell from what point it arose. He disliked this journey to Sydney, and he disliked Hakluyt even more.

Brave as any man could be, he feared for his own safety, not for his own sake, but for the sake of Isbel. Should anything happen to him what would become of her?

And there was nothing he could do. He was completely in the grasp of events. He could not refuse to perform this obvious duty that had suddenly been laid down before him by Schumer. He could not take Isbel with him, and he could not take any precautions as to his own safety beyond simple watchfulness.

He turned back from the sea, and as he turned he saw Isbel. She was standing at the edge of the grove, and the trees quite sheltered them from the sight of the people by the house. He came toward her, and they entered the grove together.

Close to the sea edge of the grove a huge tree had fallen. Rotten with age, it had crashed its way through the lesser trees and lay like a dead giant over which the undergrowth had cast its green skirts in part. They sat down upon it, and Isbel, nestling up close beside him, rested her head upon his shoulder.

Then he told her that he was going. Told her the whole thing and the reasons that held him. Told her that the separation would only be for a little while, and surely, surely he would come back, and as he talked and explained he felt her shudder as a person shudders from the cold.

CHAPTER XXVI
GOOD-BY

All that morning and all that day Schumer kept the hands busy at work bringing the shell across the lagoon and storing it aboard the *Southern Cross*. Some of it was rafted over and some brought in the whaleboat. Schumer superintended everything himself, and now that speed was urgent he proved what he could do as a driver.

Never did a Yankee stevedore work a set of hands harder. His voice acted as a whiplash, and his energy infected everybody.

Next day it was the same, so that at sundown the last of the shell was on board, the locking bars secured, and nothing remained but to take on the water.

"We can do that to-night," said Schumer, "and if this wind holds, though there is not much of it, you will be able to start at sunup. It will be slack tide about then. Now, if you will come up to the house, I will give you the last details of what you have to do in Sydney. There is nothing like having everything cut and dried."

They went up to the house, and Schumer at once plunged into accounts. He had tabulated a list of all the stores required, and he had written down the main points in Floyd's program, even to the address of a house where he could stay.

Hakluyt looked on while the two men talked, and, when they had finished, the three went out, Hakluyt and Schumer to see to the watering of the vessel and Floyd to find Isbel.

It was a night of the full moon, a hot, almost windless, night filled with the scent of flowers and the song of the reef.

The moon hung almost in the zenith, the apex of a pyramid of light, and under the silent whiteness of the moon the island lay clipping the vast pond of the lagoon in its arms as a mistress holds her lover.

Hakluyt and Schumer had taken the boat to fetch the water casks, and from away out over the water came the sound of the oars. The fellows over at the fishing camp were singing, untired by their day's work, and now and then on a stronger puff of wind a snatch of their song came over the lagoon water, and, just for a moment, as Floyd stood by the water edge, all his trouble of mind lifted from him—for a moment. The brilliant light, the beauty of the scene before him, the snatch of song from the fishing camp, and the perfume of the flower-scented wind seemed to open doors in his mind through which from some remote past came happiness. The moonlight for a moment caught some magic from the morning of the world. Then he turned and went toward the outer reef edge, where Isbel was waiting for him.

An hour before dawn the beach before the house was astir. The moon had sunk, but the stars gave enough light to work by. The water was all aboard, and now some coconuts, breadfruit, and taro roots were being taken off. Floyd was directing operations. He had said good-by to Isbel, who was nowhere to be seen. He sat in the stern sheets of the fruit boat, steering, and when the stuff was transshipped he boarded the *Southern Cross* and sent the empty boat back for Schumer and Hakluyt.

Schumer came on board, and stood chatting while the hands were at the capstan bars getting the slack of the anchor chain in. Then when the mainsail was being set and the hands were at the halyards, Schumer slipped over the side into the boat and pushed off for shore.

As the anchor came up, Floyd, who was forward superintending the men, left Joe to see to the securing of it and came aft to where Hakluyt was standing by the wheel.

The dawn was now bright in a sky that showed scarcely a trace of morning bank. It came over the reef and between the palms, whose trunks stood like bars against the brightening east. It flooded the lagoon as the schooner gathered way, and the great trapezium of the mainsail showed a tip of rose gold as they passed the pierheads of the reef. On the pierhead to port something showed white against the coral. It was Isbel.

The *Southern Cross* rose to the swell at the break of the reef just as a horse rises to a low fence, the foam roared in her wake, and the noise of it mixed with the clatter of the rudder chain as the fellow at the wheel twirled the spokes. Floyd raised his hand, and Isbel signaled in reply as the wind, now gaining its morning strength, pressed the schooner over to the tune of straining cordage and creaking blocks.

Floyd, leaning on the after rail, looked backward. The little figure of Isbel was no longer to be seen, blotted out by distance. Then distance took the reef, leaving only a trace of palm tops above the blazing water, and in an hour the Island of Pearls had vanished like a dream beyond the edge of the sea.

CHAPTER XXVII
SYDNEY

Hakluyt, despite his appearance, was a very efficient schooner captain, and as day followed day, Floyd's respect for him as a sailor rose more and more. As a man, he disliked him just as much as ever.

It was not an active dislike. His temper never rose against him, for Hakluyt, to give him his due, was perfectly easy to get on with. He neither swore at the hands nor heckled the subordinate officer. On the contrary, he seemed always endeavoring to make himself agreeable, always anxious for smooth water. The dislike that Floyd had for him was instinctive and beyond the reach of reason, but he did not show it outwardly as he would have done had Hakluyt been difficult to get on with.

The *Southern Cross* was a good deal of a Dutch ship. Hakluyt hailed originally from Amsterdam, and he brought the Dutch flavor with him. He was an eternal cigar smoker, and the food and drink on board were reminiscent of Holland, especially the De Kuyper. There was a certain slackness also, and a go-as-you-please method of doing this foreign to an English ship.

Yet she made good way without taking any risk. The great art of schooner sailing as laid down by Hakluyt was formulated by him as follows: "Carry all the canvas that you can without danger to your sticks."

And this art implied not only good handling of your vessel, but incessant weather watchfulness, at all events in the Pacific, where squalls drop on you out of a perfectly fair sky.

Three weeks brought them to Sydney, and though it was not Floyd's first acquaintance with the harbor which seems to have been made when the gods were making harbors for great fleets that have vanished, it still filled him with the same wonder and admiration and surprise.

They anchored close to McGinnis' wharf, and Floyd on the morning of his arrival found himself a comparatively free man for a few days.

"Run round the town and amuse yourself," said Hakluyt. "Id is worth seeing. Id is good to stretch one's legs after a voyage, but first come to my place and I will show you over."

Hakluyt had two places, one on the wharves and the other an office on Market Street.

The office was a dingy-looking place with wire blinds to the windows inscribed with the legend "Hakluyt & Son" done in dingy gold.

The place on the wharf was much more lively and pleasing to the mind.

It was an enormous emporium where everything was sold that could be wanted by a shipmaster. Here you could buy an oilskin coat or the provisions for a voyage round the world. It was all the same to Hakluyt. He could put you in the way of a spare anchor or a barrel of petroleum or a slush tub with the same hand that dealt out tobacco and preserved fruit. His storehouses were enormous; he victualed his own ships, and his influence in the maritime world was ubiquitous.

A man who can give you a job if you are out of work or if your board of trade certificates are not quite clear is a power. A man who can lend you money and who is willing to do it if you are on your beam ends is also a power.

Hakluyt had helped many a man. He had established that reputation, yet the men he helped had better have gone without his help, for once he touched a man in this way he held him. The money he lent always, nearly always, returned to him with heavy interest. Sometimes he made a dead loss. He did not mind that, for he was a man who reckoned up things in the large, and in the large he always profited, with this addition—he could always put his hand on a man ready and able to do a dangerous or dirty job for him.

Floyd, when Hakluyt had shown him over the wharfside store, took his gear to the house recommended by Schumer, where he obtained rooms. Then he went out to see the town, and finished up by dining at a restaurant and going to the theater.

Next morning he went down to superintend the towing of the *Southern Cross* into dry dock for an overhaul. This business held him for most of the day, and most of the next day he spent at the dock having a good look at the vessel's copper sheathing. It seemed to him that the dry docking was a work of supererogation. The *Southern Cross* was in excellent condition, and Hakluyt was not the man to waste money in frills. Why had he gone to this expense?

There were several of Hakluyt's ships in the harbor, and chumming up with one of the wharfside loafers, he managed to obtain a good deal of information as to Hakluyt and his ships.

Said the broken-down sailorman, who was one reek of rum and navy twist:

"*Southern Cross* in dry dock havin' her bottom scraped? I dunno in the nation what bee's got into Hakluyt's bonnet. There's the *Mary and Louise*—that's her lyin' by the oil tank—the weeds fathoms long on her keel and the barnacles as big as saucers on her copper, yet she's good enough to put out o' port without no dry dockin'. There's the *Boomerang*, another of his tubs. You can see her forrard, the yaller one, beyond that point. She's wrong from stem to rudder, she's held together mostly by her paint, she hasn't seen a dry dock for years, an' the sight of one would make her spew her bolts. I reckon she's just held together by the salt water she floats in, yet he docks the *Southern Cross*! Is that all his vessels? No, it ain't. D'you see that schooner out there by the whistlin' buoy? She's the *Domain*. She's Hakluyt's. Just come back from the islands a month ago. Been lyin' there waitin' for I don't know what ever since. The copra's been out of her this fortnight, and there she lays waitin' her job.

"What sort o' man is Hakluyt? Well, he's no sort to speak of. He blew in here twenty years ago out of a Dutch ship that was glad to get rid of him, and here he's stuck and prospered till he's fair rotten with money and has his thumb on the town and half the harbor side as well. He's owner and ship's chandler both. I've heard folk say he's sold his soul to the devil, but that's a lie, for he ain't got a soul to sell. The grub aboard his ships is most salt horse, and the bread bags has to be tethered they're that lively with the weevils. Go and ask any sailorman on the front if you don't believe me."

Floyd did not need to confirm this view of Hakluyt by making inquiries of sailormen on the front. He took a long look at the *Domain*, and then turned away from the wharfside and walked uptown to Hakluyt's office.

Hakluyt was in, and they went over the list of stores together.

"You leave id all with me," said Hakluyt. "I shall have them all aboard by the date of sailing. Well, and how do you like Sydney?"

Floyd expressed his opinion of Sydney. The dullest place in the world for a lone man unaddicted to bar-room festivity or horse-racing. Hakluyt gave him a pass for the theater, regretted that he could not ask him to dinner, as he was a lone bachelor, told him to enjoy himself, and dismissed him.

During the next fortnight Floyd managed to amuse himself innocently enough. He had never been much of a reading man, but, picking up a cheap edition of the "Count of Monte Cristo," he suddenly found a new world open before him. He read it in bed at night, and he took it out with him and read it by the sea front.

It occupied a good deal of his time, as he was a slow reader, and it gave him a new horizon and new ideas and a new energy.

Monte Cristo's discovery of the treasure, his escape from the Château d'If, the girl he loved, his cruel separation from her, his revenge, all these things appealed to his mind with the power of reality, as they have appealed to minds all the world over and as they ever will appeal.

When he had finished "Monte Cristo," he bought a new novel. It was about a young lady, who, starting life as a shop assistant, married a duke at the end of the third chapter. The book did not hold him, and he fell back on fishing.

There is good fishing to be had in the neighborhood of Sydney, and one day toward the end of the third week and close now to the time of the sailing of the *Southern Cross*, he met an individual on one of these fishing excursions, a joyous and friendly personage who, returning with him to Sydney, proposed drinks and led the way into a bar.

Floyd was not a drinking man, but the best of men make mistakes, and the hot air of the bar, the friendliness of his new companion, the pleasure of having some one to talk to, and the strength of the whisky had their effect. He had not eaten since breakfast.

Presently he found himself one of a mixed company. His first acquaintance had departed, yet he did not trouble about that. He scarcely recognized the fact, and presently he recognized nothing. He had been doped. One of these new friends had done the business, and an hour later he found himself lying on a couch in Hakluyt's inner office, of all places in the world, his pockets empty and his throat like a fiery furnace.

He recognized at once his position. He had been robbed and left in the street and had managed to reach Hakluyt's by that instinct for a known place common to homing pigeons and drunken men, an instinct that in the man is much more tricky than in the bird, as in the case of Floyd, who, instead of finding himself in his rooms, found himself at Hakluyt's.

His mind, as he lay there on the couch, was terribly lucid. He remembered everything up to a certain point.

It was still daylight, so that his intoxication must have passed away very quickly, as it does in those instances where it is produced by a doper and through the medium of a "knock-out drop" placed in the victim's drink; but Floyd knew nothing of this. He did not suspect that he had been doped by some scoundrel for the purpose of robbery. He only recognized that he had been drunk and incapable, and, to use the old term so unfair to animals, had made a beast of himself.

The awful depression that comes after drink or drugs had a hold upon him, and the unfair spirit that waits upon depression of this sort began to exercise its power.

It showed him the vision of Isbel standing on the reef against a background of blue and burning sea; it showed him the coconut trees and breadfruits, their fronds and foliage moving in the wind; it showed him all that was brilliant and fresh and pure in that extraordinary life through which he had passed out there, away from civilization and its dirt, and then it showed himself lying in Hakluyt's dusty office recovering from drink and fortunate in not having been jailed.

It seemed to his simple mind that he had sinned against Isbel and that he never, never could rise from his degradation and look in her face again. All his homesickness for the island came upon him like a wave, and he was endeavoring to raise himself on his arm to leave the couch when a voice from the outer office made him lie down again.

It was Hakluyt's voice. He had just entered, and Floyd, as he lay, heard the door of the outer office close.

"Well," said Hakluyt, who seemed to be continuing a conversation begun outside, "id is just so. There is noding to fear. Wait for a moment, though."

He came to the door of the inner office where Floyd was lying, pushed it more widely open, and peeped in.

Floyd, more from shame than any other reason, lay with his eyes closed.

Hakluyt stood looking at him for a few seconds, then he closed the door.

Floyd instantly opened his eyes and sat up on the couch.

Hakluyt and the other man, whoever he might be, had been talking about him. Of that he felt certain. He had no concrete evidence to go upon, yet he felt sure that he had been under discussion and that they were discussing him now. His ego had become abnormally sensitive, fortunately for him. He felt sure that his disgraceful conduct was the subject of their talk, and the overmastering desire to hear the worst that could be said of him prompted him to leave the couch, approach the door, and put his ear to the paneling. He heard Hakluyt's voice and every word that he said distinctly.

"Look here, Captain Luckman," said Hakluyt, "when I say a thing I mean id. You need have no fear. Schumer will see that there is no evidence against you. You will dispose of the young man so that no trouble will be made, no questions asked. You will not raise the price on me on that account. You run no risk. That is all Schumer's work, and no blood need be spilled. Schumer is nod the man to make any blunder. Two hundred pounds now and two hundred when you get back. That is my uldimatum, and what have you to do for that—noding, *absolutely* noding."

"I'm not troubling about what Schumer does to the blighter," came Luckman's voice. "I'm thinking of myself, and I say it's not enough. Two-fifty down and two-fifty when I get back is *my* ultimatum, and poor enough pay it is for a job like that."

Floyd heard Hakluyt laugh. Just a single laugh, mirthless as a rap on a coffin lid.

"So you would dictate terms to me," said he. "Why, God bless my soul," his voice rising in inflection, "suppose I order you from my office, suppose I say to you, 'Get clear out of this place, Captain Luckman, and never you ender id again,' hey? Suppose I say to you, 'Very well, Captain Luckman, all those papers in my hands go to the owners of the *Morning Star*. Sent anonymous.' Suppose— —"

"Oh, stow that!" came Luckman's voice. "Suppose I put the mouth of a revolver at your head and blow out your dirty brains? I'd do that same as I'd poison a rat, if you cut any capers with my affairs. You're not going to frighten me with threats. Put me beyond a certain point and I'd do you up before the authorities could nab me, and if they did nab me I'd croak you when I came out of quod. Talk like a man to a man or I'll leave your office and let you do your own dirty work. Who else is there in Sydney you could get?"

"Hundreds," said Hakluyt.

"Not one," replied Luckman. "Not one who would not either mess it or give the show away in drink sometime or another. Five hundred is my price. Two-fifty down, two-fifty when I land back. Not a halfpenny less will I take."

In the momentary silence that followed, Floyd heard a drawer opened, and then came Hakluyt's voice counting: "One, two, three, four—*and* five."

Then Luckman's:

"*And* five. Right you are."

The money was being paid over, and from the chinking sound it was being paid in gold, five bags of fifty sovereigns each, evidently.

Floyd did not wait for any more. He went back to the couch. He had forgotten his position, he had forgotten the drinking bout, he no longer even felt the headache and the parching thirst that had tormented him on waking. Hakluyt and Schumer had made a plan to get rid of him. That was all he knew for the moment. The idea excluded everything else by its monstrosity and strangeness.

The discovery that a plot is on foot against one's life is the most soul-stirring discovery that a man can make. The knowledge that one is an object of enmity is always disturbing. It unsettles the placidity of the ego, almost more than the discovery that one is an object of love. It also raises the temperature of the soul.

But the discovery that one is plotted against with a view to one's removal from the world is a heart-chilling discovery which at all events in the first moments reduces the temperature of the soul and body both.

Floyd, taking his place on the couch again, closed his eyes. He heard the two men go out; then after a moment he heard Hakluyt return.

Hakluyt opened the door and looked in on him, and Floyd, moving and pretending to wake up, rubbed his eyes. Then he sat up, asked in a confused manner where he was, got on his legs, pretended to stagger, and made for the door.

Hakluyt, nothing loath to get rid of him, followed him to the stair top.

"Where are you off to now?" inquired Hakluyt, as the other went down the stairs clutching the banister tightly.

"Going to have a drink," replied Floyd. "See you in the morning."

"Right," said Hakluyt. "Take care of yourself."

In the street Floyd turned into the nearest bar, drank a bottle of soda water, and, having sat for a moment to collect his wits, started for his rooms. He had now entirely recovered mastery of himself. His discovery about Hakluyt was finer than any pick-me-up or tonic, and his mind before the problem clearly stated by fate had little inclination for sleep.

The problem itself, though clearly stated, was intricate and in some respects obscure. If Hakluyt and Schumer wanted to clear him out of the pearl business, if they were scoundrels enough to plot his destruction, why did they not commit the act themselves without calling in a third man? He could imagine no answer to this question that satisfied him, yet there were two answers that might have been put forward by a man with a knowledge of Schumer and Hakluyt, a knowledge of psychology and a knowledge of the world.

Firstly, neither Schumer nor Hakluyt might be murderers in an active sense. Very few men are capable—God be thanked—of taking a fellow man's life in cold blood with their own hands. Schumer was without doubt a man of sensibility and parts. Hakluyt, though without parts or sensibility, was not of the active type of scoundrel. Both of these men might be capable of planning the destruction of another man, but neither would be likely to do the work himself.

Secondly, in a business of this sort it is always safer for the murderer to employ an agent than to act himself.

It is the assassin who leaves traces, the assassin who is followed, the assassin who is hanged.

Of course, he may accuse his employer, but an employer of the type of Schumer or of Hakluyt is not likely to give an agent any chance to make evidence against him. He had paid Luckman in gold, and when the job was finished he would pay him in gold. Gold cannot be traced—and that is one of the greatest pities in the world.

Floyd could see nothing very clearly in the whole of this business with the exception of the fact that foul play was to be used against him, but he saw that fact clearly enough. Leaving the problem of Schumer and Hakluyt aside, he tried to imagine what method Luckman might possibly employ. The remainder of the money was not to be paid to Luckman until his return. Return from where? There could be only one answer to that—from the sea.

Luckman would sail with the *Southern Cross*, be put on board either as mate or supercargo; and on the voyage he would do what he was paid to do.

The *Southern Cross* would most likely never reach the island. An accident would happen to Floyd, and she would return to Sydney. Luckman would be paid off for his job, and Hakluyt, taking charge of the schooner, would sail for the island and shake hands with Schumer over the fact that they two were the sole possessors of the place and its wealth.

And what would happen to Isbel?

At this thought a wave of fury rose in his soul against the men whom he imagined to be plotting his destruction.

He half rose from his bed, and had Hakluyt appeared at that moment it would have been a very bad thing for the shipowner.

Then he lay down, a deep determination in his heart to deal with this matter in the only way it could be dealt with satisfactorily, to match cunning against cunning, and force, at the proper moment, against force.

He determined to say nothing and do nothing to arouse any uneasiness or suspicion in Hakluyt, to welcome Luckman on board, and then to deal with Luckman when they were clear of the Heads.

If Luckman were put on board as mate or supercargo the matter would be easy, but if Luckman were placed over him as captain it would be much more difficult.

If Hakluyt were to suggest such a thing he determined to oppose it, to stand on his dignity and refuse utterly to give up his post as chief in command to a stranger.

Then as he lay down again the thought came to him what a miraculous and providential thing it was that he had gone out fishing that day and fallen in with the bibulous stranger. He had been robbed, it is true, of a few pounds, but that was a very cheap price to pay for his life.

Floyd, without being a professedly religious man, had a deep and intuitive belief in a God that rules the world and deals out justice and protects—though sometimes in a roundabout way—the innocent. He felt that Providence had a hand in this affair, yet he was not of the type that believes in a Providence who works single-handed. He determined that in this matter he would give Providence all the help he could, and having come to this determination he fell asleep.

CHAPTER XXVIII
CARDON

Next morning Floyd presented himself early at the office of Hakluyt & Son, and Hakluyt received him with some very bald jokes about his condition on the day before.

Floyd was not in a temper to take them, and indicated as much. Then they fell to discussing stores and the sailing of the *Southern Cross*. The stores were all on board, and the crew were ready. "I had thought of your sailing on Friday," said Hakluyt, "but Friday is not a good day; Thursday is better; that is the day after to-morrow. Will you be ready to sail on Thursday?"

Floyd asked nothing better, and said so; then he waited, expecting Hakluyt to broach the subject of Captain Luckman, but Hakluyt did not say a word about that gentleman. They talked of a good many things, but Luckman's name was never mentioned.

Floyd left the office perplexed and more disturbed than he would have been had Hakluyt announced his intention of superseding him as captain by appointing Luckman to the post.

Was Luckman to be sprung upon him at the last moment? Apparently so.

He turned down Market Street. So deep in thought was he that the passers-by were unnoticed. He walked without aim or object for some two hundred yards till at the corner of Fore Street he was brought to reality by a hand laid on his arm.

He turned, and found himself face to face with a tall, bearded man, wearing a slouch hat, roughly dressed yet somehow well-to-do looking, bronzed, hearty, and healthy with sun and open-air life.

"Captain Cardon!" said Floyd.

"You passed me as if you didn't know me," said the other, laughing. "And I'm Captain Cardon no more; plain Jack Cardon, gold prospector, and down on his luck—that's me. Where the deuce have you sprung from?"

"You don't look particularly down on your luck," said Floyd. "Me? I've sprung from the islands—let's go somewhere and have a talk."

"You come with me," said Cardon, turning and leading the way down Fore Street. "Well, this is a bit of good fortune. I was crazy for the sight of some man I knew other than the bar bummers round here. It's four years since we met, isn't it? And I owe you that five dollars still; lost your postal address, or did you give me one?"

Floyd laughed.

He had sailed under Cardon in one of the blackbird freighters, and knew him for what he was—one of the best, most desperate, and irresponsible of men. He had parted from him at 'Frisco in a bar in a haze of tobacco smoke, Cardon, relieved of his responsibilities in life by reason of a quarrel with his owners, sitting on a high stool by the counter, a full glass beside him, and leading the chorus of "A Hot Time in the Old Town To-night."

He was to have seen Cardon the next day, but they had failed to meet, and then the sea had separated them. He remembered the five dollars; they fluttered up to his mind now—ghosts of silver coins forgotten beneath the waters of memory.

Cardon was like a sea breeze to him in his present state of mind, and he followed as Cardon led the way through a garden where seats and tables were set out and into a bar where more seats and tables faced a bar counter gorgeous with colored bottles.

There were island spears and head-dresses on the walls, and photographs of towns sea-washed and backed by coconut palms.

The poetry of the islands spreads across the Pacific even to the bars of Sydney and San Francisco, where the trade winds blow in mariners bronzed by the sun and salt, where even the traders carry with them in their hands something more than copra or gold.

The place was almost empty at this hour, and Cardon, at Floyd's request, called for soft drinks. Floyd produced cigars.

"Well," said Cardon, when he had lit up, "I'm blessed if this doesn't lay over everything. To think of you and me parting at Black Jack's on the Barbary Coast four years and more ago and promising to meet the next day, and then meeting here, just as though we'd only parted yesterday—what have you been doing with yourself?"

"What have you?" asked Floyd. "You tell me your yarn, and I'll tell mine. I want a little time to think about mine, for if I'm not mistaken it will have more to do with you than you think. I may have an offer to make you; however, that will do to talk of afterward."

"If your offer has anything to do with money, I'm open to it," said Cardon. "What have I been doing since we parted? Everything and nothing. I made a fortune the next year in Brazil—mining. And I lost it six months after I got it. I was done by a partner, and pretty nigh done up. Then I took to the sea again. A cattle boat, and I was boss of it. I was tending the cattle—fact. But I didn't grumble. I like cattle; they're a long sight honester than men. Well, after that I did some railway work in Central America, and after that I went oil prospecting with a young fellow who paid for kit and accouterments and died on my hands with malaria before we got a sign of what we were looking for. He had no relatives, and he gave me all the money on him before he died, which wasn't much—some seven hundred dollars. Then I turned up here on the hunt for gold, and found none; did some more railway work and got good pay for it, straggled back to Sydney and struck you in the street. That's all."

"Well, you're looking well on it," said Floyd; "you don't look a day older than when I met you last."

"Nor I don't feel it," said Cardon. "If I'd been living in a city all the time it would have been different, but the open air keeps one alive. If I'd managed to keep that fortune, I'd have mostlike been dead by this time between wine and women. As it is, I'm liver than when I started—I don't care a hang for money."

"Well, why are you always hunting for it then?" asked Floyd, with a laugh.

"For the pleasure of the hunt," replied Cardon. "What makes a man hunt bears and spend thousands of dollars on guns and tents and guides, as I've seen some of these N' York chaps do? He doesn't love bears; he hunts them for the fun of the thing. Same with me and dollars; I don't love them, but I love hunting for them. It's the same with most men, I reckon. Well, what's your yarn?"

Floyd tipped the ash off his cigar. All this time, while listening to Cardon, he had been making up his mind. He, like Cardon, did not love money. He reckoned that his share of the pearling business and the pearls, even if he were to divide it equally with Cardon, would give him enough money to start in life at some more profitable business than sailoring. He was bitterly in need of friendship and a strong man's help, and he decided to tell Cardon everything, invoke his help, and offer him half shares.

"What I'm going to tell you," said he, "sounds like a yarn out of a book, but it's the truth. Some months ago I left 'Frisco, bound for the islands in a schooner owned by a man named Coxon. The *Cormorant* was her name. She was an unlucky ship." He told of the fire, of the island, of Schumer and Isbel, of the pearls—he told everything worth telling about the whole business; and, when he had finished, the effect of the yarn on Cardon was very evident, for that gentleman for once in his life was dumb.

"But that's not all," went on Floyd. "Something happened yesterday that puts a topknot on the whole business."

He told of the conversation he had overheard in Hakluyt's office, and of the act of treachery which he believed to be impending.

"That's clear enough," said Cardon; "they mean to do you up. Who is this Luckman?"

"I don't know him from Adam. Didn't even see him, only heard his voice."

"That's bad," said Cardon; "and you say the *Southern Cross* sails the day after to-morrow?"

"Yes, on Thursday."

"You are bound to go in her?"

"Of course."

"Has Hakluyt said anything to you about Luckman?"

"Not a word."

"Yet you are the skipper?"

"Yes."

"What's your crew?"

"All Kanakas."

"All Kanakas?"

"Yes."

"But how in the nation are you going to work her single-handed?"

"Oh, easy enough. I have a chap called Mountain Joe; he's a Kanaka, but he has picked up a bit of navigation."

"Well," said Cardon, "that simplifies matters a bit, for Hakluyt can't ship this blighter as a Kanaka, can't slide him aboard as an extra hand. He must ship him openly; most likely he'll do it at the last moment."

"That is what I'm thinking," said Floyd. "He'll dump him onto me just as I'm getting up anchor, and I can't refuse, for he's sure to make up some yarn. My only course is to take him and then deal with him when I get to sea."

"That's easier said than done."

"You're right."

"Unless you shoot him right off and chuck him overboard, which is impossible; or put him in irons, which, with a Kanaka crew, would be risky;

or maroon him on some rock or other with a beaker of water and a bag of bread, which is also a bit risky. No, I should take him right along and front him with this Schumer, tell them they are found out, and at the first sign of a move on their part—shoot."

"That's easy to say."

"Yes, easier to say than do; yet if it was me I'd do it."

"Look here," said Floyd, "will you come into this business with me? I'll give you half profits."

Cardon did not reply for a moment. He took a pull at his drink, wiped his mouth with the back of his hand, looked at the top of his cigar, and then said, quite simply:

"I don't mind."

Floyd stretched out his hand and they shook.

"I thought you would," said Floyd. "And now I'll tell you something else—it's not the money I'm thinking of so much as that girl I told you of."

"Isbel?"

"Yes, Isbel. I'm—I'm——"

"Soft on her," said Cardon, laughing. "Well, you're not the first to get tangled with a girl. All the same, I wish we were fighting this business out without petticoats in it. I have a holy dread of petticoats. On shore and after a cruise I don't mind; but they're no use afloat or where fighting has to be done."

"Aren't they?" said Floyd. "I'd sooner have Isbel backing me in a row than most men. I told you she helped me in my scrap with those scamps, but I did not tell you all. She can shoot straight, and she doesn't know fear. She backed me right through the business without turning a hair, and we were fighting half a day and the whole of a night. Fighting? Yes! I have never known what it meant before—shut up in a house with nearly half a hundred Solomon Islanders outside all yelling like fiends and mad to have one's blood."

"Well," said Cardon, "I expect you'll have some fighting to match that before we have done with this business. If this man Schumer is anything like what you say, and if this man Luckman is anything like Schumer, we will have our work cut out for us by a fancy tailor. What did you say these pearls were worth?"

"Worth? I don't know the exact figures, but Schumer has pearls there on the island now that I reckon must be at least worth twenty thousand pounds. I'm figuring on the values he suggested, and he's a man who knows something of pearls, and he's not a man who exaggerates."

"Well, I'm not going to halve your pearls," said Cardon. "I reckon my share in the business will be the whole of Schumer's."

"Of Schumer's?"

"Of Schumer's."

"But, see here," said Floyd.

"Yes?"

"You intend to take Schumer's share from him?"

"That is what I said."

"But would that be fair? He has worked deuced hard; he discovered the oyster beds— —"

"And he betrayed you, and is only waiting there on this island of yours to help to do you in."

"All the same," said Floyd, "I don't like the idea of stripping him if we get the better of him. It may be foolish, but I've worked alongside of him, and, though I believe he is the biggest scoundrel God ever put hair on, I don't like the idea of taking his share of the pearls from him."

"When we have done with Schumer," replied Cardon grimly, "I don't suspect he'll want pearls. We'll leave the matter till then, for it's on the cards that when he has done with us we won't want pearls, either. So let's not divide the stuff up till the business is over. How are you off for arms and ammunition?"

"I have a revolver at my rooms and half a packet of cartridges, and there is a rifle on board in my cabin with a hundred cartridges for it."

"Good!" said Cardon. "And I have my old friend Joe." He opened his coat and showed a navy revolver strapped in its case to his belt. He slipped the long, beautifully kept weapon from its case and stroked it lovingly. "This is him. This chap would stop a hippopotamus. He's a man's weapon—what?"

"He's big enough," said Floyd, as Cardon returned Joe to his case, "and I hope to goodness we'll pull this thing through without having to use him. I'm not a coward, but I hate killing."

"So do I," replied Cardon, "till it comes to the point. Well, now we've settled about the arms, let's fix another matter. How am I to book a passage on the *Southern Cross*?"

"I have been thinking that out the whole time," replied Floyd. "Suppose I go to Hakluyt and say that I have a friend I want to take with me, he'll buck at the idea at once, the same as if I told him I wanted an extra hand to help in the navigating; and it would be quite natural, too, for the whole of this business is a secret, and if another white man was taken on board, no matter who or what he was, it might mean the secret getting out."

"Sure," said Cardon.

"The only way," continued Floyd, "is to take you without Hakluyt knowing."

"Stowaway?"

"Yes. There are two cabins off the main cabin—the captain's and the mate's. Only one is used; for Mountain Joe, the fellow I told you about, berths with the crew. I can take you aboard to-morrow night. I'll tell Joe next morning you have gone ashore in a shore boat. You can stay in the mate's cabin till we get the anchor up."

"No," said Cardon, "in your cabin."

"Why so?" asked Floyd.

"This way: Suppose old man Hakluyt arrives off with this Luckman at the last moment. You can't refuse to take him; you don't *want* to refuse. Well, naturally, he'll want the mate's cabin, and you can let him have it without any bother."

"That's true," said Floyd.

"Luckman may be sprung on you before that," said Cardon. "In which case we must make some other arrangement about my getting on board; but, as far as we know, what we have decided on will stand."

"Where are you staying in Sydney?" asked Floyd.

"Well," said Cardon, "I only arrived last night, and I put up at a tavern on the Leicester Road. I left all my gear there. It isn't much, and it won't take many porters to fetch it down to the wharfside."

"Well," said Floyd, "you had better come and stay at my place. I can get you a room, and you can put your things among my baggage which I'll send on board to-morrow night."

Cardon agreed to this, and, finishing their drinks, they left the place together.

CHAPTER XXIX
PETER WILLIAMS

Next morning Floyd called on Hakluyt, while Cardon, who had accompanied him, waited outside the office.

Floyd was half an hour in the office, and when he came out Cardon followed till he had turned the street corner, and there joined him.

"I can't make it out," said Floyd; "I've said good-by to him, and I'm to start to-morrow morning at sunup, and not a word did he say about Luckman or anyone else, not a hint that he was going to send an extra hand on board. What's the meaning of it? Did I dream that business in the office, or was it real?"

"Oh, I guess you'll find it real enough to satisfy you before long," said Cardon. "You see, there's one solid reason behind all this that will make it work out different from a dream, and that reason is pearls. You say you have a third share in the business, which share, if the business is worth twenty thousand as it stands, would work out close on seven thousand pounds. Now, if Hakluyt is a shipowner, he's a scoundrel; and if he's a scoundrel, he'll do a lot to secure seven thousand pounds. Why, men sink ships every day for less than that; and sinking a ship is a lot more risky business than doing up an unknown sailorman. You needn't be uneasy on that score. You dreamed a real dream. You see, you are worth killing, that's the long and short of it; for not only are you worth the seven thousand, but you are worth a third of all that pearl lagoon will bring in the future, which may be a lot. I wish we could get to know something about this Luckman. Suppose we make inquiries?"

"Whom could we ask?"

"Some one who knows the port. Peter Williams, he's the man; he keeps a bar down on the waterside. I knew him in Melbourne years ago, and I gave him a call when I came here first, and he's a friendly sort of customer. Don't you do any talking; leave it all to me."

They took their way down to the waterside, and here, before a rather dingy bar with the name Peter Williams done in huge letters on the front, Cardon paused.

"This is the place," said he, "and we'd better go in separate. You see, if Williams by any chance was to know Luckman and tell him two strangers had been inquiring about him, Luckman would ask for a description of them, and might spot you. Don't pretend to know me, then we will be on the safe side."

Peter Williams, a red-headed Welshman in shirt sleeves, was leaning across the bar talking to Cardon when Floyd entered. There was no one else in the place.

Floyd glanced round him with disgust. The walls were dingy and showed a dado of grease marks above the benches where the heads of customers had rested against the wall. The atmosphere was heavy with stale tobacco and the smell of gin and sawdust.

He called for a drink, and took his seat on one of the benches while Peter Williams returned to his conversation with Cardon.

"Well, I wouldn't have him here," said Peter. "Not that I'm a prying man into another man's character, for a publican has nothing to do with the character of his customers. No, it's not that; it's my other customers I'm thinking of. If he was to come in here or be seen here regular, I'd lose my trade—and no wonder. He's never been had by the law, but he's got the name of having drowned more sailormen than is good for him. It's so. He's lost three ships out of this port alone, and God He knows how many more, and has done it so artful that the law can't touch him. And still he gets ships. What's that you say—you wonder that sailormen will sign on under him? How are they to pick and choose? Give them drink enough, and they'd sign on under Satan. And there's more than that to it. The *Baralong*, she was known to be rotten right down to her garboard strake and Huffer was her captain, and he was known to be as bad as her; and there were two jacks in here drinking and talking her over and talking Huffer over and giving them both their proper names. Well, next day both those chaps signed on under Huffer, and the day after they were off to Valparaiso on the *Baralong*. I believe some of those chaps would sooner sign on in a crazy vessel than a sound one. They seem to like the danger. All the same, when they sit down to their drinks they don't want to have the taste of their liquor spoiled by the sight of chaps like Huffer or Luckman. They'll sail under them, but they won't drink near them. That's the plain truth."

Cardon, after a little while, went out, and presently Floyd followed him.

"Well," said Floyd, when they met in the street, "you've heard Luckman's character. What do you think of it?"

"I never think about men's characters, or bother a cent about anything than the man himself," replied Cardon. "A man may have a tremendous big character—or, better, call it reputation for being a holy terror; and when you overhaul him you may find him to be a merchantman painted in imitation of a pirate, or, again, he may have the reputation of being a very quiet man indeed; then you take his lid off, and—oh, my!

"I've seen a little bit of a man who looked like a parson with the pip, a little bit of a chap with a pale face that looked as if it had been trying all its life to raise a beard and then given up the business as unworkable. Well, that chap swam out to a ship somewhere down the Chile coast, talked the crew over, and made them mutiny. With the crew he took the ship, and with the ship he took a town, and with the town he'd have taken Chile, I believe, only the Chilean government chipped in in time and sent troops and beat him in a big battle near Valdivia and then hanged him at Concepción. I saw him hanged. Benken was his name—an American from nowhere, with a past history that showed nothing except the fact that he had once been a prisoner in Numea and had escaped by raising a revolt and murdering the guards. Yet to look at him he was quite a quiet man; might have been a shopman.

"No; as I was saying, there's nothing counts but the man himself, and by the man himself I don't mean a man's character or face, but just the something that drives him on. If he hasn't got that something, he may have the face of a Napoleon Bonaparte or the character of a white lamb—it doesn't matter, he arrives nowhere. Now, from all accounts, the man I fear most in this business is not Luckman but Schumer. Schumer seems to be all there from what you tell me, and he doesn't seem to make much show. Is he a quiet sort of chap?"

"Yes, very."

"Fair spoken and easy in his talk?"

"Yes."

"That's the sort of man that gives trouble. Well, we will see what we will see when the time comes; and now I propose we go and have a bit of dinner. It's the last we'll have on shore for some time."

That afternoon Floyd, having paid off his landlord, called a porter and had his gear, together with Cardon's, taken down to the wharfside. Here they took a shore boat and rowed off to the *Southern Cross*. Mountain Joe was hanging over the rail as they approached. He and the whole Kanaka ship's company had been specially provided for when on shore by Hakluyt. He had sent the whole lot, in fact, under the guidance of one of his men, to a fishing village down the coast, there to amuse themselves till the time of sailing. He did not want them knocking round Sydney and maybe talking, though indeed they knew little enough as to the truth concerning the pearl fishery.

Mountain Joe grinned when he saw Floyd; then he lowered the ladder for them.

It was a lovely late afternoon, the great harbor like a sheet of glass, the gulls crying and wheeling above the water and the trees of the shore and the far-stretching hills green against a sky of summer. Cardon, when he stepped on deck, looked round him with approval. The *Southern Cross* was not a fast boat, as schooners go, but she was only some six years old and she had been well looked after. Built by McDowell, of Sydney, than whom no better schooner builder exists, she had been laid down to the plans of a private firm with ideas of their own, as though one were to go to Mr. Pool or Messrs. Stultz for a suit of clothes to be made according to one's own ideas of cut and style.

The result was that the *Southern Cross* turned out to be something of a failure as far as speed was concerned, but a splendid sea boat. Every bit of stuff in her was good, and spars, rigging, and hull would have stood the criticism of an English navy dockyard inspection.

Floyd took Cardon down below and showed him the main cabin and the cabins of the captain and the first and second mate.

The captain's cabin had two bunks—an upper and a lower one—and they arranged that Cardon should sleep that night in the upper bunk, which had curtains.

"If Hakluyt should turn up before we start," said Cardon, "I can lie in the upper bunk with the curtains drawn and you can say I'm some of your gear you have stowed there. There's no fear of any of those tomfool Kanakas coming and poking their noses in here?"

"No, I'll look to that. The fellow that acts as steward is a born fool, and if he did see you he wouldn't take notice; and, anyhow, you're on board, and, Hakluyt or no Hakluyt, you are going to sail with me."

He got out the spirits and some cigars, and they sat smoking and talking till the steward came in to light the lamps.

Cardon, at sight of this person, felt no uneasiness; he was of the stupid type of native—"wore his mouth open," to use Cardon's expression, and was afflicted with deafness due to adenoids.

They came up on deck after dark, and sat smoking and watching the lights of Sydney and the harbor all spangled with star reflections and the anchor lights of the shipping.

"Well," said Cardon, "if old man Hakluyt had been intending to come off for the purpose of dumping Luckman on you, I guess he'd have come by this."

"You never know," replied Floyd. "That sort of reptile is pretty cunning, and I don't give up a fear of surprise till I'm outside the Heads. Look! There's a shore boat come off, and it's making for us if I'm not mistaken."

Cardon looked in the direction indicated.

"You're right," said he.

Without another word he turned and dived below.

Floyd, quite sure as to the other's ability to take cover, remained on deck.

He could see the boat now clearly as she drew near across the starlit water.

There were four fellows rowing, and a figure in the stern steering. It was Hakluyt alone and unaccompanied by Luckman.

Hakluyt came on board and gave Floyd good evening, inquired if the crew were all right, and then came below.

Floyd, who preceded him, looked anxiously round, but Cardon had removed all traces of himself, and the door of the captain's cabin was closed.

"Well," said Hakluyt, as he took his seat and a drink, "here's luck to the voyage and a quick return with another cargo of shell, though I expect it is Schumer himself who will come next to Sydney. You will give him my very good respects?"

"Certainly," replied Floyd, "and perhaps the next time I meet you will be on the island. You are sure to pay us another visit."

"Maybe," replied Hakluyt, "and maybe not. I am getting old for sea work, but I shall always be glad to welcome you in Sydney."

He produced a pocketbook, and they went into accounts as to stores, et cetera. This business took them some half hour or so, and then Hakluyt took another cigar and talked on indifferent subjects till it was time to go.

He shook hands effusively with Floyd on deck, and wished him good luck again as he went down the side.

Floyd watched the boat draw off and the oars making rings on the star-spangled water; then he returned to the cabin, where he found Cardon released from his prison and seated at the table.

"He's gone," said Floyd.

"And no sign of Luckman?"

"Not a sign."

"Well," said Cardon, "it's beyond me. However, we're not out of Sydney harbor yet, and there's no knowing what may happen before we are."

CHAPTER XXX
THE OPEN SEA

Floyd did not take the trouble to speak to Mountain Joe about Cardon's presence on board.

Cardon got into the upper bunk at about eleven o'clock and went promptly to sleep. As for Floyd, he could neither sleep nor lie still. During his stay in Sydney, he had been restless enough at times, but he had never felt like this. Ever since his departure from the island the idea of Isbel had followed him and been with him now clear and close, now more remote and partly obscured from him by everyday affairs.

To-night she haunted him.

All sorts of fears and imaginings rose in his mind. He had never known the extent of his love for her till just this moment, on the eve of his return. Suppose when he got back he found she was not there. Suppose the natives had revolted again; suppose that Schumer, playing every one false and on the chance of a passing ship, had gone off from the island, taking the pearls with him and Isbel. Suppose—suppose——There was no end to the suppositions that rose up before his mind as he paced the floor of the main cabin and listened to Cardon snoring in his bunk.

Cardon, in his idea of passing himself off as baggage, had not reckoned on his capacity for snoring. Floyd, however, did not trouble about it; even if Hakluyt were suddenly to come on board and see Cardon in the flesh, let alone hearing him snoring, it would not much matter.

In his present frame of mind, he would have bundled Hakluyt down the main hatch and closed it on him had he appeared to give any trouble.

He came on deck, leaving Cardon to his dreams, and paced the planks, still engaged in suppositions as to Isbel.

Then the night wind, balmy and warm, blew the evil fancies from his mind and restored its tone. Nothing could have happened in the few weeks that had elapsed since his departure. Isbel was well able to take care of herself, and as for the natives, they were not likely to try any more tricks with Sru dead and Schumer in command. The real danger was to come, and its name was Luckman. That was nothing. With Cardon at his elbow, he felt able to cope with a hundred Luckmans and Schumers. He was forewarned. Fate had declared for him—or so it seemed.

He remained on deck till dawn began to break upon the harbor, then he went down and woke Cardon.

Before going down, he had stirred up the cook and ordered coffee to be sent to the main cabin; and while they were drinking this they heard a boat coming alongside, and Mountain Joe shouted down the hatchway that the pilot was coming on board.

"I reckon I'd better stay hid till we are clear of the harbor," said Cardon. "There's no use in running risks. Up with you, and interview the pilot and get the anchor out of the mud as quick as you can. Give me a word when you have dropped him. You won't have far to look for me."

Floyd went up and found the pilot already on deck. The wind was fair; all the port regulations had been complied with, and there was nothing to hold them but the anchor.

Cardon, down below, could hear the clank of the windlass pawls as the slack of the anchor chain was being hove in, the feet of the fellows on deck running to orders, their voices as they hauled on the halyards, and then again the welcome music of the pawls as the anchor was dragged from the mud and hauled, gray and dripping, to the catheads.

Instantly the schooner took the feel of a live ship, to use Cardon's words. She heeled ever so little, and, as he lay in the bunk, he could hear the warble of the water against her planking, to say nothing of the rattle of the rudder chain and the occasional creak of woodwork acknowledging mast pressure and strain.

After a while Cardon, tired with the stuffy air of the cabin, dropped asleep. When he awoke, Floyd was standing beside him, and by the movement of the cabin he knew that the *Southern Cross* had cleared the harbor and was making her bow to the Pacific.

"How about the pilot?" asked Cardon, rubbing his eyes.

"Dropped him long ago," replied Floyd. "Hop out and come on deck. The fellow is laying the things for breakfast, and a breath of air will do you good."

Cardon slipped from the bunk and came on deck.

A brave breeze was blowing, and the sea, roughed up beneath the morning sun, had a hard, gemlike look. Foam caps showed, and in the west the setting moon hung, ghostlike, in a sky that suggested millions and millions of miles of depth and blueness.

All the east was hard and bright; all the west was blue and subtle and tender; and between the east and the west lay the sea like a country carved from sapphire and tourmaline, with the green hills of earth sinking slowly but surely away beyond the foam in the schooner's wake.

Then, as the sun mounted higher, the sea lost its look of solidity, cast it back on the land, now remote and hard, black fish came walloping along as if racing the rushing schooner. The wind, freshening, blew in great, steady gusts, filling the bellying canvas and pressing like a great hand so that the lee rail was almost awash and the spray came inboard, fresh, like the very breath of the sea.

Cardon, with his hand on the ratlines, stood taking it all in while Floyd stood beside him, his clothes flapping round him in the flogging wind.

Mountain Joe was at the wheel. He showed no surprise at Cardon's presence on board, nor did any of the others. They evidently looked on him as a passenger or supercargo of some sort approved of by Hakluyt.

"She's a good sea boat," said Cardon, "and she seems to steer well; but what in the nation can have become of Luckman?"

"That's what's bothering me," said Floyd. "I've been trying to figure the thing out ever since we got the anchor on board. He can't be stowed away anywhere. He's not in the fo'c'sle, for I went down there under the pretense of seeing whether the hammocks were all right. He's not in the galley, he's not in the cabins, and he's not in the hold. He's not on board, in fact. Well, what is the meaning of it? The only thing I can imagine is that the affair has fallen through and he's gone off with the money Hakluyt gave him—either that or I must have imagined the conversation I heard."

"Oh, I reckon that wasn't any imagination of yours," said Cardon. "There was lots of reason why Hakluyt should have put the business against you. No; the only explanation is that the thing, as you say, must have fallen through. Luckman funked it and took his hook with the money. That's the only possible thing that can have happened. But it leaves the position just the same as far as you and I are concerned."

"How do you mean?"

"Just this: The plot was made against you, and it wasn't made in Sydney. It was all arranged on the island between Schumer and Hakluyt."

"Yes, it must have been."

"Well, then, the question turns up, are you going to go on working with this Schumer, who has made all the arrangements for doing you in and who would have done you in had not the thing fallen through?"

"Never!" said Floyd. "I have finished with Schumer."

"Oh, no, you haven't!" replied Cardon. "Not by a long chalk. There remains the question of the pearls, and the question of punishment. Schumer has got to pay for his villainy, and pay through the nose. But there's the fellow bringing breakfast aft. Let's go down, and we can talk the matter out below."

They went down, and when breakfast was over Cardon lit a pipe, settled himself comfortably on the couch at the starboard side of the cabin, and, after a moment's silence, turned to Floyd, who was lighting a cigar.

"You have got to get even with Schumer, and from all you have told me of Schumer you will have your work cut out. I know the type. The Pacific is full of it. This chap is a trader and a sailor and a fighter all rolled in one. I know the sort—able to do anything, from playing a tune on a fiddle to playing a dirty trick. I know them."

"Don't you be too sure," said Floyd. "This man Schumer is not one of the ordinary sort of traders and swindlers. He's a very big man. He ought to have been anything, and the wonder to me is he has never risen to something in the world better than what he is."

"There you have his weakness," said Cardon. "I admit he may be a big man, as you say; and yet, as you say, he is only a little one as far as the world is concerned. There's something wrong somewhere in his make-up. He doesn't drink?"

"Not he!"

"Well, there's some crack in him we must try and feel for. I expect the chap is such a rightdown wrong one that he has failed in life just because of that. I don't say I'm not a failure in my way, but I have failed mostly through taking things easy and trusting in men. But Schumer hasn't those weaknesses, if I can judge by what you have told me. No; I suspect his disease has been a pretty general one. He's a wrong un. I'm not a man given to moralizing, but I've seen a lot of the world, and I've seen that men who don't run straight don't get on. It's funny, but they don't. Now look at old man Schumer's case. He fell in with a pearl lagoon; he has taken twenty thousand pounds' worth of pearls out of it, and maybe more by this. He had a partner named Floyd. He couldn't run straight with that partner, but must lay plans for his wiping out. Floyd discovers his trick, and now Schumer is going to lose pearls and lagoon and all; and when he's lost them he will go back to his old way of life with his feathers clipped, and men will say: 'I can't understand that Schumer; he ought to have been anything, and yet there he is bumming around in bars.' That's what they will say. Honesty is the best policy, and that's God's truth and no copybook story, and that's what I'm going to teach Schumer."

"But, look here, you say he is going to lose pearls and lagoon and all——"

"I? He may keep the lagoon—we only want the pearls."

"Yes, but——"

"I know what you are going to say—we have to get them before we keep them. I know. The thing to worry out is how we are to get the weather gauge on him. You have taken me into this affair as a partner, offering me half your share. I don't want that. I want Schumer's share. The man is a murderer, and deserves hanging. I am only going to fire him, but I admit the thing will be difficult.

"If we sail into the lagoon and declare war openly with him, he'll fight, and he'll be backed by all those natives he has got there."

"He will, and besides there's the—the girl."

"Just so; you don't want her injured."

"Cardon," said Floyd, "I tell you the truth as between man and man. She's everything. I don't care a straw about the pearls, about money, about Schumer. I don't care about life itself where she's concerned. She's the only thing I have ever cared for really."

"And yet," cut in Cardon, "if you care for her like that, it's all the more important for you not to be done out over the pearls. Pearls are money. Well, do you think you don't want money? To a single man, money is useful, but to a man with a woman in tow, by God, it's a blank necessity! What are you to do with her as a sailor? Leave her in some seaport while you are off sweeping the sea for tuppence a week in some dirty hooker owned by some dirty owner who feeds his men on salt horse and sends them to the bottom through overloading or for the sake of the insurance money? No. If you care for a woman, put a pistol to her head before you turn her into a sailor's wife, depending on a sailor's pay. You have got to get the money that's owing to you from Schumer, and you have got to get your satisfaction from him. I don't know how yet, but I'll find out by thinking over it."

"You are right," said Floyd. "I have got to get the money, anyhow, even if I don't get the satisfaction. But there's another point: Suppose I do get the pearls; there's always a difficulty in selling them."

"You needn't worry about that," said Cardon. "I've got the means of selling anything that is come by honestly. I have a good name among a good set at 'Frisco. Now I'll tell you something you can't easily believe; but if I wanted to borrow money in 'Frisco, I could do so to the extent of thousands and thousands of dollars. There are two men there, rich men, who would let me draw on them for what I liked; and yet I have often borrowed a few dollars from a poor man—you remember that five dollars I got from you and which I owe you still, by the way. No, sir, I have never tapped those rich men because they are under an obligation to me, and because they are my friends, and because I know that they would be only too pleased to lend to me. Men are funny things, and I guess I'm a man. Anyhow, that's how things stand. Now, if I were to go to those men and say: 'Look here, I have got a fortune in pearls, and I want to turn it into dollars,' those fellows would put all their means at my disposal to get me the best price, and ten to one they'd buy the stuff themselves, and my difficulty would be to stop them from paying too big a price. One is Kane, of the Union Pacific Company; the other is Calthorpe, the grain man. I knew them first twenty years ago, when we were all dead beats together. Kane started life as a newsboy, selling books on the cars of the Reading Railway. He builds them now. Calthorpe started in life on the docks at 'Frisco, helping to load sacks of wheat. They don't load wheat in sacks nowadays; his elevators do most of the work. Well, they are white men, and though they have wives and daughters and carriages, they are always glad to see me at their offices, and they are such gentlemen they have never offered to start me in life. They take me as one of themselves, and we have a clack and a smoke and a drink. I generally stand the drinks, and I know they are green with envy of my stomach, for they are both eaten up with dyspepsia. Now those chaps have succeeded in life, but they haven't succeeded in keeping up their pleasure in life. I have, and I reckon, when all's said and done, the account is on my side. They are pretty well done to death with worry, living in stuffed-up rooms, fighting every moment of the day to keep what they've got, taking their food like medicine, and with gold teeth in their heads to help them chew it; and here am I with every tooth in my head and an appetite like a shark, clear two hundred, without an ache or pain, breathing God's good air, and sailing to belt a chap over the head and collar a pearl lagoon. I guess they'd change places if their wives would let them."

"You have never grown old," said Floyd.

"I'm forty-five," replied Cardon, "and I don't want to grow any older, and I wouldn't be an inch younger for worlds. A man only begins to live properly when he's forty, and at forty-five he has just about found himself. Well, I'm going on deck to have a breath of air. She seems to be going a bit steadier; I expect the wind has fallen."

When they got on deck, they found that the wind had lost its gusty character and had settled down into a steady blow. The land was very far away, and only one sail was in sight—a full-rigged ship, almost hull down on the horizon and white like a flake of spar. The *Southern Cross* was heading northeast, on a course that would leave Norfolk Island some two hundred miles to port; and before her lay that great, empty zone of sea which stretches from the Kermadec Islands to the Tongas, and from the Australs to the Isle of Pines.

Some ten days out from Sydney, they hailed a steamer; she was the mail boat from Auckland to Fiji, and the last trace of her smoke was the last sign of man for many days.

The weather was perfect and the wind favorable, though moderate, as they stole northward toward the line. Each day the sea became of a deeper and deeper blue, and each day the sense of remoteness from the world as we know it grew more intense.

The nights were tremendous with stars, and the days were scarcely days, as days are reckoned with us. They left on the mind only one enduring impression—great spaces of radiant blueness, infinite distance where there was nothing but the send of the sea and the blowing of a tepid wind.

One day, breaking the sea line on the starboard bow, came an island—a dream of the sea, foam-stained and waving palms to the wind, the tepid wind still blowing steadily and ceaselessly like the moist, warm breath of million-leagued Capricorn. It was Rarotonga.

It faded away, and at sunset it had vanished. Next day, toward noon, the Hervey Islands showed right ahead, and, like a white gull coming from the islands toward them, a schooner. She passed only a few cable lengths away, her canvas luminous and honey-colored with the sun. She was a trader bound for the Tongas, and in an hour she was a speck to the southward, while the Hervey Islands loomed more fully ahead, only to be passed with the sunset and wiped away utterly by the night.

One evening Floyd, who had been working out the reckoning, said to Cardon:

"To-morrow, if this wind holds good, we ought to arrive—somewhere about noon, I should say."

"Good!" said Cardon. "And now I'll tell you of the plan that's been in my head for the last couple of days. We have no longer to reckon with Luckman; he has evidently miscarried. Still, Schumer will give us all the work we want. My plan is this, and it's simple enough. When we drop anchor, he's almost sure to come on board. Well, you must receive him on deck and ask him down into the main cabin. I'll be ambushed in your cabin.

"Out I'll step, put Joe's muzzle to his head, and say, 'Hands up!' When he's disarmed, we'll give him a fair hearing and a fair trial; you'll be judge, and I'll be jury. Then we'll lock him up in your cabin to pray for his sins, and I'll keep watch on him while you go ashore and collect the pearls and the girl.

"You'll bring them off, and then we'll put to sea. Outside the reef we'll put Schumer in a boat and let him row ashore. Then we'll upstick back to Sydney, and there you and I will have an interview with Hakluyt, fling Luckman and all that business in his teeth, and gag him with it. Then we'll make for 'Frisco by the mail boat. You see, we must take the schooner back to Sydney, or else be had, maybe, for stealing her. Well, what do you think of the plan?"

Floyd was silent for a moment.

"Suppose," said he, "Schumer doesn't put his hands up when you tell him. Suppose he goes for his revolver?"

"Then I'll shoot."

"Suppose he comes on board with half a dozen of those natives and brings them armed? It's not likely, but Schumer is just the man to do an unlikely thing of that sort."

"If we see him coming off with a boatload of those scalawags, we must change our plan. I can hide till we are able to get him onto the schooner alone; but there's no use supposing too much. What we want is a plan to go on, and that's the best I can think of."

"Well," said Floyd, "I don't like it, and that's the truth. It's a good enough plan, no doubt, but there seems to me something treacherous about it. I don't mean that in a nasty way, or as reflecting on you. All the same, it's a plan I'd hate to carry out."

"Well, and who forces us to use treachery, as you call it? If you hide behind a bush to shoot a tiger, is that treachery? No, it would be if you were dealing with a man; it isn't if you are dealing with a tiger. Schumer is a tiger; or, more like, a polecat; and if you don't use treachery, he will. He has already, in fact."

"He'd still have the lagoon," said Floyd, wavering.

"Yes, we'd leave him the lagoon—not for love, but for our own sakes. I've been figuring the thing out, and we'd better let the lagoon go. If we tried to cling to it, we would have to tear Schumer's claws loose from it, not to speak of Hakluyt's. If we leave it to them, it will be a sop in the pan and will stop them from making any worry. We only want the pearls already captured. They'll do for us."

Floyd heaved a sigh. He could not but see the force of Cardon's reasoning. Schumer deserved punishment, beyond all question; he had plotted with Hakluyt, and the plot had only failed to materialize owing to some accident or some rascality on the part of Luckman toward his fellow conspirators. Still, he hated the idea of the whole business. Inveigling a man into the cabin and then clapping a pistol to his head was a plan of action that would never have occurred to him. Cardon was thicker skinned. All the same, he could not help feeling that Cardon was right.

There are some men whom it is impossible to deal with as gentlemen, just as there are some men whom it is impossible to fight with according to the rules of the prize ring. Schumer was one of them.

Floyd thought the matter over for a moment, and came to the conclusion that Cardon was right. "I have no right to criticize your plan," he answered, "since I haven't any plan of my own to offer instead of it. We'll leave it at that, and trust to luck, and if it comes to doing what you say, I will, of course, back you, unless I hit on any idea between this and to-morrow."

He went on deck. The *Southern Cross,* carrying every stitch of her canvas, was making a good ten knots, and the foam in her wake had a phosphorescence as though she were leaving behind her a cloud of luminous smoke that clung to the water and refused to rise. Never had he seen the stars more wonderful, or a night more lovely. There was little of the heaviness and languor of the tropics; and but for Canopus and the Cross blazing overhead it might have been a night of June in northern latitudes.

Floyd stood by the fellow at the wheel for a little while, and then he walked forward, and, leaning against the lee rail, looked over the sea. From the fo'c'sle came the sound of a concertina, faint and indistinct; that and the creak of cordage and the slashing of the bow wash were the only sounds in all that infinity of night and silence.

He was thinking of Isbel and the island invisible, but surely there beyond the rim of the sea. There were moments when the whole thing seemed a fantastic dream—Schumer, and the pearls, and the island, and the woman he loved. Was it possible that he would see her on the morrow?

CHAPTER XXXI
THE ISLAND

Next morning early, Floyd was on deck and aloft with a glass. He knew it was impossible, at their rate of sailing, that the island could show up before noon. They might not even sight it before sundown. Yet, all the same, he was on the lookout. There was nothing; nothing but the great wheel of the sea. Not even a gull showed in the whole of that blue expanse.

He came down, disappointed, and was gloomy and absent-minded at breakfast, though Cardon was cheerful enough.

Toward eleven o'clock, when they were on deck smoking and talking, a great bird passed them, flying straight ahead.

"That chap is going twenty knots," said Cardon. "I reckon he could make forty if he wanted to. He's not much of an indication that there's land about, for a thousand miles to him is less than a thirty-mile walk to you or me. Say, Floyd, how would it be if we couldn't find your island? I heard a yarn once of a chap who spotted a guano island. He said it was a solid slab of guano a mile wide, and he started for 'Frisco and got up a syndicate to work it, and they chartered a schooner and had a champagne breakfast to start on; and when they reached the spot, the darned thing had gone—sunk into the sea."

"Rubbish!" said Floyd. "And I wish you wouldn't start those sorts of yarns just now; it's not lucky."

"Oh, I am only joking. Your island is there, safe enough, with Schumer on top of it. That sort of chap never sinks into the sea; it's only the good men Davy Jones troubles about. He's a mascot, sure."

Floyd did not answer him; he was staring right ahead.

"When I sighted it first," said he, "I was in an open boat that gave very little horizon, and what struck me first was the sky. It was pale, just a patch of it, a sort of glittering paleness that was caused by the lagoon. Have you ever seen that mark in the sky above a lagoon island?"

"Can't say I have, but then I'm not so used to the Pacific as you are. Do you see anything now?"

"No," said Floyd. "I wish I did."

Cardon whistled gently to himself, tapping the ashes out of his pipe against the rail and refilling it. He was just as anxious as Floyd, but his anxiety had not such a keen edge and he hid it better. There were times when he, like Floyd, almost doubted the reality of the island.

He was bending in the shelter of the bulwark to light his pipe when a hail came from aloft.

Floyd had stationed a lookout in the crosstrees, and it was his voice that came, high and clear, like the call of a bird.

Next moment the two men were swarming up the ratlines and looking forward in the direction to which the fellow was pointing.

"It's the island!" said Floyd.

Cardon looked.

All he could see at first was a tiny mark on the sea line, a mark no larger than a pin head; then, as his eyes grew more accustomed to the dazzle, another tiny mark appeared close to the first, and then another.

Then these marks became fused together, forming a faint line.

The lookout had a glass with him, and Floyd, taking it, found that it gave scarcely any better definition than the naked eye. The shimmer of the sea formed a veil more impenetrable than the veil of distance.

He handed the glass to Cardon, who was clinging to the ratlines below him.

"It's land, sure enough," said Cardon, "and another hour will bring it right up. We'd better go down and wait on deck; no use sticking here."

In less than an hour the palm tops showed clearly through the glass, and in two hours' time the reef could be made out and the white thread of the foam breaking upon it.

It was the island, surely enough, though still a great way off—so far that from the deck and with the naked eye nothing could be seen but a faint smudge that might have been a trace of smoke clinging to the sea line.

The wind had fallen a bit, and now, as if beneath the weight of afternoon, it was falling still more.

Floyd hove the log. They were making seven knots, and he calculated that it would be sundown before they could make the break in the reef.

Dinner was served, but they could scarcely eat; the weather held all their thoughts, and the dread of the wind falling to a flat calm was on both their minds.

At four o'clock, however, the wind was still steady, and the land ahead was visible now clearly from the deck.

Floyd, who had gone aloft, suddenly hailed Cardon, who was on deck, and the latter came up to him.

"Look out and tell me what you see," said Floyd, handing him the glass he had been using.

Cardon looked through the glass.

"By gad," said he, "there's a vessel in the lagoon."

The glass showed the reef and the grove on the right of the break distinctly. The break in the reef was not so clear, as they were heading slightly to the south of it; but very clearly indeed could be seen the threadlike masts of a vessel anchored in the lagoon. She was stripped of canvas. She was a schooner.

Cardon handed the glass up again to Floyd, who took another long look; then the two men came down on deck.

"That's Luckman!" said Floyd.

"'Pears so," said Cardon, "unless it's some vessel blown in by chance."

"No, it's no chance. I feel convinced of that. He started ahead of us, and maybe laid over us in sailing. Let's go down below and have a talk over this."

They went down to the cabin, and Floyd took his seat at the table while Cardon took the couch.

"You see, it explains everything," said Floyd. "Explains why Luckman did not sail with us, and why Hakluyt looked so cheerful, which he wouldn't have done had his plans fallen through."

"If what you say is right," said Cardon, "it makes everything a lot worse, for why should these scoundrels employ two ships unless they are determined to lose one of them? You may bet the *Southern Cross* is insured to the hilt and over. You say Hakluyt had her into dry dock and spent money having her scraped when she did not want it. That was all part of the plan to allay suspicion, for what would the ordinary fool say but that a man wouldn't spend money like that on a ship he was going to lose."

"Besides," said Floyd, "if Hakluyt had sent Luckman with me, what reason could he have given me for sending him? We don't want another white man in this business—well, what excuse could Hakluyt have given me for shoving Luckman in?"

"None," said Cardon, "that I can see; but that's not saying a clever rascal like Hakluyt couldn't have found some excuse."

Floyd suddenly struck the table with his fist.

"The *Domain* wasn't at her anchorage when we left," said he. "I noticed it, but I never thought of it as being connected with us."

"The *Domain*? What vessel was she?"

"One of Hakluyt's, a schooner. She was pointed out to me as belonging to him, and before we started I noticed that she wasn't at her anchorage. I thought nothing of that, for a shipowner doesn't keep ships to anchor them out and leave them to rot. But there's the fact, and I'll bet my life that schooner in the lagoon is the *Domain*."

"You're probably right," said Cardon. "Anyhow, we'll soon see. Now let's talk of my share in the business. If Luckman is really here, it means that your destruction has been plotted and planned to the last tip end. It means that there must be no quarter for Schumer."

"If Luckman is here," said Floyd, rising and pacing the cabin, "Schumer will get no quarter from me. Not a ha'porth of mercy."

"I'm glad you are beginning to see things in their proper light," said Cardon. "And now to business. I must keep hidden; I can stay in your cabin, and you must get these two fellows on board as quick as possible. It may be that Schumer will board us right away when we get into the lagoon. He's almost sure to. It may be that he will bring Luckman with him. Now I think the best plan, if Schumer boards us right off and by himself, is to deal with him at once, lock him up here, and then land and deal with Luckman."

"Maybe you are right," said Floyd.

"I'm sure I am. There's nothing like grasping your nettle right off, and it will give them no time to conspire together. Of course, if they both come aboard, so much the better. You speak to them fair, and bring them down here, get them seated at the table before some drink; then I'll open the cabin door and enter, smiling. Directly you see me, draw your gun and cover one of them. Cover Luckman; that will be pleasanter for you, seeing that Schumer is known to you and was once your friend—or pretended to be. When we have disarmed them, we will tie them up."

"Suppose they succeed in drawing their pistols?"

"In that case we must shoot first, and shoot to kill. There's no use in putting on kid gloves in this matter. Your life has been planned against; these two chaps are out against you, and they've got to be scotched. Do you feel equal to the job? If not, we had better 'bout ship and make back to Sydney."

"God help me," said Floyd, "but what I would have shuddered at a few days ago leaves me now without the least feeling. It's finding Luckman here, I suppose, finding that the plot against me is absolutely true. I don't know. But the idea of killing those men seems no more to me than the idea of killing a pair of scorpions."

"That's right," said Cardon. "You'll do all right. And now up with you on deck—I don't appear till the business begins. If I were to go on deck now, there's no knowing that I mightn't be spotted through a glass. Give me your fist."

The two men shook hands.

Then Floyd went on deck, where the hands were crowded forward, gazing at the island, which was now so close that the individual trees could be distinguished, the coral, and the surf breaking on the outer beach.

Floyd's heart leaped in him at the sight. He took the glass from its sling near the wheel and examined the shore through it. Not a sign of life could be seen.

The house was, of course, hidden by the grove, and it was quite unlikely that any one might be here on the seaward side of the reef; still, the absence of all signs of life struck a chill to the heart of Floyd, the illogical heart of the man who loves.

The wind was still holding steady, and the *Southern Cross* was making good way.

Now they were so close that he fancied he could hear the tune of the surf on the coral; and now they were opening the break of the reef, and the lagoon showed mirror calm as compared to the sea.

Floyd took the wheel.

The schooner held for a moment on her course; then, answering to the helm, made full for the opening in the reef. The tide was with them, and like a white cloud the *Southern Cross* passed the pierheads of the reef and entered the lagoon.

Floyd handed the wheel over to Mountain Joe, gave his orders to the fellows at the halyards and the braces, and walked forward. There was, indeed, another vessel in the lagoon, and she was the *Domain*. He could not be mistaken. She was anchored a good way out from the shore, and he maneuvered to get the inner berth. Even as he did so, his eye caught sight of a figure that had just emerged from the grove. It was Isbel.

He ran to the bulwark rail and flung up his arm just as the roar of the anchor chain through the hawse pipe cut the air. Isbel waved her hand in reply. She was alone. Not a sign of Schumer or Luckman was to be seen, and Floyd, half mad with delight, started orders for the quarter boat to be lowered, and helped with his own hands at the falls.

When the boat touched the beach he sprang out knee-deep in the water, waded ashore, and caught her two hands in his.

Then he remembered the fellows in the boat and the possibility that Schumer might be watching from some post of observation. He released her hands and led the way up to the house.

"Schumer?" said he. "Where is Schumer?"

Isbel nodded toward the fishing camp.

"Over there," said she; "he and the new man. They will only know that you have come now. I saw you very far at sea, but I said nothing. I was to light a fire if I saw a ship, but I knew it was you, and I did nothing."

They had entered the house, and were safe from observation.

"Isbel," said Floyd.

He held her apart from him for a moment; then he caught her in his arms.

She clung to him, holding him about the neck with her naked arms, telling him in a broken voice and a half whisper how she had waited and watched always for him; how she had prayed to the sea to bring him back, and the stars to light him on his way. Then holding him from her she told, in short, hot sentences, fierce as stabbing spears, of his danger.

A new ship had come into the lagoon only the day before; a new man had joined Schumer, a terrible man. They had talked last night, and she had listened. No sooner had this strange man shown his face than she suspected danger; he "carried danger with him." So she had listened. They had not talked in the house; they had gone together and sat by the grove edge. She had crawled through the trees and listened. At first she could not make out what they said, they spoke in so low a tone; then, feeling safe and forgetting caution, they spoke louder. Even still she could seize upon nothing definite, as they spoke in a general way as if about some prearranged plot, but she gathered enough to know that Luckman had come to the island to wait for the man she loved, and then, with the help of Schumer, or, more properly speaking, the connivance of Schumer, to do away with him.

As she told this her gaze seemed to turn inward, as though she were looking at some mental picture, and a long shudder ran through her as though from some vibration of the soul. It was not the shudder of fear or cold; it was the shudder of hate, and Floyd, who had never seen it before, felt for a moment almost afraid of Isbel. He recognized, and not for the first time, that this being whom he loved belonged to a world of which he knew little. She was a person from another star, the child of another race. In her love for him a whole unknown world was rushing to meet him. It was this that completed her fascination and made him, now heedless of Schumer's menace, seize her to his heart and cover her face and throat with burning kisses. Taking fire she returned them, and then, holding him apart from her again, and still speaking in those sentences, short and hot like stabbing spears that have already tasted blood, she went on to give him all that she had gathered and all that she suspected. She knew for certain that Luckman and Schumer were expecting Floyd, for they had mentioned him by name, and she knew for certain that they had designs upon the life of the man they were expecting, and here lay her great grief; she could not fathom the nature of their design. She had, however, gathered enough to understand that the Kanaka crew of the *Southern Cross* was to be brought ashore as soon as possible.

"Yes," said Floyd, "they are going to do away with the schooner. Well, we will see. We will see which of us is the cuter and which the stronger. Isbel, I am not alone."

"How?" said Isbel, looking at him with wide-open eyes.

"I have a friend with me."

"A friend!"

"Yes, a friend. Providence sent him, I think." He began to tell her about Cardon, how he had met him in the street in Sydney, how Cardon had joined in the venture and was ready to assist against Schumer, and how he was now on board the *Southern Cross* awaiting developments.

He had reached this stage in his story when a sound from outside made them both turn. It was the sound of oars in rowlocks.

Floyd sprang to the door. A boat that had crossed the lagoon from the fishing ground was within a few yards of the beach. It was the boat bringing Schumer from the fishing camp.

A man was seated beside Schumer in the stern sheets. Was it Luckman?

If indeed it was Luckman, then Luckman was a most formidable individual. This person seated beside Schumer was immense, a great four-square built man beside whom Schumer had the appearance of a youth.

As the boat touched the sand Schumer leaped out, and, half wading, made up the beach toward Floyd, who had come down from the house. Isbel had remained indoors.

"So you're back," cried Schumer, as he held out his hand. "I knew nothing till half an hour ago over there at the fishing ground I turned my head and saw the *Southern Cross* coming into the lagoon. Isbel should have spotted her hours ago and given us a signal. Oh, I forgot. I have a new man to introduce you to, but you've seen his vessel; it ran in here yesterday for water. It is the *Domain*, of Sydney, owned by—who do you think?—Hakluyt, and here's her captain; Luckman is his name. Luckman, this is Mr. Floyd."

Just as Floyd held out his hand toward Luckman a curious sensation struck him, as though for a moment he were clairvoyant, as though for the hundredth part of a moment some glimpse had been given him of his psychic surroundings, a glimpse of the soul of Schumer, of Luckman, and incidentally of Hakluyt. It was Luckman's appearance, perhaps, that influenced him.

Luckman, though a very big man at a distance, was a very little man seen close to. In other words, he had nothing to recommend him but his size. He had, no doubt, been all that the barkeeper had hinted. He had, no doubt, sunk ships in his time and lost the lives of innumerable sailormen and escaped from the law himself by a miracle. All the same, from the crown of his flat head to the sole of his flat feet, the man was a duffer, a mass of brute force—nothing more. And the thing that struck Floyd most keenly at that moment was the thought that Luckman, like himself, was in the toils of Schumer and Hakluyt; that Luckman might be used as a tool against him—Floyd—but would be inevitably flung away when used by Schumer and Hakluyt. That they would take the opportunity not only of getting rid of the *Southern Cross* at a high insurance and of their troublesome partner, but also of Luckman, their tool and assistant.

The fact that Schumer had taken Luckman to the fishing ground and let him see the secret of the island with his own eyes, that fact seemed to Floyd to be Luckman's death sentence.

"Glad to meet you," said Luckman, holding out a fist like a ham.

"It's funny that you should have turned up here," said Floyd, "for only a very little time ago I parted with Mr. Hakluyt, your owner."

"Yes," said Luckman, "it's funny enough to see two of Hakluyt's vessels in the same lagoon, considering the many lagoons there are in the Pacific. I was bound for Upolo, and was blown a bit out of my course, then I picked up this island and put in for water, and when Mr. Schumer here found Hakluyt was my owner he *was* surprised—weren't you, Mr. Schumer?"

He laughed as he asked the question, and Schumer laughed as he replied in the affirmative.

"The strange thing is," said Floyd gravely, "that I left Sydney, came straight down here, and here I find the *Domain*, who has missed Upolo, which is a good way out of the line, been blown out of her course, and yet has arrived here only a day before me."

"And how is that strange?" asked Luckman.

"In this way: I saw the *Domain* in Sydney harbor two days before I left, riding at her anchor. How the deuce has she managed to go through all those experiences you speak of and yet arrive here only the day before me?"

"And what date was it when you left Sydney?" asked Luckman.

Floyd gave the date.

"Well, all I can say," said Luckman, "is that the *Domain* left ten days before that. You must be thinking of the *Dominion,* which is also owned by Hakluyt. She's a sister of the *Domain,* built on the same slip, owned by Shuster, she was, till he went bankrupt and Hakluyt picked her up for an old song. That's the vessel that's in your head. I left her anchored in Sydney harbor when I left." Floyd said nothing. Luckman's manner was so assured and plausible that had he not overheard that fatal conversation in Hakluyt's office he would have been entirely taken in. He turned to Schumer as if to change the subject.

"Well," said he, "how has the luck been going?"

Schumer took him by the arm and led him away a bit along the water edge.

"I'm glad you are back," said he, "before that man Luckman leaves. It's a nuisance, his coming. Of course he's one of Hakluyt's men, else I'd have made him clear out of the lagoon when he'd taken his water on board. As it is he knows all about the pearling. He scented it at once, and spoke to me of it. You see, he's an old island hand, so I just told him, and, what's more, took him right over the grounds. I did a bit of trade with him, too. He had some timber and corrugated iron on board, and I bought it of him, and we've been rafting it over all yesterday and to-day. I'm going to put up huts over at the fishing camp. The rains will be here soon, now, and I want to get the fellows under cover."

"Oh, is that so?" said Floyd.

He could not make out all this in the least, but he determined to say nothing and wait for more indications.

"Yes," said Schumer, "it's most important for us to keep these fellows fit and well, and tents aren't much use against the rains, especially in an exposed place like the grounds over there. Seems like Providence, doesn't it, that fellow Luckman happening along with his building material just at the moment?"

"Schumer," said Floyd, "are you sure it's all right about Luckman?"

Schumer turned on him with a surprised look. "Why, what could be wrong?"

"Well, I could have sworn I saw the *Domain* in the harbor two days before I left."

"In Sydney harbor?"

"Yes, in Sydney harbor."

"My dear chap," said Schumer, "you heard what he said—what could be wrong? Even if Hakluyt were to try to get the better of us in any way what could Luckman do? Steal the pearls? Well, I reckon he'd have his work cut out, considering we are two to one. No. You have made a mistake. It was the *Dominion* you saw. Mind you, I wouldn't trust Hakluyt farther than I could see him, but it's against common sense to think that he is trying to play any game against us. You see, the crew of the *Domain* are all Kanakas, and not fighting Kanakas, either, but a soft lot; otherwise it might be different. Then again Luckman is off to-morrow. Oh, you needn't be a bit scared of Luckman; I'm sharp enough to smell a rat, as you very well know, and I'm satisfied."

"Very well," said Floyd.

"Now as to the building business," went on Schumer, "I want all the *Southern Cross* chaps to get to work on it first thing to-morrow, so we may as well get them over to the fishing camp to-night."

"To-night!"

"Yes, they'll be able to stretch their legs before setting to, and they'll want to put up tents for themselves while they are working."

"Very well. I can send them over in the whaleboat."

"That will do after supper," said Schumer.

The sun at this moment was just setting beyond the reef, and a thin wreath of smoke was rising near the grove where Isbel was busy lighting the fire and getting supper ready. Luckman was seated on the sand, near the house, smoking and seemingly oblivious to everything but the beauty of the scene before him.

The crew of the *Southern Cross* were fraternizing across the water with the crew of the *Domain*. Their thin, high-pitched voices came across the lagoon water and mixed with the crying of the gulls who were flocking around the vessels, picking up scraps from the rubbish that the fellows had hove overboard. Then, as the sun sank, the crying of the gulls died down and silence fell on the island with the night, a silence only broken by the song of the surf and the blowing of the night wind in the foliage of the grove.

Isbel, having prepared the meal, had disappeared, and the three men found themselves alone by the flickering camp fire. It was the night before the new moon, and beyond the zone of firelight the lagoon showed all shot with stars, and the two schooners gray black with their anchor lights shining in the twilight of the stars.

Schumer had produced a bottle of wine in honor of Luckman, but despite the wine and Schumer's attempts at conviviality the talk hung fire.

Floyd was thinking hard.

Schumer's suggestion that the crew of the *Southern Cross* should be landed over at the fishing beach was plausible on the face of it. The men would work better after a night on shore; they would be on the spot in the morning, and so no time would be wasted bringing them across the lagoon, and it was certainly necessary that no time should be lost in putting up the huts, if they were to be put up, for the rainy season was fast approaching. All the same, he felt that there was more in the proposition than what met the eye.

He did not like the idea of being left alone here with Schumer and Luckman. It was true that the crew of the *Domain* would be on board their vessel, but she was anchored a good way out. The conviction came to him that whatever these two men had in mind was to be carried out that night, and that the *Southern Cross* would be the object of their plans as well as himself. Most possibly they would sink her at her anchorage after having disposed of him.

He determined, come what might, not to sleep ashore, and as they were finishing supper he made up his mind to state his intention at once.

"Well," said he, "I suppose I'd better get off and send those fellows across to the camp. I'll give them the whaleboat; it will hold the lot."

"Yes," said Schumer, "I'll come with you and start them off, and maybe you'd better sleep on board for to-night, as I've put Captain Luckman up in the house and there's only two beds."

"Yes, I'll sleep aboard," said Floyd, relieved, yet somewhat surprised at Schumer suggesting the very plan that was in his mind. "I've got all my tackle there, besides—well, shall we start?"

He looked round, on the chance of seeing Isbel, but she was nowhere about; then they left Luckman, smoking by the fire, and, going down to the lagoon edge, pushed off the quarter boat which was lying by the dinghy. They would have taken the dinghy, only that she had developed a leak. Schumer explained this as they rowed, and Floyd scarcely heard him; he was thinking of Isbel.

He could not possibly take her off with him, and she was safer ashore in the dangerous business that he felt was developing. He had no fear of harm coming to her left alone with Schumer and Luckman, for she was well able to take care of herself, and she was armed. She had told him so. All the same his heart felt heavy as lead at leaving her, even though they were separated only by a couple of cable lengths of water.

On board, he gave orders to Mountain Joe for the landing of the crew, and in a moment the deck was swarming. The idea of getting ashore set the fellows chattering and carrying on like school children just set free, and there were no hands wanted to assist at the falls.

In a moment the whaleboat was lowered and alongside and the crew tumbling into her. Schumer helped in the lowering of the boat and shouted directions to Mountain Joe, who took the stern oar.

"They'll find canvas enough over there if they want to make tents," said Schumer. "As like as not they will prefer sleeping in the open on a night like this. There they go."

The whaleboat had pushed off, and was now out in the lagoon, making good way despite its heavy load.

It looked like a huge, heavy-bodied beetle crawling across the surface of the lagoon.

Schumer turned away and followed Floyd down to the cabin for a drink. Floyd had shipped some Bitter Water at Sydney, and he opened a bottle now and produced glasses from the swinging rack by the door. He also brought out a box of cigars.

Schumer took a cigar and a drink, and sat down at the table, placing his hat upon it.

Floyd took his place opposite to him, and they sat smoking and talking on indifferent matters, Floyd trying to keep pace with the situation and at the same time to appear his ordinary self.

Should he deal with Schumer now and at once or let him go ashore and then have a consultation with Cardon?

Cardon, he knew, was listening to every word of their conversation, and he had a great respect for Cardon's judgment. He determined to explain the situation to Cardon now and at once and through his conversation with Schumer.

"It was a good idea of yours to send all the crew ashore at the fishing camp so as to have them on the spot for working in the morning," said he. "Of course that only leaves me on board, and I'm a jolly sight too tired to stand an anchor watch. However, we don't want an anchor watch in this lagoon. There's nothing to look out for but sharks."

"That's so," replied Schumer.

"Luckman is off to-morrow, you say?"

"Yes, he'll be off to-morrow if this wind holds."

"Well, I'm glad to have met him. He didn't give me a very good impression at first sight, but he improves a bit on acquaintance. He must be a powerfully strong man. I'd sooner have him at my back in a fight than against me."

"Yes," said Schumer, "I reckon he could hold his own against any two men, or maybe three, but he's all strength, not much intelligence."

"And it's the intelligence that counts nowadays," said Floyd. "You see, if a man has a gun and some intelligence, brute force doesn't count for much, or even numbers. I had an adventure once that proved that to me. I was held up in the cabin of a ship by two ruffians—it was off the South American coast—and I didn't resist simply for the reason that a friend of mine was close by whom I reckoned to be a much cleverer chap than myself. He was lying in his bunk, and the fellows couldn't see him. I waited for his lead. His name was Cardon, and I determined to let him decide whether I should put up a fight at once or just sit still and let myself be robbed. It was the funniest sensation, sitting there and waiting for another man's brains to work out the situation, but I was right. The upshot was I recovered my money." He yawned, and then suddenly, switching off the subject: "There's no fear, is there, of Luckman getting too close to the pearls? Mind you, I'm not going against your judgment about the man. All the same, temptation is temptation, and it's as well to be on our guard."

"The pearls are all right," said Schumer. "They are in the safe, and the safe is in the inner room of the house, and I sleep there."

He rose to go, flicking the ash of his cigar onto the floor. Floyd rose also.

There was no sign from Cardon, so he knew that wily person had decided to let Schumer go ashore. Then he accompanied the other on deck.

The boat in which Schumer had come was alongside. He got into it, bade Floyd good night, and rowed ashore. Floyd watched him land. He saw Luckman come down from the house to help in beaching the boat, and then the two men walked up to the house. They entered it, and closed the door, and then beach and reef and grove lay deserted under the starlight.

Floyd left the deck and came down to the cabin, and there, at the table, Cardon was seated.

"You've done well," said Cardon. "I was afraid you would open the game too soon. Sit down there and give me a few points. What's Luckman like?"

"Like a beast," said Floyd.

"I heard all you said," went on Cardon. "Schumer has got all the men off the ship, hasn't he?"

"Yes."

"That's their first move, and they mean business to-night—when you are sleeping. They won't act for an hour or two yet, so we have plenty of time."

"What's their game, do you think?" asked Floyd.

"It's as simple as sin. They mean to row off, steal down here, knock you on the head, and then scuttle the schooner. They'll reckon to take you sleeping. That's their game, and as like as not, when the business is done, Schumer will do Luckman in and sink him with the ship."

"Good God!" said Floyd. "I was thinking that myself to-night, and yet you who have never seen Schumer suspected it, too."

"Simply because I have studied out the whole proposition while I was lying in that stuffy bunk. Can't you see how it stands? They must get rid of Luckman. The only thing that gravels me is this: Why did they ever bring Luckman into the affair at all? Why didn't Schumer knock you on the head, do the thing off his own bat, so to speak?

"I can only work it out like this: If he had done that there would have been witnesses sure. The crew of the *Southern Cross* would have smelled a rat. There's nothing more likely to pop out than murder if there are any witnesses that know the murdered party. Schumer wants to break off from the island and every one connected with the pearling. Most likely he suspects the lagoon is beginning to give out. Anyhow, he has got a big lot of stuff, and it's my belief that his plan is to cut his stick instantly you are out of the way, leave the island and the lagoon and the niggers to look after themselves, and set sail in the *Domain* with the boodle he's got. That's why he has landed the crew."

"You mean to say he will desert the island and never come back?"

"Yes."

"But surely if he did a thing like that it would only mean losing a good property. I don't believe the lagoon is giving out. There was no indication of it."

"I only suggested that. It may be giving out or it mayn't, but there's this fact, you must admit—the lagoon is not real estate; you have no title to it. Suppose an English man-of-war shoves her nose in and asks you what you are doing here. What will you say? That you are looking for mushrooms? English, French, or German, the first ship that gets wind of the business does for you. They'll mark it down on their chart and say to you: 'This is our island; get out!' Suppose even a trader comes along and sniffs you. Do you think they're going to leave a jeweler's shop like this severely alone? Do you think they won't say 'half shares or we split'? No, sir. You and Schumer have had a very good swig at this cornucopia. It's amazing you haven't been interfered with before this. The common-sense thing is to take what you've got and do a bunk, cut all connections with the business, and don't leave a rag of yourselves behind. That's what Schumer is going to do. Of course he'll have to play fair with Hakluyt so as to get rid of the pearls and have no trouble about the schooner. Then there's the insurance money on the *Southern Cross*. That will be a nice penny for them to divide."

"I suppose you are right," said Floyd. "It's hateful—the whole thing. The world seems suddenly to be filled with devils, not men. I could never have fancied such villainy if I hadn't gone through it."

"Oh, you'll be pretty tough to this sort of thing when you are as old as I am," said Cardon, "and when you have knocked about the west American seaboard a dozen years or so. You don't know these chaps as I do. A sailor doesn't know anything. You must leave the sea and stick for a few years to the land as I have done to find the truth, and the truth about the Pacific coast is that quite a lot of people don't give a cent for the life of a man if it's worth a dollar to them.

"Now, there's no use in sticking down here any longer. We'd better be getting up on deck and taking our position. I've got a plan in my head which you'll see put in work before long. Have you got your gun?"

Floyd showed the butt of his revolver.

"Right!" said Cardon. "And now, first of all, let's make everything straight."

There were three glasses on the table, his own, Floyd's, and the one Schumer had drunk from. He renewed his own glass, looked round to make sure that he had left no trace of his presence anywhere, put out the light, and led the way on deck.

At the top of the companionway he turned to Floyd, who was below him.

"Don't show yourself above the bulwarks," said he. "Crawl along the deck after me to the caboose. That's the place for us to hide and wait for them."

"Right!" said Floyd.

They crawled along on hands and knees till they reached the caboose door. It opened to the starboard, and as the *Southern Cross* was swinging to the incoming tide, with her nose to the break in the reef, the door of the caboose faced the *Domain*, and consequently could not be seen from the shore.

Cardon opened the door, and they went in, closing the door behind them.

The place was terribly stuffy and filled with the smell of grease and cooking. The copper was still hot, which did not improve matters, and cockroaches were in evidence even in that darkness.

There was a scuttle giving aft, and in a moment Floyd had opened it. It gave a view of the whole of the deck aft, and though there was no moon the starlight showed everything. The main hatch, with its cover of tarpaulin, the saloon hatch, the bulwarks, and the planking of the deck so clearly that the lines of division between the planks could be traced, and even the dowels that fixed the planking to the beams.

It was a noisome hole to be cooped up in, but it was a splendid post of observation, though, from the size of the scuttle, only one man could keep a lookout at a time.

"We'll take it turn about," said Cardon, "and the chap that's off duty can sit on the copper and keep it warm. We haven't a watch, and a watch would be no use to us, as we daren't show a light; so we'll have to guess the length of the trick. Ten minutes each will be the length of the lookout as far as we can make it. I'll take first, if you don't mind."

Floyd had no objection, and he sat on a ledge by the copper, listening and waiting in the dark while Cardon stood on watch. The ship was full of sounds. On deck everything seemed bathed in dead silence, but here, listening in the dark, all sorts of little noises came to greet the ear and imagination.

The outside sea sent a vague, almost imperceptible, swell into the lagoon, and as she moved to it she creaked and muttered and groaned, masts, spars, and body timber all finding points of greater and lesser tension and every point a tiny voice.

The rudder shifted now and then slightly, and the rudder chain clicked in response. There were rats on board, and they made themselves audible, and there was a nest of young rats somewhere under the planking, and their thriddy voices came in little bursts now and then, telling of some disturbance in the nest. Floyd pictured to himself the old mother rat suckling them while the father was out on business seeking food, and he philosophized on the idea that even the timbers of a ship may hide all sorts of interests and ambitions, affections and hates.

An hour passed, during which he and Cardon relieved each other at the lookout post several times, and it was during Cardon's watch, some twenty minutes later, that the event occurred.

Suddenly a sound made itself heard that was not a sound born of the ship. A faint splash came from alongside, followed by something quite unmistakable—the sound of an oar shipped and laid along the seats of a boat—incautiously. It had probably slipped from the hand of the rower as he laid it inboard.

Floyd, who had heard the sound also, tipped Cardon's leg with his toe, and Cardon, reaching out with his heel, signaled that he knew.

A few seconds passed, and then Cardon saw a form coming over the side. It was Schumer. He had never seen Schumer, but from Floyd's description he knew that it could not be Luckman. Then, surely enough, came Luckman in all his immensity.

Neither man wore either boots or stockings, and their bare feet, wet with the bilge water of the boat, shone in the starlight. Those glistening feet fascinated Cardon. All the tragedy of the business seemed focused in them, and, strong and brave though he was, they exercised such a powerful psychological effect that for a moment he could have retched.

The two men did not pause for more than a second. Soundless as shadows, they made for the saloon hatch, while Cardon, who thought the moment for action had arrived, moved slightly as if to leave his post.

Then he stopped.

Schumer and his companion, instead of going down below, were bending over the hatch. They were closing it.

Cardon drew in his breath.

He saw at once their object. Instead of going down to kill the man they imagined to be below, they were bottling him up. No man, however strong, could force his way on deck through that hatch once closed.

Again he felt Floyd's toe, as if it were inquiring if all was right, and, again reaching back, he signaled an answer. His eyes were glued to the malefactors, who were now at the main hatch removing the tarpaulin.

It did not take long. Then they worked the locking bars loose and removed the hatch with scarcely a sound. He saw Schumer produce something. It was a lantern. They lit it, and Schumer, with it in his hand, vanished down the main hatch into the hold. He was there a full minute that seemed a full hour to the man at the scuttle; then he reappeared. The hatch was closed, but the tarpaulin was not replaced, and, leaving it, they came forward, Schumer carrying the light and Luckman following him. They passed the caboose, and were lost to sight.

"Now is our time," whispered Cardon, turning from the scuttle. "We've got them forward in a close space. Cock your gun and follow me."

He opened the caboose door and found a vacant deck.

For a moment he thought that the two men had gone overboard; then he saw the truth. They had gone down into the fo'c'sle. Floyd saw the situation and the chance in the same flash with Cardon, and in a moment they had flung themselves on the fo'c'sle hatch cover and driven it to.

The men who fancied they had bottled Floyd were bottled in their turn.

They had imagined a vain thing, and the fact was evidently borne in on them now to judge from the sounds coming from below.

The cover of the fo'c'sle hatch was placed at such an angle with the fo'c'sle companionway that it was impossible to make much noise by striking upward from below, and its thickness was well demonstrated by the feebleness of the noise of the men who were now shouting at the top of their voices.

"They're fixed and done for," said Cardon, "and I reckon Schumer will start repenting in a minute that he sent the crew ashore. Come, we have no time to waste here."

He ran to the port rail, followed by Floyd.

The boat Schumer and Luckman had come in was alongside. Every plan they had made and every preparation seemed working now for their destruction and for the success of their enemies. The thought crossed Floyd's mind as he followed Cardon down into the boat, but there was little time to think in, and, taking the stern oar while Cardon took the bow, they pushed off for the shore.

Having beached the boat, Floyd led the way up to the house, and as they approached it a figure came out of the grove into the starlight. It was Isbel. Floyd ran up to her as Cardon entered the house; then, as he was holding her hands and trying to tell her all that had occurred, Cardon appeared at the house door with a lighted match in his hand.

"There's no safe here," said he.

He lit another match as they followed through the main into the inner room.

There was nothing there at all, except the bed which Schumer slept on and the tossed blankets. The safe, which had stood in one corner of the room, was gone.

"That does us," said Floyd. He had fancied that the pearls were a secondary consideration, that Isbel was the one and only thing. Now he knew different. Isbel was not the only thing. Without the pearls and the money they would fetch he was nothing. Nothing but a sailorman earning a few shillings a week, tossed hither and thither about the world at the will of an owner.

For one terrible minute before the loss of these things he felt his poverty, and there is nothing much more terrible than that if one loves. What had stricken him would strike Isbel. Where could he take her? What could he do with her, he who had no home but a sailors' lodging home, no resources but a miserable pittance only to be earned at the cost of separation from her?

Cardon brought him back to himself.

"No, it doesn't," said Cardon, "but it saves us a lot of trouble. Can't you see? The pearls and the safe are on board the *Domain*?"

"On board the *Domain*?"

"Where else? Didn't I tell you Schumer was going to shin out of here in the *Domain*? Well, he has removed the safe there, and all we have to do now is to go aboard the *Domain*, up anchor, and get away. He has played into our hands all through, and every point he made against us has turned against him. Don't you see?"

Floyd did. This last act of Schumer's put the finishing touch to the business. Not only had he saved them the trouble of carrying off the safe, but he had destroyed all qualms in the mind of Floyd. All Schumer's plotting, so skillful, so carefully weighed, so intricate, and so powerfully backed by Hakluyt with his ships and money had been brought to naught by one little flaw, one accident—Floyd's surprisal of Hakluyt's conversation with Luckman.

"Come!" said Cardon.

They hurriedly left the house, Cardon walking first, Floyd following with Isbel, whose hand he was holding.

It was their good-by to the island. In that short walk from the house door to the lagoon edge the fact that he was leaving what he nevermore might see was brought vividly to the mind of Floyd. Never had the place seemed more beautiful from the piers of the reef to the far-off fires, where the pearl fishers were holding a revel beneath the palm trees with the crew of the *Southern Cross*.

As they rowed across the lagoon, passing under the stern of the *Southern Cross*, they could hear the songs brought by the wind across the water from the fishing camp. Not a sound came from the schooner, where the trapped men were no doubt fumbling in the fo'c'sle for some means of escape, and not a sound came from the *Domain*, where the whole crew, anchor watch included, were fast asleep. As they came alongside the *Domain*, Cardon hailed her, and a fellow rousing on deck came to the bulwark rail, rubbing his eyes. He cast a rope, and the boat was made fast.

Then they came on board.

Three men had been sleeping on deck, the bos'n and two of the hands, and when Cardon gave the order to rouse the crew and get the anchor up just for a moment it seemed there was going to be trouble. Then Isbel saved the situation.

"It is by Luckman's orders," said she, speaking in the native. "He is staying here; the ship is to be taken where he wills," she finished, pointing at Cardon. Had there been any resistance on the part of the bos'n or the crew Cardon would have promptly dealt with it, but there was none. They were an unsuspicious lot. There had been no sign of disturbance on shore, and whether the ship sail under Luckman or under Cardon did not matter a button to them. Besides, it was due to sail. The water was on board, and Luckman had told them to be ready to weigh anchor at any moment.

The wind was blowing steadily for the break in the reef, and now, had you been ashore, you would have seen the mainsail of the *Domain* rising like a black wing under the stars to the creaking of blocks and slatting of canvas; then came the sound of the capstan pawls as the anchor chain was hove short, and Floyd's voice ordering the jib to be cast loose. The tide was near the turn, and it was just approaching the moment of smooth water at the reef opening.

Floyd, before starting to work the vessel, had run down to the cabin, where, sure enough, the safe was standing against the couch which ran along the starboard side, and between it and the table.

Not only was the safe on board, but Schumer had also brought off the tin cash box holding what remained to them of the money of the *Cormorant* and *Tonga*.

He had made a clean sweep, only to sweep it all into Floyd's pocket.

Floyd was thinking this as he stood on deck now giving orders for the securing of the anchor which had left the water and was being hoisted, dripping, to the catheads, and now as the mainsail filled to the wind he took the wheel himself.

As he turned the spokes and got the feel of the ship answering to his hand a faint, hot, acrid smell came on a puff of wind, a smell of burning, though from where he could not say. He glanced back at the far-off fires of the fishing camp, and fancied it might be coming from that quarter. There was nowhere else possible for it to come from except the *Southern Cross*, and the *Southern Cross* showed no sign of smoke or fire as she lay there mute and somber, her spars cutting the starlit sky and her hull blackening with its shadow the starlit water.

So gently did the *Domain* move that, viewed from the deck, it seemed that past her, lying stationary, the reef and the trees were gliding aft.

Then the pierheads of the reef passed like ghosts or shadows, and the *Domain* rose to the swell of the outer sea and sank, bursting the foam away from her bow like snow.

Floyd gave the wheel over to the bos'n, and stood for a moment looking aft across the sea; then he turned and went below, where Isbel was waiting for him in the cabin.

Cardon, left on deck, paced up and down, now with an eye on the binnacle card, now glancing aft, as though on the watch for something he expected to appear in the wake of the schooner.

The wind had freshened, and the *Domain* was making a good eight knots. Not a cloud was to be seen in the star-spangled sky, nor a sail on the sea line, nor a sign now of the island.

The atoll island does not show up well at night. It is less an island than a kink in the sea over which a vessel may trip just as a man trips over a kink in a carpet, and, looking back now as Cardon was looking, nothing could be seen of the shore they had left.

Till suddenly Cardon drew in his breath, clutched the after rail, and stood motionless and gazing at a pale orange-colored glow marking the sky on the sea line they were leaving.

Even as he watched the glow deepened in color to an angry red.

A great fire was in progress over there. One might have fancied that the whole of Pearl Island had caught alight and was blazing like a torch in the wind. But Cardon knew better. He knew that what he was watching was the destruction of the *Southern Cross*.

When he had seen Schumer going down into the hold with the light he had guessed what was forward. Schumer had fired the vessel, and then, to make sure, he had gone into the fo'c'sle with Luckman to fire her in a fresh place.

The fire had proclaimed itself now, and Schumer and his companion, bottled up in the fo'c'sle, would by this be beyond praying for.

Cardon had said nothing to Floyd of his suspicions, and now as he watched them verified he determined to keep the matter still to himself.

There was no use in troubling the mind of Floyd. As for his own mind, he was not in the least troubled.

What Schumer had prepared for another he was receiving himself, and Cardon was not the man to pity a traitor and a murderer or to quarrel with the justice of fate.

But it was strange beyond imagination to watch that steady, silent, distant glow, knowing what it meant.

He watched it increasing to a certain point and decrease to a certain point. Of a sudden, with a heave and flicker, it went out, and the stars burned clear where the glow had been.

The *Southern Cross* had sunk at her anchorage, and Cardon, turning away, left the deck and came down to the cabin where Floyd and the girl were seated.

ENVOI

Some three weeks later the *Domain* cast anchor in Sydney harbor, and Cardon, after the port authorities and the health officer had been on board, took a shore boat for the quay. Floyd and Isbel did not accompany him. He was going to interview Hakluyt, and he judged that he would do the business better if he did it alone.

He waved his hand to them as he rowed off, and when he reached the quay he made straight for Hakluyt's office.

Hakluyt was in, but was engaged, and Cardon waited in an outer room patiently enough for some twenty minutes. He was in no hurry, and when at last he was shown into the room where the shipowner was seated at his desk he showed no hurry to begin the business he had on hand.

He was studying Hakluyt.

"Well, sir," said Hakluyt, after the pause that followed Cardon's announcement and while that person was comfortably taking his seat, "and what can I do for you?"

"Nothing," said Cardon. "I have come to tell you that Luckman has burned the *Southern Cross,* according to arrangement with you, and that I have all the evidence in my pocket, that he tried to do away with Mr. Floyd according to agreement, and that I have witnesses of the plot. In other words, my dear man, that your game is up and that it rests entirely with me whether I close my fist on you or let you go free."

Hakluyt said nothing.

"All your pearls are gone," said Cardon, lighting a cigarette. "Floyd has got them. They are worth a good many thousand. I have taken your schooner, the *Domain,* and you have here and now to make out a paper selling her to me for the sum of—shall we say five thousand?—not one penny of which you will ever receive. I am going to take her to 'Frisco, and if you make one kick or give one squeal or try one dirty trick I will put you in quod as sure as my name is Jack Cardon."

"This is blackmail," said Hakluyt, sweating and grinning at the same time, and in all his life Cardon had never seen anything stranger than that grin.

"This is blackmail!"

"Of course it is," replied the other, "but what I want to point out to you is that there is no resistance. You are absolutely tied up. I have Luckman and Schumer in the hollow, of my hand, a whole island full of Kanaka witnesses, *and* the sunken schooner; also Floyd and a native girl. Well, what do you say?"

"Where is Schumer?" cried Hakluyt, who seemed now like a person dazed by a blow.

"He's with Luckman, and I can only say this—he can be produced when wanted." Then, suddenly bursting out: "He is where you sent him. Dead in the fo'c'sle of the ship that he sank. He, and Luckman along with him. Blackmail! Do you think if I were working this thing for my own hand I would stoop to blackmail *you*? No, sir. I'm working this for Floyd, who is a soft-shell Englishman, as good as they make them, but a child against ruffians of your cut. I'm squeezing you for him, and if you don't like my loving embrace say so and I'll call in the law to do the business. Now I give you one minute to decide. Do you stick out or do you give in?"

"I give in," said Hakluyt.